Death by Design

For John, Janet, Colm and Douglas

By the same author

AN END TO FLIGHT (Faber & Faber)

Vincent Banville

Death by Design

No Exit Press

1993

No Exit Press

18 Coleswood Rd

Harpenden,Herts,AL5 1EQ

First published in Ireland by Wolfhound Press 1993

A CIP catalogue record for this book is available from the British Library.

I S B N 1 - 874061 - 16 - 5 Death by Design

Printed and bound by Cox & Wyman, Reading.

Prologue

IT WAS EIGHT o'clock on a raw April Sunday morning, the sun playing hop-scotch with the clouds but mean so far with warmth. Over the River Liffey the sound of early Mass bells tolled forlornly, and Dublin city, from any vantage point, looked grey and unwelcoming.

Down in Fishamble Street, the tramp was oblivious to any such shadings of feeling. He was craned over, gazing earnestly into a builder's skip. The skip was painted yellow and had the name of the carrier, Cesspit Waste, stencilled on the side in blue letters. There was also a telephone number, but the tramp didn't look as if he were interested in taking it down with a view to using it.

The street was bow shaped and curved down to the river. At the top end the plexi-glass frontage of the seven-storeyed bunker that housed the city corporation offices was pitted and scored by the hundreds of stones thrown by street-wise urchins with time on their hands and vandalism on their minds. The view didn't get any better further down: most of both sides was bordered by decrepit buildings, or by hoardings that advertised attractions that had come and gone. On one panel someone had taken the trouble to spray paint, in surprisingly good script writing, the legend 'Tomorrow is cancelled because of lack of interest'.

Only at the bottom did the street take on any hint of individuality, where a red-bricked, turn-of-the-century sprawl lurked behind high metal railings. Formerly the home of a Chief Secretary at the time of British rule, it was now the Star of the Sea rest house for indigent men and women. As such, it exhibited an outer aura of serenity which gave way inside to a Dickensian confusion of noise and babble.

The tramp, a bulky figure clad in plus fours, a shabby brown hacking jacket and wearing a bowler hat, shifted his position to get a better look into the skip. Reaching in, he pulled out what was either a broken light fitting or a piece of abstract art. He scrutinised this carefully, turning it this way and that. Obviously it didn't meet with his approval and he threw it carelessly over his shoulder and began to rummage further.

The street had been deserted, but now an even odder figure than the tramp began to move slowly up the slope from the direction of the river. This character had wrapped himself completely in a number of clear plastic sacks — he even had one over his head with eyeholes cut in it to enable him to see where he was going. He moved with a stiff-legged gait, like an astronaut who had just got out to stretch his legs on the moon, his arms out wide on either side, his shoulders jerking to force himself along.

When he got to a point level with the tramp he paused and leaned against a poster of an amply endowed exotic dancer. It didn't seem to bother him that he had his hand planted right between her spectacular breasts.

The tramp, sensing that he was no longer alone, stopped his prying search and looked carefully over his shoulder. He squinted eyes that resembled the proverbial pissholes in the snow, then gave a phlegmy chuckle that started somewhere down around his knees. 'You ... you ..,' he ground out, pointing in the direction of the newly appeared apparition and shaking his head.

The other man moved in his jerky fashion out into the middle of the road. 'You see something funny?' he asked from behind his plastic mask. 'You see something that tickles your funny bone? You should take a look at yourself. Why, you could've fallen right out of that skip and no one'd be the wiser. You get my drift ..?'

'Wha ..?'

The tramp blew the word out in a hiccup of surprise. He squinted his eyes again, the hacking laughter breaking off abruptly. He transferred his gaze and looked up and down the street, but they were alone. Away out over the river a scattering of gulls squawked perfunctorily, and a few early Mass goers, dots in the distance, were making their way to the Franciscan Friary whose bells had been summoning them a little time before.

The tramp looked back again at the man confronting him. A slight tracing of worry was beginning to etch itself onto his grizzled features. There was something here beyond his comprehension, a whiff of menace that signalled more than the foretaste of an argument or a trading of blows. In the tramp's mind the basic instinct for survival stirred: he would be better off out of there as fast as his feet could take him.

The other man, as though sensing his companion's thought, moved in closer to him. 'What d'you say, Jockser?' he inquired. 'Want to go a round or two with me? Good for the morning constitutional ...'

The tramp stared, then set his jaw pugnaciously. His way of escape was blocked, so attack was obviously the best form of defence. He came forward, his arms spread wide.

In spite of his former awkwardness, the other man was suddenly light on his feet. He flicked his left hand into the whiskered face in front of him and, when the head leaned away involuntarily, he slashed across the exposed throat with the open razor he held hidden in his right. Bright blood fountained out through the suddenly sunlit air and whacked audibly against his plastic covering. The tramp did a little dance, like a marionette on strings. Before he could fall, the other man caught him, then, holding him against the side of the skip, he began levering him into it. When he had most of him in and only his feet visible and sticking up in the air, he stepped back and made the sign of the cross in the air. 'Go with God,' he muttered — 'Or the devil,' he quickly amended it. 'Whichever is the quickest ...'

Fastidiously he wiped the razor on the dead tramp's flapping trouser-leg, then set it carefully on the edge of the skip. He began to strip off the plastic sacks, keeping them at arms length in order to avoid the blood. Rolling them individually between his gloved hands, he laid them in a neat pile. He worked slowly and meticulously, in no particular hurry, and he whistled tunelessly between his teeth as he did so.

When he had divested himself of the plastic, he was revealed to be attired in a three-piece navy suit with a discreet reddish stripe. His shirt, pristine white, glinted in the morning light, and his dark tie had diagonal maroon bars to match the piping in his suit. He threw the bags in on top of the tramp, wrapped the razor in a handkerchief, the newness of whose folds he had to shake loose, and put the whole lot in his jacket pocket. Then he stood back to survey the scene.

He frowned, as though everything were not to his satisfaction. There was a 'Private. No Parking' sign fixed to a gate to his left, and he pulled this off and propped it against the protruding legs of the tramp. Once more he stood back, then nodded his head contentedly.

Briskly, but not overtly hurrying, he moved off down the hill. There was a jauntiness in his step as he walked along in the early morning sunlight.

1

I WOKE UP that Monday morning to find a shaft of sunlight poking me in the eye. I knew immediately where I was, which was not as easy as it seems. Sometimes I come to thinking I'm Puff the Magic Dragon, my breath hot enough to burn the paint off the ceiling. Unlike Paul Muni in *I Was a Fugitive from a Chain Gang*, who stole, I drink.

But only really in the last year, since Annie my wife left me. Before that I was a sociable drinker, not a loner, and alcohol made me into a merry drunk. Now it had the effect of turning me into a nettle that flailed out at anyone who so much as brushed up against me.

Heigh-ho, so much for that. I tried napping for a while longer, but the fuzzy finger of light kept following me about and finally I gave up and got up. The house was quiet, so I went downstairs and made some tea in a mug, using the last remaining teabag. Then I took it back up with me, intending to shower and shave.

One of my lodgers must have taken a late night bath, for the towels were damp. I stood for a long time under the shower, letting the water rat-a-tat-tat on my head. I found this a pleasurable sensation, as it cleared my brain and caused me to think. This morning my thoughts were a boy's thoughts — long, long ones. But there was nothing original about them: invariably they followed their own tail and came back again to centre on Annie. It had been her habit to share the shower with me. Now, when I closed my eyes, I could feel her presence as palpably as though my hand were sliding down the long curve of her back ...

Such thoughts were leading me nowhere fast, so I got out

of there, wiped condensation off the mirror and began shaving. It was hard to avoid my eye in the glass. I stood back for a moment to take stock. John Blaine, six foot two, 220 lbs., light brown hair shaved close in a crewcut, grey eyes, an old hurling scar puckering one eyebrow into a quizzical expression, long jaws, a dimple in the chin. I grinned at myself without thinking, then hurriedly shut my mouth when I realised I hadn't yet put my plate in.

Once upon a time I had been young and fit, able to glory in the power of my body. Now, at thirty-three, I felt about in the same shape as Christ had up on the cross. People pointed out to me how quickly athletes went to seed when they retired: my pods had already germinated and were sending out tender little shoots of fat.

I did a few half-hearted knee bends and arm jerks, then got into my clothes and went downstairs again. There was still no pitter-patter of tiny feet so I set off the house alarm and let it ring for as long as I could bear it.

Its strident call netted me Marty Lynch, the would-be millionaire. He staggered into the kitchen wearing the bottoms of a pyjamas and a vest that had faded to a fetching shade of mouse grey. He was small and rotund, sort of egg-shaped, with a domed head and short bandy legs. Normally his thatch of brown hair was neatly combed over his bald patch, but this morning it was disordered and a gleam of pink skin showed like a rock above the water line. He was also unshaven, his face having a hue slightly lighter than his vest. He looked like something the cat had dragged in to play with later.

He stopped moving when his pot belly met up with the edge of the kitchen table. He leaned on it and began to groan. I looked around for a clean mug, found one that didn't stick to my hand, put the used tea bag into it and poured in boiling water. I shoved the mug into Marty's limp paw, then went and released the venetian blind. The blast of daylight almost knocked Marty over.

'Oh God ...' he whimpered, ducking his head. He would

probably have shielded his eyes except that he needed one hand to balance the mug and the other to hold up his pyjama trousers.

Marty worked in the stock exchange, a regular nine-to-five man. On Saturday nights, however, he shed his respectable patina, decked himself out in designer clothes and went cat-on-a-hot-tin-roofing. Sundays were for sleeping it off, but obviously this weekend had provided him with a little more than he'd bargained for.

'You shouldn't have spent all that fun in one go, Marty,' I told him. 'You should've cut a strip off and kept the rest for next week.'

'Don't I know it.'

I lit the first cigarette of the day and blew smoke out the open window. I had one other lodger, Kate. In her early thirties, she was a buyer for one of the more up-market stores in the city. She appeared each morning lacquered and veneered like one of the models she helped to dress, but her room, which as landlord I felt justified in peeking into from time to time, was as sleazy as the rest of the house. Since Annie had decamped, the whole place had slowly been turning into a rubbish dump.

I moved away from the window, fished the teabag out of Marty's mug, put it in mine and poured some more water over it. The resulting liquid was as pale as a ghost's sweat. I abandoned it and lit another cigarette.

Marty got up and did a shuffling round of the table, then sat down again. He hugged himself hard. 'What time is it?' he asked me.

'Time to be out earning a crust.' I looked at my watch. 'It's almost ten o'clock.'

'Christ,' he groaned, 'another late. And I'm on my last warning.'

'I thought you were your own boss in there,' I said, showing him no sympathy.

'You're the only one who believes that, if so ...'

'Well, at least you've a steady salary.'

For a moment I brooded on the state of my own finances, which fluctuated like a hypochondriac's health: from poor to bad to pass me the sal volatile and let me go and lie down. The bank manager had had a revolving door installed in his office just for my benefit.

'Anything good coming up in the market?' I asked him, not that I would have had anything to invest if there had been.

He shrugged, then shook himself like a dog shedding water. 'The market's as quiet as an altar boy's fart,' he said. 'It's like a reach of swamp water — not a ripple.'

'Just thought I'd ask.'

I took up the mug and drank some more of the tepid tea, but it still tasted like stain remover. I gazed at Marty, slightly concerned about him. He was a survivor, one of that legion of rather inoffensive people who huffed and puffed a lot but would never do anyone any real harm. He harboured no soaring ambitions, having come to terms with what he was capable of achieving and settling for it. Acceptance was his forte, he knew he wasn't going to turn the world on its head, but neither was he going to let it get him down. Normally he would have perked up by now, his natural humour being one of wry optimism.

'Is there something bothering you?' I asked him.

'It shows, does it?'

He glanced at me, then as quickly away. In the brittle stream of light from the window, he looked sick and distraught. As I watched, his hand made chopping motions in the air as though beating out the rhythm of thoughts he was rehearsing in his mind but couldn't quite put into words.

I didn't hurry him. I lit a third cigarette, blew out the wooden match, dropped it into a convenient saucer. I leaned a hip against the white deal dresser that Annie's mother had given us as a wedding present, and did my best to think about nothing in particular.

Instead I saw Annie, in a red bandanna, a green tee shirt,

and faded jeans. She was ironing, her tongue between her teeth in concentration, tendrils of auburn hair curling in the steam. I could even hear the sibilant hiss and the slight crackle as the cloth stretched under the hot triangle of metal. It was always the same: the moment I let my attention wander in that house, she was there. It contained too many memories of her, and yet I hadn't the heart to put it up for sale.

'So, Marty,' I said, shaking off the mood, 'are you going to get it off your chest?'

'Huh?'

'Whatever's troubling you. Are you going to unburden yourself, rip it off in one go like a bread poultice?'

'Give me a minute.'

He got up and did another round of the table, the pyjamas still drooping, likewise his face. I stubbed out my cigarette and drained the last of the tea. Immediately I felt as though I'd been poisoned. The combination of it and Marty shuffling dolefully round the table did nothing for my patience level.

'You'd better get a move on,' I told him.

Obviously misunderstanding me, he broke into a trot, causing me to laugh and him to glare reproachfully at me.

'What's so funny?'

'Nothing. It's just that I've got to be downtown to kick around a few matters of state.'

'Oh, that's typical.' He shook his head. 'A few minutes to listen to a friend's troubles and you're suddenly in a hurry. Time enough to sit around and chew the fat about every topic under the sun, but when a little consideration is called for the hat is on and the feet are legging it out the door ...'

'I like that ... feet legging it ...'

'I'm serious.'

It was hard to believe him. In the get-up he was wearing even an undertaker on the end of a no payment for services rendered would have had difficulty looking serious. Still, I guessed that he really did have something on his mind and that it would help him to talk about it, so I sighed and prepared to sacrifice another few minutes in the cause of, well, friendship I supposed.

It wasn't to be. Just then the kitchen door was pushed open and Kate O'Hara came in. Thin and angular, she had high, arched eyebrows, green eyes, a good nose, a wide mouth, and a long, unfortunate jaw. Her hair this morning was jet black and it was pulled so tightly back from her face that it caused her eyes to squint. Her fingernails were long enough to slice bread.

She was wearing a severe, powder blue suit, the shoulders high and padded, the skirt coming to just above her knee. She had good legs, but the rest of her just missed out on that womanly softness that responds so well to an exploring hand. We fooled around together from time to time, but neither of us had ever been desperate enough to go the whole way.

Now she looked at Marty with distaste, winked at me, and began fussing about, looking into cupboards, rattling plates, peering into the refrigerator. In the end all she came up with was some stale bread and a lump of questionable cheese.

'It appears,' she said in her rough smoker's voice, 'that the larder's empty.'

'It took you long enough to find out,' Marty said nastily.

'Oh, we are grumpy this morning, aren't we?'

She perched herself on a stool, crossed one leg over the other and jiggled her foot about. Marty and herself did not get on. They had moved into the house on the same day and immediately had begun squabbling over which room should be whose. On a number of occasions I had tried to make the peace, but eventually gave up when I realised that they were getting a perverted kind of enjoyment out of their running battle. It seemed to put a certain amount of colour into their lives.

I knew that once she'd arrived all of Marty's attention would be given over to trying to score points off her, so I decided to take my leave of the two of them. Whatever was troubling Marty, he'd have to put it on hold until I had a chance to talk to him alone.

I left them bickering and went out into the April sunshine. The cherry tree at the gate was already beginning to shed its pinkish blossoms, and there was a drift of them under the front wheel of my ancient Renault 9. I scooped up a handful and winnowed them through the air. They reminded me of confetti, and that made me sad.

2

THE TRAFFIC WAS heavy along the Cabra Road and on down into the North Circular. I had time to admire the passing parade. At Doyle's Corner a girl in running shorts leaned against the traffic lights, waiting for them to change. She saw me watching her. I was about to give her a smile when she put up her hand and gave me a vertical middle finger.

I drove on, reflecting that there was a time in this city when people greeted one another in the mornings, and a friendly salute was accepted for what it was and not as a possible prelude to a mugging or worse. I could even remember when you could help old ladies across the road without having them turn on you and beat you about the head with their umbrellas.

In Parnell Square there was such a foul-up that I turned off into Bishop's Lane, found a spot and put up my bogus 'Doctor on Call' sign. I walked down into O'Connell Street and bought an *Irish Press*. Three soldiers and a nun had been blown up in the North and the politicians were coming out with their usual platitudes.

The other headline concerned the finding of yet another murdered tramp, the third one this month. All of them had been similarly slaughtered by having their throats cut.

I checked the sports pages. My old team, Wexford, had won another National League hurling match and were now into a semi-final against Cork. The local soccer matches seemed to be generating all the excitement of a temperance wake, while the horses I'd backed on the Saturday were still running now on the Monday.

My office is located on a side street off the main thoroughfare. The building it is housed in wouldn't be impressive even if you were blindfolded and had to rely on touch. Downstairs the Roxy video shop is tatty with posters of horror movies and teenage sex comedies. There was a quick turnover of business in this area: a striped barber's pole marking the video shop out for what it had been some months before.

To get to my little corner of heaven one turned into an entrance beside the shop, climbed up a flight of rubber-tipped steps and, hey presto, you were there. Most people who bothered to ascend the stairs soon wished that they hadn't: the surroundings are about as salubrious as a bus shelter on a wet Sunday.

I turned in and was about to go up when Batt O'Hanlon, the proprietor of the Roxy, called out to me. I paused, undecided, then stuck my head in the door. Batt was ensconced on his usual high stool behind a narrow, formica-topped counter. In his sixties, he was wiry and lean, a flinty little man who had spent most of his life as a professional soldier. When he had been within a couple of years of retirement a demonstration grenade that he'd been about to throw anticipated him and blew his arm off. Now he sat on his stool, argued with his customers, and tried to trip me up on questions about old films.

I nodded at him, then waited.

'I've got a good one for you,' he told me. 'Are you listening now?'

I nodded again, but said nothing.

'At the end of the film, *Some Like It Hot*,' he intoned, looking below the line of the counter as though reading it off something, 'what did Joe E. Brown say to Jack Lemmon?'

'Come again.'

'Lemmon was dressed as a woman and Brown had asked him to marry him. What'd he say?'

'Who?'

Batt began to look exasperated, a common expression with him. 'Are you dense or what?' he asked me. 'Maybe you're playing for time ...'

'Maybe.'

I knew the answer, but I wanted to drag it out a bit. So I stared at him with my mouth open. Time passed, and I could hear the rumble of traffic out in the street behind me. Now a look of alarm began to furrow itself onto Batt's features. Maybe he was beginning to think that I'd been struck dumb by the complexity of the question.

'So, what d'you think?' he coaxed, then: 'You don't know, do you? I've got you this time.'

'Well,' I said, shrugging, 'nobody's perfect.'

Batt recoiled, the smile on his face firming into a grimace. I had just given him the correct answer, but it took him a moment to acknowledge it. Then he dredged up a scrap of paper from below the counter and began to tear it into pieces, using his body as a fulcrum while he shredded it with the fingers of his one hand. 'Fuck you,' he muttered, but whether he meant it for me or the paper I didn't stay to find out.

My office, as I choose to term it, is really one room partitioned into two. It belonged to a dental mechanic before I inherited it, and he must have left in a hurry because quite an amount of his equipment, including rows of jars of false teeth, was still there when I moved in. There was also a kind of serving hatch beside the frosted glass door, but I decided early on that the sight of me looming up in it might not be conducive to a build-up of confidence with my clients, so I had it boarded up.

The flooring in the ante-room creaked, but I left it like that to prevent anyone from creeping up on me. There is also a line of straight-backed chairs, an ashtray with a sliding top incorporated into a free-standing glass pyramid, a low table ornamented with back copies of *In Dublin* and 'Phoenix' magazines and, on the wall, a calendar sent to me by an order of nuns that I'd had occasion to help when they had been troubled by a land speculator.

In the misguided hope of imposing my personality on the inner office, I had thrown out the departed dental mechanic's equipment, but I kept the false teeth. I went down the quays and bought a second-hand desk — real mahogany, none of that veneer stuff, with only a suspicion of woodworm round the back. It had a corrugated, pull-down top, and a lot of little pigeon holes that I could stuff with bits and pieces of paper, mostly bills.

I stuck that in a corner to give the place atmosphere, then bought a more conventional-type flat desk with glass inserts to sit behind, and a padded swivel chair to afford me fluidity of movement. A straight wooden chair served for my visitors, who only came one at a time anyway. I placed a Walter Osborne print of two little girls making a house of cards on the wall, and sat a second-hand pulldown blind that kept slipping its moorings over the room's only window.

For the first few months I was as happy as a cat in a sandbox, but then the décor and the lack of paying customers began to pall on me. It had seemed like a good idea, after losing my job as an insurance claims analyst, to set myself up as a private investigator, confidential, discreet and utterly honourable. My former occupation had given me an insight into the grey underbelly of urban life, the little scams, the laundering of stolen money, the leaning on small shopkeepers, publicans and bookies by hard-faced men in mohair suits with a line in dialogue that would make the funky gibbon sound erudite in comparison.

I considered that a good living could be made out of jollying cranks along, a bit of debt collecting using gentle persuasion rather than arm and leg breaking, bringing back errant wives — and more often errant husbands — by the scruff of the neck: it was part of my mistake to forget that it was the Irish way to keep such things within the family circle or to send for the priest. My former colleagues in the insurance business sent me the odd bit of fraud investigation; I had a couple of friends in the police detective unit who nudged me in the direction of making a few bob; but generally I sat in my office, twiddled my thumbs, and thought about life, destiny and who put the overalls in Mrs Murphy's chowder.

Eventually I began to feel punchdrunk, so I splashed out and bought a telephone answering machine, installed it, left it to fend for itself and spent most of my time either drinking with old cronies from the hurling days or at home, smoking and listening to Janis Ian tapes. When I lost my job for refusing to turn a blind eye for the umpteenth time to chicanery, Annie had accused me of being too honest; now she accused me of being too lazy, too self-indulgent, too bloody-minded to get out and find a decent occupation that befitted a thirty-three-year-old graduate in economics and English literature, who still had some of his own teeth, a full head of hair, and enough self-pity to fill a barrel and still have some left over.

I couldn't believe it, at first, when she left me. But it had been building up for a long time. I had met Annie when we were both in University, and we had outraged the moral code of the time by moving in with each other. We had been happy-go-lucky and drifting with the good times. I was just beginning to make a name for myself as a hurler: by the age of twenty I was already an Allstar. But the Wexford team of the late seventies and early eighties had never got anywhere; we could never make the breakthrough, win the provincial title and hence progress for a tilt at the All-Ireland Championship. It was our bad luck to come up against some very good Offaly and Kilkenny outfits, and in the end we lost heart and began to blame our lack of success on poor management, lack of facilities, anything in fact except ourselves.

But even though we did badly, I was still the star of the team. What about that Blaine who plays for Wexford, the newspaper headlines would trumpet, and the sporting public came to love me for my do or die efforts, my determination in adversity, my grace in losing. And to make it worse, I began to believe in my own publicity: I saw myself as a heroic figure, the personification of triumph in the midst of mediocrity. No more was I a team player, now I went it alone, never passed the ball, never looked for a team mate in a more advantageous position than myself. In the end I became so puffed up with my own importance that no one close to the team could stand me.

Annie and I were married by then, taking the plunge on a whim and living to regret it. We were both free spirits and needed the shoulder-flexing space to do our own thing in our own way. Strangely enough, with no contract of marriage between us, we had lived in closer harmony than after pledging our respective troths.

Still, when she left me, I refused to accept that she meant it. I kept ringing her up at her mother's place, asking her when she was coming back. Then, after she moved in with Harold, the body builder, I committed the unforgivable sin of laughing at her. Here was this musclebound yob, with a body like lumpy porridge, and she was letting herself be seen in public in his company. My wife! I ask you!

I waited, feeling secure in our house, with all the mementoes of our courtship, our marriage, our life together, laid out about me. But the months went by and she never did come back. Eventually I begged, I grovelled, but all to no avail. I telephoned, I sent flowers, letters, a lock of my hair — I even considered hacking off my ear in the manner of Van Gogh and sending it to her. Finally I came to a kind of fuming acknowledgement that for the immediate future she was lost to me, but I cossetted myself with the thought that in the end she would see the error of her ways and would sidle back, penitent, loving and more than eager to make amends.

In the meantime, here I was once again sitting in my office, my sensible brown brogues propped up on the desk, my jacket off, my waistcoat unbuttoned, all ready to apply my grey matter to a little sleuthing. More out of boredom than anything else I flipped on the answering machine. The first message was from my landlord reminding me that the rent was overdue. Then there was a call from my father down in Wexford to tell me, among other things, that the weekend gales had whipped a number of slates off the family house roof, but that I wasn't to worry because as soon as the winds abated he'd be up there replacing them. My father is eighty-three years old!

With the third taped message I hit pay dirt. An eminently confidential voice came on the wire and informed me that I would learn something to my advantage if I were to call, immediately if not sooner, on Mrs Joseph Walsh-Overman at the Cottage, Howth Summit. The voice went on to whisper instructions on how to get there, wished me good morning and gently clicked off.

I sat for a time listening to the hum of the machine as it ran down. Could this possibly be Mrs Joseph Walsh-Overman of the Walsh-Overman chain of department stores that was summoning me to her presence? The reclusive lady who was rumoured to be worth more than her weight in gold, and then some? Sounded like it.

I got up, buttoned my waistcoat, put on my jacket and looked around for my hat. What hat? I never wore a hat. Cautioning myself not to get too excited, I half ran, half fell down the stairs, waved to Batt and started up O'Connell Street at a rate of knots. If I could have known what was in store for me, I'd have headed off equally snappily in the opposite direction.

3

THE COTTAGE MAY have been just that, a cottage, once upon a time, but over the years it had grown up and now it was almost a fully fledged castle. It had battlements and turrets and those narrow leaded windows that you have to stand sideways to look out of — all that was missing was the moat, but the wide sweep of gravel that led up to it and encircled it may have fulfilled that function in the days when visitors were less well disposed towards its inhabitants than I was.

The extensive grounds that I drove through to get to it had hinted at no ordinary two up, two down. There was an artificial lake, a par three golf course, and enough shrubs and bushes to give a gardening enthusiast an orgasm.

The lawns in front of the house were the colour green that you see in brochures advertising Ireland as the Emerald Isle, and they were as smooth and level as snooker tables. A fountain, presided over by a stone lady with a rather knowing expression on her face, squirted parabolas of iridescence into the April sunlight, and a few courting birds flew about, whistling at one another and generally being cheeky.

I parked my 1980 Renault 9 beside a brand new, maroon BMW, on the side away from the house so that no-one looking out would see it. I straightened my tie, sucked in my belly and wondered whether it might seem just a little too subservient if I were to go up to the door on my knees. The view from where I was standing was spectacular, the horseshoe of Dublin Bay clothed in about the right amount of smoky sunlight, a couple of toy-like ships way out on the wrinkled sea, nearer to hand the red and white striped Peggy's Leg of the Bailey Lighthouse.

Tearing myself away from all that splendour, I climbed the

steps and leaned on the bell. Cultivated ivy grew thickly against the face of the building, and I ripped off one of the veined leaves and rubbed it between my fingers. I was smelling its tattered remnants when the door opened and a character in a black jacket with velvet collar and lapels, a white shirt, bow tie, dark trousers with a shiny stripe down the sides and patent leather shoes, stood looking out at me disdainfully.

He was about my age, early thirties, but fitter and more muscular. His thin, high cheek-boned face was prevented from being more regular by a large fleshy nose, and he had very red lips that were made to look even more so by the dead white pallor of his skin. It was his hair that caught the attention first, though: it was pale and wispy and stitched like a small bush of fibreglass onto his bony skull as though to keep it warm. I'd have considered him to be an albino except for his eyes, which were blue and no way pinkish. In spite of the twee way he was dressed I had the feeling that he could be a tough cookie if provoked.

I put the hand holding the ivy leaf behind my back and straightened up to my full six foot two. He didn't seem impressed. 'You were seeking?' he inquired, in the same voice he'd used on my telephone answering machine and, not for the first time, I saw a lip curl.

'An audience, I suppose,' I said. 'My name's Blaine. John Blaine, private investigator. I was summoned.'

'Ah.'

He looked me up and down, in no hurry, taking in my brogues, my slightly rumpled three piece beige suit, my milk chocolate coloured shirt and matching tie. He might have been registering me and tucking me away for future reference.

'You like?' I asked him. 'If you wind the key I'll do a jig and sing Mother Macree in A flat ...'

He ignored that one, although plainly not liking it, and stood aside to let me in. The entrance hall was not quite big enough to bivouac an army, but a troop of boy scouts would have been quite comfortable in it. The floor was highly polished parquet, the rugs Arabian, the furniture antique, and the cost of the tapestries on the walls would have fed the starving people in Somalia for a month. At the back, an imposing stairway rose towards the higher regions, and the vault of the ceiling was fluted and moulded to a theme of nymphs and shepherds being coy with one another.

Red Lips turned and walked away from me and, presuming I was meant to follow, I tip-toed along in his wake. He led me to a massive oak door which yielded smoothly to his shoulder and slid inwards as though on castors.

The room I came into was high ceilinged, dimly lit, and as ornately and impersonally furnished as a room in a show house. It had the slightly musty air about it of ancient evenings, as though at some stage it had become paralysed in the past. It didn't surprise me too much to note that the gloom engendered by the drawn curtains was relieved, not by electric light, but by standing oil lamps. They cast a subdued, golden glow that was reflected in surfaces, the crystals of the huge chandelier, the glass fronted bookcases, the porcelain figures nestling in every nook and cranny.

Although the sun was shining outside and it had become quite warm, a lively little coal fire was burning away in the grate. Sitting close to it in a brocaded armchair was an old lady with beautifully coiffured hair and a lived-in face that was as seamed and fissured as the bottom of a well in the dry season. As I came towards her, she looked at me out of eyes that belied the rest of her: they were as shiny as agate stones and twice as lively.

'The private investigator you requested, madame,' the character in the major domo's outfit intoned, extending his arm in my direction as though to say, 'Take it away, Ramsbottom.'

I nodded, then feeling my response to be rather inadequate I said, 'Mrs Joseph Walsh-Overman, I presume?'

'You know me?'

Her voice was like the wind rippling over autumn leaves, a dry rattle haunted by the shades of too many years.

'I know of you,' I said. 'Who doesn't, on this small island?'

'Oh.' She sounded vaguely pleased. 'It's nice not to be forgotten. It's so long now since I played a part ... All those able young people who look after my interests ... they are so ...'

'Capable?'

'Yes. I find it rather sobering. When I was their age I was more interested in dancing and music and young men ...'

'You could probably afford to be.'

Beside me Red Lips suddenly cleared his throat. 'Will there be anything further?' he asked, putting just the correct amount of disinterested insolence into his tone. We both turned to look at him.

'No, I'm quite comfortable, Saunders,' Mrs Walsh-Overman answered him. She transferred her gaze to me. 'Perhaps Mr Blaine would like something? Tea? Coffee? A drink?'

'Some tea, I think. And Saunders,' — stopping him dead in his tracks — 'I like it weak, with no sugar and just a suspicion of milk.'

He let that one pass too, but the set of his shoulders and the bunching of his neck muscles told me that I was well on the way to ruining a beautiful friendship before it had even started.

At Mrs Walsh-Overman's invitation I sat down on a straight-backed, handsomely carved chair that had been placed facing her. Her hands were gnarled and stiffened by arthritis, and she was endeavouring to hide the condition by wearing black lace gloves. She was dressed in the fashion of maybe fifty years ago, long black taffeta gown and a little bonnet like a maid's cap. If it were not for the darting eyes she might have been cast in wax, a Grandma Moses, emblematic of all our yesterdays.

I thought about a cigarette, but stifled the longing. It would be as out of place as breaking wind or spitting in the fire. I might be a down-at-heel, not too successful private investigator, but I knew my place, and that place right now was sitting looking at one of the richest women I was ever likely to meet.

Along with her husband, the late Joe Overman, she had built up a chain of cut price department stores that was now tentacled countrywide. Joe had provided the hard-headed Jewish business acumen, she had been the one with the initial capital and the brains. Together they made a perfect team and, when Joe died — popping off rather noisily, it was said, when a chicken bone got stuck in his throat — she had continued as usual as though still in touch with him by celestial messenger.

'I suppose we should get down to business,' she now said, in that dry murmur of a voice. 'I want you to find my eldest boy for me.'

'Boy?'

'My son. I suppose it is rather a misnomer to call him a boy. He must be well on in years by now — let me see, what would he be? I think ... why, fifty at least.'

'A fine age,' I agreed.

'I have two sons,' she went on, 'and they've both been a great disappointment to me. Redmond was always a rebel, taking stances against this and that. For years he refused to speak anything except the Irish language. Wore homespuns and a kilt. Then marrying that very common woman just to spite his father and myself.'

'Yes,' I encouraged her.

'And then Charles. Well, you know what Charles is like,' she said, giving me her basilisk stare. I waited for her to elaborate, but she didn't.

'Which one of them do you want me to find?' I asked her.

'Redmond, of course. Charles is not missing too, is he?'

'I've no idea.'

'Catch him leaving his mother's coat tails,' she said waspishly. 'He knows which side his bread is buttered on. Of course he can be very attentive when he wants to be. Usually heralds one of those nasty messes he keeps getting into.'

'Who plays Laurel to his Hardy?'

'I beg your pardon?'

'A comedy duo on the silver screen. One of them was

always getting the other into fine messes.'

'I seem to have heard of them ...'

At that moment Red Lips Saunders came in with the tea, and we both waited while he fussed about distributing cups and saucers and serviettes. There were some dainty little triangular sandwiches to titillate the palate, and some slices of tipsy cake that looked as if they were suffering from a hang-over. Not exactly a feast fit for a king, but the old lady appeared to take it as normal. At her age food was probably as important as a ten-mile run.

Saunders hovered for a moment or two, maybe watching to see that I didn't pocket the family silver, then he left as silently as he had entered. I drank some tea and ate a sandwich. Just as I thought: chicken paste. I also thought about the tipsy cake, but came to no conclusion about it one way or the other.

'Your son ... ah, Redmond ...' I looked at Mrs Walsh-Overman. 'When did you last see him?'

She stopped fiddling with her sandwich and gazed back at me. 'In his true persona of my son, hardly ever. Certainly not since he was a young man. I've seen him in various guises over the years. He always had great difficulty in sorting out his real role in life. I never understood him. I doubt he understood himself.'

There was a finely carved escritoire beside her chair, and she pulled out a drawer and extracted a folder done up in red ribbon. 'I've got all the information here,' she explained, handing the slim package to me.

'And a photograph?'

'Yes.'

She took a photograph from where it had been stuck down beside her in the chair and handed it over. It was a two by four, in colour, of a dumpy guy in a skirt. He was also wearing a hat with a feather and a kind of tartan sash held together on his shoulder by a gold pin done in Celtic design. It was a three-quarter shot, and I could see his knees sticking out under the skirt. His face was shadowed by the hat, but he had Joe

Overman's prominent snout, a feature that had always shown itself off to great effect in the many publicity photographs of him that I'd seen.

I slid the photo into the folder. 'I'll read this of course,' I told the old lady, 'but a person comes more alive when he or she is talked about. Give me some insight into how Redmond thinks, what his habits are, the places he might be inclined to frequent.'

Mrs Walsh-Overman took a tiny lace handkerchief from her sleeve and dabbed at her face with it, but it was more playing for time to collect her thoughts than any attempt at remedial action: the years had scored her features too deeply for that. Eventually she said, 'I suppose Joe and I were partly to blame, we never seemed to have the time to devote to our children. They were shifted around from place to place. And then there was the tragedy of my daughter's death ...'

She paused, and once more I waited for her to elaborate, but with the same result as before. 'The pursuit of money, Mr Blaine,' she went on, 'can be a terrible thing. Neither Joe nor myself ever wanted anything except to possess it. It was like a contest between us, to make more and more money; and the more we made, the more we sought. He was more like a business partner than a husband, and in the end desire between us came in blocks of pound notes.'

She did some more dabbing with the handkerchief, this time at her eyes, but if there were tears there they weren't ones of sentiment: 'I'm telling you this so that you will have some feeling for my son, and for his predicament. Redmond had an inquiring mind, unlike Charles, whom I sometimes think has no intelligence whatever. It was Redmond's Garden of Gethsemane that he postulated the possibility of happiness without ever being able to realise it. But it wasn't money that was going to bring that happiness about. He had no time for the trappings of wealth, and we had very little else to offer him. That's one of the reasons he took up with that awful woman, I suppose.'

'You keep referring to that awful woman, Mrs Walsh-Overman, but you don't say any more about her.'

'What else is there to say?'

I spread my hands. 'I don't know. But if you could tell me something about her ..?'

This time the eyes were as hard as tungsten. 'I'd prefer not to talk about that side of things,' she said. 'You'll find it all there in the dossier, the whole muddied story.'

I looked down at it. 'Okay,' I said, 'but maybe you'll tell me the last occasion you saw Redmond.'

'He came to his father's memorial service. He was dressed, if I could call it that, like a tramp. In cast-off clothes. As far as I could see he came to solicit money from the mourners ...'

'And that was when?'

'Five years ago? Maybe more ...'

I gazed at her, then I asked: 'Why d'you want to find him now, Mrs Walsh-Overman? You've let a lot of time go by.'

There was a longer pause this time before she answered: 'I'm eighty-seven years old, Mr Blaine. I look out at the trees and I see them budding into leaf, and I wonder if I'll live to see those leaves wither and fall. In the mornings when I awake I lie with my eyes closed and wait for pain, my constant companion, to abate. More and more I find the days distasteful. I'm a very wealthy old woman, but everything about me is turning into ashes. I have no friends, merely acquaintances. My younger son, Charles, has always been lost to me. My daughter died young. Is it any wonder that I wish to see Redmond one more time before I die?'

I took out a cigarette and put it in my mouth without lighting it. Like her voice, she herself was becoming more insubstantial by the minute. The heat from the fire was oppressive, the furniture dark and brooding, the porcelain figures garish and almost threatening. The house was like a mausoleum, a cold, echoing vault devoid of human sounds. No matter how many fires were lit, an impersonal chill would always permeate the place. I wondered if it had ever rung to the sounds of children's laughter, if it had ever been encompassed by the warmth of family love.

'So, Mr Blaine,' Mrs Walsh-Overman said, 'I presume you will take on this commission of finding my son. I want the affair handled with tact and finesse. You are that kind of person?'

'Indubitably,' I assured her.

'And your charge?'

'Fifty pounds a day, plus expenses.'

'The expenses will be kept within reason?'

I eyed her warily: the hardness wasn't merely in the flintiness of her gaze. And that set me to wondering at this sudden longing of hers to reacquaint herself with her long lost, prodigal son. Tramps were in the news at the moment, and their mortality rate wasn't as high as a Corgi's belly button. Maybe more than his mother was looking for Redmond Walsh-Overman.

Answering her about the expenses I said, 'Sometimes I use a bicycle to get about. And I tend to regurgitate breakfast instead of buying lunch.'

She looked at me grimly, her mouth just another line in the wrinkled face. 'There is no need to be impertinent,' she said. 'There are other investigators in the Yellow Pages, you know.'

'I'm the best, though,' I said, lying between my teeth. 'There's a long list of satisfied clients waiting to testify as much.'

This seemed to satisfy her, for she took out a sheaf of new fifty pound notes from the drawer of the escritoire and peeled off four. She considered for a moment, and I thought she was going to put them back. Then she unshackled two more and handed the six of them to me. 'You've three hundred pounds there,' she told me.

'I'll take your word for it,' I said, barely refraining from counting them in front of her.

Next she took out a small, leather-bound notebook and made me sign a receipt. If she had asked for my birth and baptismal certificate I wouldn't have been in the least surprised. No flies on this old lady, even if she did consider herself to be teetering on the edge of the grave.

'You'll report to me when?'

'I'll come out and see you on Wednesday evening,' I told her. 'Maybe sooner, if anything crops up. I don't see any difficulty in finding Redmond. When I do, I'll talk to him. Then I'll come out and see how you want it handled.'

That seemed to be about it, so I put the cigarette back in my mouth and jiggled it up and down again. Mrs Walsh-Overman closed her eyes and appeared to go into a trance.

But she must have pushed a bell or signalled to Saunders in some fashion, for he suddenly made another of his silent entries, gestured towards the door, and I followed him out. Behind us either the fire or the old lady gave a satisfied little hiccup.

4

WHEN I GOT outside the only thing that had changed was that the ships were a little further out towards the horizon. The sun was still shining, the birds were still mating, the lady in the fountain still had the supercilious expression on her face.

I had walked down the first flight of steps when I heard Saunders behind me call, 'Hey you ...'

I turned and looked up at him. 'Are you addressing me?' I asked him, 'or are you practising for the next hog calling contest?'

'There's a difference?'

'Ha,' I said, but I knew I'd walked straight into that one.

We stared at one another, then I took out a wooden match, ran it along the stone balustrade and lit my cigarette. The smoke was very blue in the still air. Saunders walked down and stood about a foot away from me. We were the same height, give or take a centimetre, so eye contact was on the level. I wondered how it was that two people could take such a dislike to one another so quickly. Normally it took me some little time to form judgements, but with Saunders antipathy was instantaneous.

'Who recommended me to her?' I asked him. 'Was it you?'

Taking his time about answering, he pursed his red lips into a grin that was meant to annoy. It did. 'Yeah,' he said eventually. 'I stuck a pin in the Yellow Pages and you fell out. What's it matter? A job's a job.'

'You don't think I can pick and choose?'

'Frankly, no.'

I shuffled my feet a little, and something flickered in his eyes. He would have liked me to take a poke at him. Instead I said, 'Tell me, is that hair your own? It looks like a bird's nest that fell out of a tree.'

Again the muscles bunched along his jaw line. I could see the effort it took him to remain nonchalant, but he managed it. 'Don't push your luck, fella,' he counselled me. Then he took a different tack: 'The money's good, isn't it? You could rummage around in a few dustbins, then come back and tell her you can't find him.'

'You think I can't?'

'Can't what?'

'Find him?'

'Maybe you can, and maybe you can't. What would you say if I told you I didn't want you to find him?'

'I'd tell you she's paying me, so she calls the tune.'

I could see him making up his mind to be nice to me — it was as plain as the nose on his face, and that was pretty plain. He said, 'You know, she's an old lady. She's had a lot of unhappiness in her life. And most of it was caused by her family.'

'So?'

'It wouldn't do any good for her to see him again — Redmond, I mean. It'd just cause her more grief and pain.'

I gazed at him thoughtfully. The humanitarian role didn't sit right, so I decided to annoy him a little. 'So what're you setting yourself up as?' I asked him. 'The old family retainer? Jeeves you're not ...'

'No?'

'Nope. That magician's suit you're wearing doesn't fool me. You're a minder, a hard man. You've been hired to throw a scare into unwelcome callers, and maybe to dunk cat burglars and the like in the shit. That's the kind of peace of mind you owe the old lady, not keeping her from her nearest and dearest.'

Mildly he said, 'You don't work in a place for over ten years without forming some attachments. I can see the kind of anguish it causes her to have a prick like Charles about the place ...'

'Yeah, and that's another thing. What's it about this Charles that makes everyone's nose wrinkle at the mention of his name? Halitosis? BO? Flashing at the dinner table?'

Saunders shrugged. 'You've a treat in store for you. Wait'll you meet him.'

'My knees are all a'tremble ...'

We both took a breather. I pulled on my cigarette, Saunders tried to outstare me. Then he made one more supreme effort to be nice, 'Look, I'm asking you politely to take the money, buy yourself something, and come back in a few days and tell her you had no luck in finding Redmond. That's not asking too much, is it?'

'It's asking more than you're going to get.'

He stood back a little, perhaps to get me in longshot. This time I could see it dawning on him that maybe he'd misjudged me, that I wasn't going to be the pushover he'd thought. He tapped me on the upper arm, not hard but not easy either. 'Come on,' he said, 'what's the matter with you? She's happy knowing you're looking. You've told me you've other jobs to occupy you ... What d'you say?'

I put my head back and looked at him through half-closed eyes. 'I can't help thinking,' I told him, 'that there's more here than meets the eye. I may be wrong, but my impression of you is that you wouldn't give a fiddler's fuck if the old lady fell into a vat of acid. All this talk about indulging her by having me pretend to look for her son is a crock of horseshit. You come on, and tell me the real reason you don't want Redmond found.'

This time I had really got to him. He sucked his teeth. He rolled his eyes. He twitched his shoulders. The only part of him that didn't move was the artificial thatch on his head. It was like watching a volcano trying to make up its mind whether to erupt or not.

'Cat got your tongue?' I asked him. 'If you don't want to say it out loud, you can whisper it into my pearly ear.'

The look he gave me suggested he'd like to bite my pearly

ear right off my head. 'I'll make it worth your while,' he said, reluctantly reaching into his breast pocket.

'Save it,' I said airily. 'Don't you know there's a vow of trust between a PI and his client that is sacred? Where d'you think I'd be if I went around betraying the people who hire me?'

'Up shit's creek without a paddle?'

'Got it in one.'

He stepped in closer to me. I could smell his aftershave, and I marvelled again at the dead white pallor of his skin. Was he wearing some kind of face powder? A closet Bela Lugosi admirer, maybe? Yet there was an aura of menace about him that went deeper than mere bluster. I wouldn't like to meet him in a dark alley around the midnight hour.

Now, through gritted teeth, he said, 'Just two minutes alone with you in a confined space ... Just two minutes, that's all I wish.'

As we were standing out in the open, sunlit and in plain view, I felt that it was safe enough to grin at him. 'Well, you know what they say,' I told him: 'Wish in one hand and piss in the other and see which'll fill the fastest.'

We eyeballed one another for a little while longer, but we both knew that there was nothing to be gained from it. Neither of us was about to budge: me on agreeing not to look for Redmond, he on the real reason he didn't want him found. It was stalemate, a stand-off, an irresistible force and an immovable object. The only thing left would have been for me to ask him to dance, but then we'd have had the problem of deciding who would lead.

Finally he stepped away. He didn't like it, but he moved back and allowed me to do the same. 'Be seeing you,' he said quietly, but his eyes held a look that'd make a barking dog turn tail and run.

I waved, and went down the steps without looking back. The Renault, in the shade of the BMW, was cool inside, but I was sweating and I ran the window down. I turned the car, the wheels crunching in the gravel of the drive. On the par three golf course a fat guy in a bright shirt and plus fours was leaning on a golf club and watching me as I drove by. Wondering if it was the mysterious Charles, I gave him a wave. He didn't wave back.

5

I DROVE CAREFULLY down the switchbacks from Howth Summit, enjoying the warmth of the sun and the nice crinkly feel of Mrs Walsh-Overman's bank-notes in my breast pocket. The sky was calm and blue, although out towards Bray Head a little cloudmass was building up. The city itself bled back from the bay into the foothills of the Dublin Mountains, a gauze of smoke-related smog trailing over it like an attempt at a disguise.

I hummed a little tune as I motored along, in by Sutton and then on to the Clontarf Road. Even the stench from the muck-filled basin, where the tide was out, didn't impinge on my sense of well being. At the pedestrian crossing at Vernon Avenue, a tiny girl in a bright dress led an old man across the road. The sight bolstered my faith in human nature: maybe when I got back to the office my landlord would have left a vase of flowers instead of a final demand for his rent.

There was a note stuck under the door of the inner office: it was another film question from Batt O'Hanlon and read: 'At the end of the film *Casablanca* what did Claude Raines throw into the wastepaper basket to show his contempt for the figure-head French government?' I thought about it, then I wrote 'A bottle of Vichy water' on the back of the note. I went down the stairs, but Batt had closed for lunch, so I pushed it in under his door.

As I was back out on the street again I decided I might as well get some food myself. Mrs Walsh-Overman's postage stamp sandwiches had merely tickled my fancy.

Over in Middle Abbey Street there's a pub called 'Destry's', but *habitués* know it more popularly as 'The Septic Tank'. Easy to see why. A huge, barn-like building with a minimum of furnishings, the smell of spilled beer, stale cigarette smoke and mouldy air catches you by the throat as soon as you enter and causes your eyes to water.

It does a cheap line in pub grub, however, and if you can hold your breath long enough to get it into you the after effects are slightly less than fatal. I went over there, saluted Batt, who was stuck in a corner with a group of degenerates known as 'The Geriatrics Club', and ordered Shepherd's Pie and a mug of coffee.

While waiting for my food to arrive I selected my also-rans for the afternoon's race meeting and asked Cedric, the barman, to put the money on for me. An accommodating chap, old Cedric. He had a wooden leg that he sometimes allowed customers to throw darts into in order to astound non-regulars. He also kept a piranha fish in a large, brightly lit tank, and it was the highlight of the evening when Cedric dropped in a live goldfish to be gobbled up by the toothy predator.

I finished my food and swapped some chat with him, and let an hour drift away. I was in no particular hurry to read Mrs Walsh-Overman's file. I had become so used to having nothing to do that the thought of bestirring myself was an ordeal. Inactivity can get to you, the days and the weeks floating like bits of paper down a stream, and you find yourself not caring much about anything. What advantage has one day got over another? You can sit in a room, look at the walls and bite your nails. Or you can run out onto the green sward of Croke Park on All-Ireland Final day before eighty thousand chanting spectators and spend the next hour making a fool of yourself. But time drags you through it ... you can't get away from it, time ...

Before I bored myself to death with such dreary philosophising, I got up, went over to the phone and rang Annie. When she picked up the receiver, I pinched my nose between two fingers and said, 'Hellew? Is that the lady who advertised for sale the genuine moving statue?'

'What?'

'Did you hear the one about the statue of the Virgin Mary that was found in bits up on Constitution Hill? She was knocked down crossing the road.'

There was a pause, then: 'Blaine? Is that you?'

'No, it's you. Aren't you Mrs Blaine?'

'Ex.'

'Ex? What d'you mean ex?'

'Ex marks the spot and you're on it. What about that wife support money you owe me?'

'You've just told me you're my ex-wife. Make up your mind, which is it to be?'

'You're bored again, aren't you? You only think of me when you're bored. I said to Vic, "There's the phone, I bet it's him, bored out of his twist again ...".'

'Who's Vic?'

'Victoria, one of the girls in the office. My co-worker. Oh heavens above, I've mentioned that terrible four letter word that sends you into a frenzy: work ...'

'Ha, very funny. Who's she named after, the queen or the station? Why couldn't she have chosen a typical Irish name like Sylvia or Jacinta?'

'Because she's not Irish. She's English — Liverpool English.'

'Well, we won't hold that against her.'

There was a silence, and we both listened to the wind whistling down the wires. 'How's Uther Pendragon?' I asked her, when the pause was beginning to tickle my ear.

'Don't call him that. His name's Harold.'

'Childe Harold to the gym did go ... Has a Byronic ring to it, don't you think? Has he got you pumping iron yet?'

'Not yet.'

'I must drop around for a rub down.'

'Harold'd be glad to give you a massage. He does a very good line in massages.'

'Well, you should know.'

I thought about Harold running up and down her back with his tippy-toe fingers and my blood began to boil. Some day soon I'd have to get out my hurley stick and go over and pay Harold a visit.

We were drifting into another pregnant pause, but Annie took up the slack by asking me: 'So how's the detective business? Go down any mean streets lately?'

'Well, I could tell you about the whalebone corset caper, but it turned out to be a suicide: fat woman squeezed herself to death. And then there was the case of the constipated Cardinal who blew himself up in church ...' I let the wire hum for a minute, then I said, 'Annie, I miss you ... God, how I miss you ...'

Immediately her voice became guarded: 'Now don't go starting that up again ...'

'You're an itch that I can't scratch,' I told her. 'You know that spot on your back that you can't ever seem to reach? High up between the shoulder blades ..?'

'That's charming. I'm an itch now, am I?'

'Come on, I'll bet you feel an old tingle yourself. And when you wake up in the dog hours of the night? Don't you remember ..?'

'I warn you, I'm going to hang up.'

'You wouldn't dare. Not with me telling you how much I love you ...'

'Go stick it in your left ear.'

And she did hang up on me, just like she said. I looked at the receiver in my hand, then at Cedric who was a little way down the bar. Slowly, ever so slowly, he shook his head warningly from side to side. He was remembering the last time, when he'd had to get the phone repaired after I'd torn it out of the wall in temper. Then, if my recollection was correct, she'd told me to stick it in my right ear.

I had a quick Bushmills to deaden the taste of unrequited love, collected my betting slips and went back to the office. Batt was back in position behind his counter, but I hunched down low and did a Quasimodo up the stairs. The outer office was empty, the rows of chairs silently keeping guard over absolutely nothing at all. I unlocked the inner sanctum and sat down behind my neatly functional desk.

Placed exactly in the centre of it was Mrs Walsh-Overman's file, so I picked it up and opened it. The first thing to greet my eye was the photograph of Redmond in his kilt. It didn't do anything more for me this time than when I'd originally seen it, so I put it to one side. I read the two neatly typed sheets of A4 that came with it. I learned Redmond's date of birth, where he had been baptised, where he made his first communion, his confirmation, and I was also appraised of the fact that the little finger of his left hand was missing. Ah, a distinguishing feature ...

I read on. His marriage to a Bernadette Anne Mordaunt was mentioned, and there were a few derogatory comments to the effect that Bernadette was a fortune hunter and that she'd been more intent on coming to grips with Redmond's fortune than with Redmond himself.

There was a second photograph, this time of the two of them on their wedding day. Neither of them looked too happy. From what I could make out, Bernadette was a well padded blonde, with lazy eyes, bee-stung lips and a little snub nose that just cried out to be kissed. She looked voluptuous, but also possibly the type who would put on weight at the mere sight of a cream cake.

A list of people that Redmond had known over the years followed, along with a list of addresses. The resumé ended with the rather cryptic note that he had dropped out of sight some five years before and it was believed that he had joined the community of travelling people.

I sat there, idly thinking about this rather sketchy and impersonal account of one man's life. It had probably been dictated by his mother, with Saunders doing the typing — although he didn't look like the typing type. I read it again, trying to get beneath the surface a little and understand what Redmond was really like. There wasn't much to go on. Had he had many happy days? I wondered. I remember his mother mentioning a daughter, Redmond's sister, and some tragedy connected with her. There was no mention of it in the file.

I poked his photograph towards me and gazed at it. Nothing to help me there in that blank-eyed stare. He might have been getting ready to do a Highland sword dance and wondering whether he should count his toes before or after performing.

I was still sitting there, becoming cross-eyed from looking at his likeness, when the floor in the outer office creaked and the man himself peered in around the door at me. I blinked, thinking I was having an hallucination, but no, he was still there. He came in and stood in front of the desk and fidgeted. It wasn't Redmond, of course, I should have such luck. But the man in front of me possessed a definite likeness to him. Without any great effort on my part, I realised who he must be. I'd seen him that morning on the par three golf course as I'd left the estate in Howth. It was the fat guy, the brother, Charles.

I nodded and waved at the customer's chair and said, 'Take the weight off your feet. Have a pew.'

He hesitated, critically eyeing the chair. Then he took a silk handkerchief out of his top pocket and spread it on the seat before sitting down on it. He put his two plumb knees together and rested his closed hands, with thumbs parallelled, on them.

He had the arch, crimped look of the settled gay, the type who has given up all pretence at being one of the boys and has come out of the closet with banners waving. Now I knew what Mrs Walsh-Overman had meant when she'd said, 'Well, you know what Charles is like.' Still, it takes all sorts, and far be it from me to condemn him on that score.

In appearance he looked a little like a two minute egg: he was all soft and jiggly and had the kind of unhealthy, translucent skin that if you put your hand against it and pressed you'd expect to leave finger marks. His features, eyes, nose, mouth, were all too tiny for the rising moon expanse of face, and his body generally had the folded-in, rubbery look of the Michelin Man.

All that blubber was encased in what had once been an

immaculately tailored white Armani suit, but was now as creased as an unmade bed, a crimson shirt, a slash of whey coloured tie, and enough jewellery to make a high society matron get down on her knees and drool. To complete the ensemble he carried a red and black malacca cane tied to his left wrist by a gold cord. He looked like an over-weight action painter whose enthusiasm had got the better of him.

'You are Mr Blaine?' he asked me, in a high, fluting voice that sounded as if his string vest was throttling him. Then, in diminuendo, he gave three dainty coughs.

'That's what it says on my passport,' I told him.

'Yes, quite.' He shifted his bulk and the chair squeaked ominously. 'I have a little proposition to put to you,' he went on, 'one that entails no effort whatsoever on your part, but that can lead to quite a satisfactory amount of financial reward.'

'You want me to drop my hat on the floor and pick it up without turning my back to the wall?'

'I beg your pardon!'

I looked at him, then I lit that old standby, a cigarette, and blew smoke across the desk at him. He wrinkled his pert little nose and coughed again, this time discreetly and behind a chubby hand. 'Don't worry about it,' I told him. 'It goes with the persona. Everyone expects a private investigator to be quick with the one liners. What is it you want me to do?'

'Perhaps I should tell you who I am ..?'

'No need for that, Mr Walsh-Overman,' I interrupted, to impress him. He looked about as impressed as a tax inspector listening to a hard luck story.

'Yes, well, I know you've been hired to find my brother, Redmond. Isn't that so?'

'You said it.'

'But you were out speaking to my mother this morning.'

'I could've been looking over the property with a view to buying it.'

He gazed about him. 'You don't look to me as if you've enough money to buy a tent.'

'But that's why you're here, isn't it?' I encouraged him. 'To help out with my financial fluidity?'

'Providing we can come to an understanding, yes, certainly. My brother has caused my mother nothing but heartache. Did you know he was partly responsible for my sister's drowning? No, I can see you didn't. Then again he was forever making liaisons with odd people. He espoused republican causes. And he married that common woman ...'

'Yes, good old Bernadette. I know about her. I've been briefed. He also liked to sport a kilt, and the little finger on his left hand is missing. About the only thing I don't know is which side he dresses on.'

'Is that relevant?'

'It is if he's wearing another man's trousers.'

This got some reaction and he blinked. But it was obvious that my attempts at humour were lost on him. 'This is a ridiculous conversation,' he chided me. 'What I've come here to find out is if you've discovered his whereabouts.'

'I might have.'

We stared at one another, both of us doing our best to look inscrutable. This was the second person in a matter of hours who was seeking to dissuade me from something that my natural inertia would most probably have prevented me from doing anyway. If they had enough sense to go away and leave me alone, I'd most likely have messed about for a day or two and then gone and told Mrs Walsh-Overman that her son had done as good a disappearing act as Ambrose Bierce when he walked into the Mexican desert and forgot to come back. By coming on to me in this fashion they were prickling my curiosity into life and causing me to wonder at their motives.

'Now,' Charles said, as though about to seal a bargain, 'I'm prepared to offer you a tidy sum if you'll tell me where my brother is, and if you'll then forget everything you know about my family. I'll deal with this situation as I deem fit, and you'll be the richer by the sum I'm about to mention, plus whatever my mother paid you to look into the matter in the first place.

How does that sound?'

'Like music to my ears,' I conceded. 'But I can't help asking myself why you don't want me to tell your mother when I find Redmond. All she wants is to see him one more time before she takes off for that great department store in the sky. Why deny her that?'

Petulantly Charles blew some air through his nose. 'Haven't I made it plain to you,' he said, 'that seeing my brother again would only upset Mumsie, maybe even make her angry? He's always had that effect on her.'

'Then why does she want to see him?'

'Who knows?' He waved his hands in the air and for a moment I thought he was going to hit me with his malacca cane. 'She's an old woman, her brain cells are running down. She doesn't know what's best for her anymore.'

'And you do?'

'Of course.'

I pretended to think about it, chewing on a fingernail, my brow furrowed. I felt like telling him to buzz off, but the thought of making some extra money was also very appealing. 'Your hiring me would be in direct conflict with my earlier agreement with your mother,' I said. 'You must see that?' I waited while he pondered that one. 'Now, on the other hand,' I went on, 'if you wish to put me on a small retainer to inform you, slightly in advance of telling ... ah ... Mumsie, of your brother's whereabouts, when and if I find him, then that's entirely your prerogative.'

He stared at me, a crafty expression struggling with his normal one of bland perplexity. Neither of them won out. He closed his mouth, then opened it again, breathed deeply, and said, 'You're telling me that at this moment in time you don't know where my brother is?'

'Only a temporary state of affairs,' I assured him. 'I've a number of operatives working on it as of now, and I'm expecting a report at any moment.'

He looked around the office, at the paint peeling walls, the mottled ceiling, the jars of false teeth.

'How many operatives?'

'Well, let's see now. There's Joe on the organ, Patsy on the accordion, Jackie on the guitar, and Jamie on the nose flute. How many does that make?'

That took a while to sink in, then: 'You're having me on,' he said.

I threw my hands in the air in mock supplication. 'As God is my judge ... Look, I'll tell you what I'll do. You give me, say, fifty pounds, and a number where I can reach you, and as soon as I turn up anything I'll let you know. Could I be fairer than that?'

A suspicious look was now added to the others jockeying for position on his platter puss. 'You'll give me a receipt?' he asked, showing a little of his mother's business acumen.

'Certainly.'

I took a receipt book out of the desk drawer, wrote one for the sum of fifty pounds, signed it George Bernard Shaw, folded it and handed it over. He took it without looking at it and put it in an inside pocket.

Suddenly he was all business, as he gave me the money in five pound notes, the telephone number in hushed tones, and an instruction not to call too late at night with a simper.

That seemed to be that. He stood up, folded his handkerchief and replaced it in his top pocket. He nodded, looked around the office one more time, sneered, and went out.

I sat for a time smelling his perfume, then I opened my secret bottom drawer and took out the bottle of Bushmills I kept there for medicinal purposes. Optimistically noting that it was half full rather than half empty, I put it to my head and tossed one back. It sloshed around my teeth, bounced off the back of my throat, and coursed south with a whoop and a holler. God bless whoever invented whisky.

I thought about another one, but decided against it. It was time to be out and about on Mumsie's business. My only regret, as I went down the stairs, was that I hadn't taken Red Lips Saunders' money as well.

6

NUMBER 19A, Gardinia Place, the last known address, according to my file, of Mrs Bernadette Walsh-Overman, nee Mordaunt, was a bed and breakfast establishment, a terraced, Georgian house like its neighbours, but even more run down, with shredded lace curtains dimly visible behind dirty windows, and a facade that got its last lick of paint about the time that Michael Collins was cycling past on his way up to Vaughan's Hotel. I looked down into the basement before climbing the three steps up to the entrance and was immediately sorry that I had: the least offensive object down there was a dead cat.

The front door had been given many a kick in its time and was obviously tired of fighting back. I turned the large brass knob and pushed and the door opened inwards with the same sound that a fat man's trousers makes when he bends down. I stepped in cautiously and, behind me, the door did its turn again, only in reverse order this time.

A glaucomatous electric bulb hung from a high ceiling in the foyer and gave some light, but a band of desperadoes could have been lurking in any of the corners and I wouldn't have seen them. There was a boomerang-shaped desk fitted into the wall of the stairs, and I went over and bellied up to it. Behind it was a curtained recess, and in the upside down vee of the badly hung drapes I saw framed a pair of trouser-legs, and feet encased in fluffy slippers.

I cleared my throat, tapped on the counter and called 'Shop'. I might as well have been spitting into the wind, all I got back was my own echo. Then I noticed an ivory bell set into a claw-shaped embrasure in the wall beside the desk. I leaned over and gave it a hearty jab with my thumb.

The result was thrilling. There was a strident screech from a fixture somewhere overhead, a couple of doors slammed, and the legs and feet behind the curtain rose up as though levitated by some divine force. I have to admit I gave a fair old buck jump myself.

The drapes undulated with the motion of whoever was behind them coming down again, then a head pushed itself out and a pair of eyes regarded me reproachfully. The head was bald, had bushy eyebrows, Bing Crosby ears, and a prize-winning nose with nostrils big enough to hide a brace of Lord Lucans and enough foliage to keep them hidden for a year and a day. The guy that all of this belonged to wasn't in the least bit glad to see me.

'I know,' I forestalled him, 'that was a rotten thing to do, but it just came over me all of a sudden. Please forgive me, and take this five pound note as a token of my repentance.'

I put one of Charles' fivers on the desk, but kept my hand on it. Philanthropy is fine, but one shouldn't rush into it.

Old Hairy Conk sidled out of his hidey hole with all the care of a disillusioned ferret. He was dressed in a boiler suit a few sizes too big for him, and he exhibited the exaggerated dignity of someone who had anticipated the cocktail hour by at least a couple of weeks. His breath came at me in waves — the kind you get in Boozer's Paradise.

I liked that. Drinkers always welcome a little extra cash, it causes them to see gin bottles revolving under haloes of sparkling light and blinds them to the other, more mundane things.

'You the owner of this ... ah ... establishment?' I asked him, at the same time waggling the fiver under his proboscis.

'Haw.' He hawked and spat into something out of sight under the desk, hopefully a spittoon. 'Name's Millington. Call me Milly. Everybody else does. I'm the manager. Mr Clanton is the owner ...'

'I take it he's down at the OK corral?'

The old guy, Milly, looked at me, worried at my remark,

then let it drop. He was more interested in the money in my fist and what it might buy. 'You want a room?' he asked me. 'We're just about full up but I think I can squeeze you in. Rates are reasonable, but you've got to pay in advance.'

'Well, I'll tell you ...'

I leaned forward confidentially. Unfortunately he did the same and I found myself looking up the twin barrels of his nose. If they fired I wouldn't stand a chance. Hurriedly I went on: 'I'm more interested in having a conversation with Mrs Bernadette Walsh-Overman. I was told she lives here. A matter of an insurance policy. You know the kind of thing ...'

'Fallen behind in her payments, has she?' he observed, giving me an insight into his guest's financial status.

'She's here then?'

'Well, there's a Bernadette. Didn't know she was called Walsh ... whatever it is. Been here on and off for years.'

'But is she here at this present moment? Alive and kicking and up in her room?'

'That's it. You want her room number?'

This was proving to be easier than I'd hoped. 'I'd appreciate it,' I said. I was beginning to think that I'd been a bit previous in offering him the money.

'Let's see now.'

He shuffled some papers about, picked up a hard bound copybook, put it down again. Leaning on the desk, he sighed, then he looked at me blankly.

'The room number,' I encouraged him.

'Ah.'

He went through the paper shuffling routine again, and this time he made his point. I handed over the money and immediately his amnesia vanished. 'She's up in 23,' he said. 'Two flights, then down the corridor. Door at the end. If she doesn't answer, give the door a kick. She'll think it's me.'

'You go up there often, Milly?'

'Now and then,' he said warily. 'My legs ain't what they used to be.'

'What about the rest of you?'

This time he stared at me a little longer. 'Are you in ... insinuating something? I do her messages for her. You know what she's like' — he considered that one, then shrugged. 'Sometimes I sit down with her and we have a few drinks and talk ...'

'Does she get many visitors?'

'One or two.'

'Which?'

'Huh?'

'One or two?'

'Well, not so's you'd notice.'

His train of thought had gone into a long dark tunnel, showing how tired and emotional he was beginning to feel. 'There was a fella last Saturday,' he said, wrinkling his brows with the effort of remembering. 'Did he ask about her like you ..?'

'I don't know, I wasn't here.'

'Sure he did.'

'He did?'

'Then again maybe he didn't. Excuse me a minute.' He went in behind the curtain and I heard the gurgle as liquid played hopscotch with his Adam's apple. When he reappeared his face had a nice high flush and there was a sparkle in his eye.

'Rub of the relic?' I asked him, and he winked at me companionably.

'Now what was that again?' he said. 'Yes, the guy last Saturday — or was it Sunday? — went up to visit with Bernadette ...'

'How long did he stay?'

'Long enough.'

'Long enough for what?'

He tried to wink again, but his eyes got mixed up and he blinked instead.

'What was he like?' I said, trying a different tack. 'Was he dressed as a knight of the road?'

'Wha?'

'Like a tramp ...'

'Naw, not him. Smooth character. Nice suit. Didn't give me anything for my trouble.' Milly scratched his head reflectively. 'Come to think of it, he didn't even ask me what room she was in. I followed him up to see where he was going. He looked a bit funny ...'

'Funny ha ha?'

'Naw, he had this white skin. Real weird ...'

'Plastic hair and red lips?'

'Yeah, that's him,' Milly said. He looked pleased. 'You know him?'

'On and off. He'd like to drain off a little of my blood to stop me getting over-excited.'

'No kidding?'

'Didn't say what he wanted? With Bernadette, I mean.'

'Hey, what is this?' Milly asked me, a look of suspicion beginning to form in his eye. He'd become a little meaner since he'd imbibed of the juice of the grape — a bit like a dead body when it gets the first squirt of embalming fluid. 'This is like twenty questions. Why don't you go on up there and ask her yourself? Stop bothering me ...'

'I think I'll do just that,' I told him. 'Room 23 you say? Two flights, then down the corridor? I should be able to manage that.'

'Yah,' he said, surly now and in need of another suck from his bottle.

I left him and began to climb the stairs. When I got to the first landing I paused and looked down. He was still below me, his hands spread out flat on either side of him on the desk. Reluctantly I resisted the urge to drop something heavy on his bald head; I might need him to help me with Bernadette if she proved to be awkward.

7

THERE WAS A LARGE window on the second landing. It was begrimed with the dust of years and on the outside question marked with bird droppings. But with the evening sun behind them the encrustations gave it a stained glass effect that was not unpleasing. I notice things like that: sometimes I even pause to reflect that they also serve who only stand and wait.

This time I was on business, however, and I went down that corridor counting doors until I came to number twenty-three. It was like all the others, a plain wooden door with the numerals in chipped white enamel nailed to it. I put my ear against it and listened, but I could hear no sound of movement within.

I tapped, gently at first, then a little harder. Down the hall another door opened a couple of inches and an eye peered out at me. I winked at it and it disappeared with the suddenness of a camera shutter closing.

I waited. Nothing else happened, no other doors opened; there were no sounds of feet scuttling away. I tried the knob of number twenty-three and it clicked and turned. The door moved inwards with a dry, scraping sound. I stepped in and closed it behind me.

The room I was in was blindingly lit, so much so that it took me a few moments to adjust my eyes to it. When I got my bearings the first thing I saw was the woman sitting directly in front of me. She was tilted over to one side, head bent, mouth open, her slack jaw resting on her left shoulder. In deference to the harsh light she was wearing dark glasses which meant that I couldn't see her eyes, but I presumed they were closed. She looked quite peaceful, her bosom rising and falling, little snores percolating out and bursting in the air like invisible bubbles.

The light gave a grainy texture to everything in the room. It hardened edges, highlighted surfaces, accentuated shabbiness and dust. The woman was laid out on an off-white, velour sofa; there were also two matching chairs, a glass-topped table at her knees, another table, this time in brass with folding wooden legs, a veneered cabinet in dark stain containing some crystal knick-knacks and a set of firestone delf with shepherdesses herding their sheep painted on the sides of the cups and on the edges of the saucers and plates.

In one corner an attempt had been made to set up a religious shrine: on a shelf a garish statue of Christ cradled his bleeding heart and in front of it, and screwed to a projecting bracket, was a glowing red electric lamp, its colour reduced to an etiolated pink by the fierceness of the overall glare.

This flare of brilliance was provided by the unshaded high watt bulb hanging from the ceiling, by two standing lamps and by another smaller one with a flowered globe on the brass table. There was enough light in there to have illuminated a fair-sized football stadium. It was obvious that Bernadette wasn't too happy about being alone in the dark.

I looked at her more closely, squinting to get her in focus. Her face was caked with make-up. Whoever had applied her lipstick must have been suffering from St Vitus Dance. She was fastened away in a black shiny dressing gown with gold dragons on it, but a reasonably shaped leg had escaped and was glinting suggestively at me. I doubted the gown was pure silk, but the leg was the real thing. She also had a lot of blond hair, most of it twisted into a thick plait that trailed over the shoulder her chin wasn't resting on, a pearl necklace, long hanging jade earrings, an expensive-looking watch and rings on every one of her fat fingers.

Even with the lopsided jaw and the dark glasses, I could still recognise her from the wedding photograph Mrs Walsh-Overman had given me. I had been wrong about her running to fat, though. She'd managed to keep herself pretty much in shape, although she was still a fair armful. I guessed she was about fifty, but a well preserved and high kicking fifty if I wasn't mistaken, and I didn't think I was.

The room was obviously her sitting room; there was another door set slightly off-centre in the wall to my right which possibly led to her bedroom. There was a curtained alcove in another corner — the kitchen? — and a window latticed by a Venetian blind faced me in the back wall. She was comfortable enough and able to afford a suite, but the furnishings were functional and cheap: there was nothing there that looked as if she would cry over it if it got up and ran away.

I sat down on the arm of one of the easy chairs and lit a cigarette and gazed at her. Bernadette Walsh-Overman, nee Mordaunt, quite a mouthful. I wondered if Redmond ever dropped by to lay his head on that well upholstered bosom. I had the feeling she was the type of woman who wouldn't be without a man for long.

In front of her on the grubby tabletop was a tumbler that contained a small amount of a milky white liquid. I picked it up and sniffed. It had a liquorish odour — Anis or Pernod, I guessed. Now I could see the reason why Milly might come up and keep Bernadette company: they were both fond of the gargle.

I put the tumbler back gently on the table, but some instinctive fear of being deprived of her medicine must have seeped through into Bernadette's brainbox, for she suddenly straightened up and reached for the glass. Our hands touched and she gasped. The dark glasses peered up at me and she said, 'Larry?'

'Afraid not,' I told her, holding onto her hand in case she decided to take a swing at me. 'My name's Blaine, John Blaine. I did knock,' I assured her. 'Milly down at the desk told me to go right on in if there was no answer. Said he'd vouch for me ...'

The woman relaxed and I let go of her hand. She grunted good humouredly and said, 'Vouch for you? He couldn't vouch for a posse of priests with their cassocks on.' She had a light, young woman's voice with a musical lilt to it and no discernable accent. She spread her hands and said, 'Take the weight off your feet. Not too often I get company, except for old choosey chops down below. Loosen your waistcoat and throw your hat in the corner.'

She reached down and freed a bottle that had been imprisoned between her and the sofa. Pernod was her drink all right. She fumbled around, found the glass, topped it up, then stirred it with her thumb. She waved the bottle about in the air, inviting me to join her, but I didn't take her up on it. Raw Pernod wasn't exactly my idea of a social drink.

'You're wondering about the light and the dark glasses, aren't you?' she asked me, after taking in a sizable portion of the contents of the tumbler. 'I'm not too good on the peepers, so I try to fool myself by turning on more and more lights. Cataracts, they tell me, but I'm going for an operation soon and then it'll all become crystal clear.' She leaned back, then sniffed the air. 'Is that cigarette smoke I smell? Light one for me, will you?'

There was a packet of Carroll's Number One on the table, so I shook one out and lit it. When she took it from me her hand appeared to linger with the suggestion of a caress. Then again, I might have imagined it.

While we smoked I told her that I was a private investigator and that I'd been hired by her mother-in-law to find her husband, Redmond — 'She's been hearing heavenly bells and she wants to see him one more time before she kicks off.'

'Heavenly?' Bernadette snorted. 'More likely the other place. The old witch ...'

'You don't like her?'

'Now that's an understatement if I ever heard one. I'd tear her balls off and feed them to the cat if I wasn't afraid they wouldn't poison it.'

'Balls?'

'You think she hasn't got any? She's got balls all right, I'll give her that.'

To calm herself down she poured the remainder of the Pernod down her throat, licking experimentally round her lips to see if she had missed any.

'Be that as it may,' I went on, 'you could help me if you've a mind to.'

'Help you to do what?'

'To find Redmond.'

'Why should I? Is there something in it for me? To top up the housekeeping, like ...'

I shrugged, forgetting she couldn't see me. 'I've no authority to promise you anything,' I told her. 'I can let you have ... ah ... twenty pounds if you'll give me some clue as to where I might find him. That's from my own fee, you understand.'

'Amn't I lucky? I'm in the company of one of the last of the big spenders.'

'It's better than a slap in the pus with a wet rag.'

'True.' She paused and stuck out her jaw. 'That wouldn't be a threat, would it?'

'Come on, Bernadette, I'm not like that. I'm a gentleman to my finger tips. And you don't mind if I call you Bernadette, do you?'

'Be my guest. I've been called worse.'

She grinned, the crazily lipsticked mouth opening to show some teeth. Then she took up the bottle again and shook it. 'If you go over to the cabinet,' she instructed me, 'and look in the bottom drawer you'll find another bottle of Pernod. Bring it over and we'll do it some damage.'

I went over and got the bottle and poured her a libation. While she disposed of it, I lit us two more cigarettes. I wasn't getting anywhere very fast, but then that was one of the drawbacks of my line of business. An awful lot of patience was needed to gain what was usually very little.

'I was a dancer once,' Bernadette mused, blowing a thin stream of smoke into the brightness of the room. 'I danced in the Theatre Royal and in the Capitol before they tore them down. To tell you the truth, I wasn't much good, but it opened a few doors for me. That's how I met Redmond. I was brought along as window dressing to a function by a politician who really fancied young men with sulky looks and the kind of backsides you have to lever open with a tin opener. The party was for some old fart who'd donated a few Civil War bits and pieces to the nation. Redmond was there, wearing a kilt and a funny little hat with a feather in it. He was kind and attentive and he kept his hands to himself. I liked that, you know what I mean?' She smiled around the dark glasses. 'And I liked it even better,' she went on, 'when I found out the kind of money he could call on. That sounds terrible, doesn't it? But for a girl like me, dragged up in Old Shop Street in the Liberties, sleeping four to a bed and washing from a communal cold water tap, the chance of bagging a rich husband was like catching a falling star and bringing it home to decorate the mantelpiece.'

I grunted and watched as, dispensing with the glass, she put the bottle to her head and knocked back a snort. It was obvious she intended getting to the point in her own good time.

'Well, we did get hitched,' she continued, a slight slurring of her words now becoming evident, 'and we went out to live in that crypt in Howth. We walked the dogs. We went round and round the cliff walks. We watched the horizon, but no rescue ships ever came to carry us away. In the evenings we sat and gazed at herself and himself counting their money, then played cards for matchsticks. So help me, for six years I slept in a bed with a canopy over it and little hanging curtains that you pulled down when you wanted some privacy for a bit of how's-your-father. Not that Redmond was really into that kind of thing. He preferred arm wrestling and watching me run around the bedroom in the nip.'

'A bit kinky, was he?'

'They all were. The brother Charles was as highly spiced as a German sausage. The Da kept to himself. What he did for a bit of slap and tickle I never found out, but I'm sure the old dragon didn't provide it. There was a story that Redmond did in his sister. Seemed they were out boating, the boat capsized, the sister went down, and only Redmond returned to tell the tale. But no one would talk much about that ...'

She took another slug from the bottle. I had never seen anyone drink raw Pernod straight from the font like that before and I wondered how long it would take for her to suddenly stiffen and lapse into a coma. She teetered a bit as she replaced the bottle on the table.

Taking up the story again, she said, 'I got bored. I needed a bit of razzmatazz in my life, so I started playing around. Redmond didn't notice, but it wasn't long before the old lady copped on. She told the husband and between the two of them they gave me the bum's rush. To tell you the truth, by then I didn't really mind. I was tired of that echoing old house and the people in it. They packed me off, settled a lump sum on me, and told me not to show my snoot around there again. Redmond surprised me by making a scene. He's got a ferocious temper, you know.'

'No, I didn't know that.'

We sat and thought about things for a while, and I realised that I was beginning to feel depressed. The bright light irritated me. Hearing Bernadette unburden herself threw gloom like a net over my sense of wellbeing. I could be out doing something significant, like reading poetry or watching the grass grow. My aged father in Wexford was probably up on the roof fixing slates. In the past year I'd listened to an awful lot of sad people tell an awful lot of sad tales. And what made it even worse was that most of them were lies.

'So Redmond doesn't come around much anymore?' I suggested, trying to hurry her along.

'Well, now, I wouldn't say that.'

'So what would you say?'

'I'd say you're getting a mite impatient with a lady who's passing a bit of time reminiscing about the past ...'

'You think so? Well, I already know about the past. I've an aged parent who's obsessed with it. Don't you know the past is a different country? Forget it. It's over. Let's look to the future ...'

'You see what I mean?'

I sighed, crossed my legs, stuck a used match in my mouth and began to chew it. 'Okay,' I said, 'have it your way. I'm a captive audience.'

Once more Bernadette refreshed herself from the bottle. If it had been me, I'd have been floating up somewhere near the ceiling by now. She had the capacity of an oil tanker. 'You said something about twenty quid,' she prompted me when she'd ceased at the bottle. 'Let's see the colour of your money.'

I took four more of Charlie's crisp fivers out of my inside pocket, kissed them goodbye and handed them over. She took them from me, stuffed them down her frontage, gave a little wiggle and sighed pleasurably. Nothing like a bit of lettuce to keep the ferret happy.

'You know,' Bernadette said, her tone reflective, 'if you don't have something, you don't miss it. But give a girl a taste for the good life and she can't ever shake it off. I never thought I'd miss breakfast in bed, especially from china plates and with real silver knives and forks. Or the feel of satin underwear against my pleasure domes. Or a drawing room to sit in big enough to accommodate a brass band. I used run through all those rooms just for the sheer joy of feeling all that space about me.'

'*Lebensraum.*'

'Come again.'

'German for room to breathe. That's why Hitler said he invaded Poland. He might've had only one ball, but he needed a mighty big piece of territory to bounce it in.'

'You don't say ....'

'I do. And I have.' I leaned forward until my face was only six inches from hers and I was sure she could see me. 'But none of this gets me any closer to finding Redmond. This is just kicking for touch. Won't you give me something, Bernadette?

A hint, a nudge in the right direction? To get my clock ticking over ...'

She inserted the bottle between us and glug-glugged. When she came up for air she said, 'It might not be too healthy looking for Redmond. Did you ever think of that?'

'Why? Because of his temper?'

Ponderously she winked at me. 'That too.'

'Listen, Bernadette,' I said urgently, 'since I was hired earlier today by Mrs Walsh-Overman to find her son I've had a number of people advise me to drop it. Now I'm by nature a curious individual, and the more I'm warned off something the more I want to poke at it to see if its arse is painted blue. I'm going to find Redmond with or without your help ...'

'Well, if that's how you feel about it ...'

'It is.'

'Try a dosshouse up in Fishamble Street called "The Star of the Sea". That used to be his town house. When he goes to the country there's a school boiler shed that he kips down in. Where is it now ..? Out near Fairview Park somewhere.'

'That's it?'

She looked at me with what I presumed was surprise. The drink really was beginning to get to her now, laying down a film of drunkenness that made every expression seem the same. 'What'd you expect for twenty green ones?' she asked me. 'The key to my chastity belt?'

I stood up. 'If Redmond drops in over the next day or two, maybe you'd get Milly downstairs to give me a ring,' I said. I took out one of my business cards and carefully balanced it on the rim of the empty glass. 'I'm leaving you my number. Tell Redmond his mother needs to know where he left the grandfather clock. She wants to pull the pendulum ...'

'Here, pull this,' Bernadette said, but she was mumbling now.

I was about at the end of my tether myself. My eyes felt as though the lids were being propped open by sharp pointed toothpicks. You don't get used to bright light like that, you drown in it.

I was heading for the door when I had a thought. I had forgotten to ask her about Red Lips Saunders who, according to Milly's description, had called on her earlier in the week. Also she had mentioned a name when I'd first entered the room and startled her from sleep. 'Who's Larry?' I asked her, but I had left it too late. She was back firmly in the arms of Morpheus and even a gallon drum of Pernod trundling in the door wouldn't have woken her. I'd have to pay her another visit when the tide had receded if I wanted to find out Larry's name, date of birth and serial number.

I went back along the corridor and down the two flights of stairs. Milly was back in position behind the arras, his fluffy slippers peeking out as coyly as ever. Another stray lost in the dreaming.

When I got outside the sun was still shining, but it was low in the sky and just about to call it a day. It had the right idea. I collected my car, started it up, turned on the radio and headed for home.

8

THE MONDAY NIGHT traffic was as bad as the Tuesday night traffic, or any other night's traffic for that matter. I drove up Gardiner Street in the inside lane, my windows tightly closed against a city that has too many cars, too many fumes, too many light-fingered kids eager to reach in and steal your money, your belongings, the wax out of your ears.

Once upon a time it hadn't been like that, but then, when was once upon a time? I remembered my father talking about the famous Animal Gang, who operated in Dublin before and during the Second World War. They had pitched battles with the Guards, ran extortion rings, had every bookie on every race track in and around the city terrified. As Brendan Behan said of them, they were engaged in armed begging.

The poverty in Dublin between the wars was worse than in any other European city, and it lingered, like the whiff of an outdoor toilet. One has only to view Neville Johnson's grainy black and white photographs of the fifties to appreciate the kind of squalor that existed not fifty yards from the main thoroughfare, O'Connell Street.

When they started knocking the city down in the sixties and the seventies, though, they didn't know where to stop. Okay, get rid of the teeming cobblestoned side streets and the fetid tenements, but what about the Molesworth Hall and St Anne's Schools, the Theatre Royal in Hawkins St, Frascati House in Blackrock? And they built a concrete bunker on the site of the Wood Quay Viking excavations to keep all those slumbering civil servants from public view.

There are ways and means of renovating and bringing a city up to date without tearing the heart out of it, but speculators were given carte blanche by the so-called custodians of Dublin with the result that no proper system of preservation was set up. Blocks of concrete and glass have been placed in the most inappropriate of settings, road widening has swallowed up some of the most exquisite of historic buildings, and big business, banks, insurance companies, supermarkets, condominiums, have chewed up the innards of the city and regurgitated them as freezeframe vomit that becomes ever more depressing.

I drove up by one building, thankfully, that has remained intact — the Mater Hospital — through the lights at Phibsboro and past St Peter's Church. The descending sun was painting everything pink, the long sweep of road tunnelling away from me to become the highway to Navan and other points north. Running parallel with me was the North Circular Road, which opens, after a set of ornate gates, into the broad plains of the Phoenix Park, the largest stretch of commonage in Europe. At least that remains unspoilt, although cars and lorries continue to fart their way through it, leaving the air reeking of petrol fumes and defective exhaust pipes.

Outside my house there was a greyish blue Nissan Bluebird parked half on the road and half on the path. I manoeuvred my way around it and pulled into the driveway. For some reason the front door was standing open, and the lights were on in all the upstairs rooms. I got out, locked the car and went inside. From the hall I could hear the murmur of voices above me. Suddenly the voices grew in volume, there was a thud and then a cry of pain.

I suppose, being a private detective, I should have immediately bounded up the stairs pulling my .38 colt revolver from its shoulder holster. Seeing as I don't possess the shoulder holster, not to mention the .38 colt, I decided to be a little more circumspect about matters that might endanger my health and lead to bruises and contusions. First I went softly out to the garage and got my trusted hurley stick: it was old but still serviceable, my father having given it to me when he still harboured hopes of my leading the purple and gold of Wexford to All-Ireland success.

Next I started creeping up the stairs, taking them one step at a time and praying that they wouldn't creak. The door leading to Marty's room had been pushed back against the wall, so I stuck my head around it and had a look.

Marty was standing between the two single beds, packaged between two characters who looked as if they were about to have him for their supper. One was short and broad, the other was tall and broad; both of them had a rough, unformed unanimity as though recently quarried out of cut stone. I knew the type, I'd seen them come into small businesses in the city centre and cause instant diarrhoea. They were the people you sent for when you wanted a fire to break out in your well-insured warehouse, or if you had a debt to collect that needed some pain and intimidation to make it bear fruit.

I drew my head back to consider my plan of action. I could go quietly back down stairs and over to the local pub for a drink. I could turn the television set up loud to drown Marty's cries of pain. I could have my tea, read a book, go to bed.

Ah, to hell with it, I thought, and I marched on in there, my hurley held discreetly down beside my leg.

The taller of the heavies had Marty by the right ear, and he didn't let go as they all three turned as one to stare in my direction. Feeling that it was up to me to lead for the defence, I said, 'Marty behind in his Legion of Mary contributions again? I keep reminding him to pay up and help bring a homeless girl back to God.'

The two thugs gazed at one another and kind of wrinkled their foreheads. Marty stood between them on tippy-toes, hanging by his ear. 'Who's dis guy?' the shorter one inquired, addressing his question to the grimacing Marty, but all he got by way of reply was 'Ow, ow.'

Again believing that it was up to me to proffer an explanation, I said, 'I'm the St Vincent de Paul man. He owes us too.

Would you like me to get in line, or will we all have a go at him together?'

They exchanged that look again, then nodded knowingly. 'A smart arse,' the short one said. He came around the end of the bed, his maulers clasping and unclasping. When he was within range, I kicked him in the knee, and when he bent down to have a look I hit him on the side of the head with the flat of the hurley stick. Whatever damage was done to his head, the hurl was demolished: it just disintegrated in my hand. The short, broad gorilla fell over on the floor, but now his bigger companion was coming at me, having let Marty drop onto the floor like an empty sack.

Thinking I had better make some effort, I put my hands up and curled them into fists. King Kong merely reached out and enclosed them in his. It was as if I had stuck my hands into a meat grinder: pain shot up my arms, into my head, and out my ears. I went up on one leg and began a pirouette, which was abruptly terminated by my partner flinging me away from him like Nureyev in a temper. I went into the wall leading with my head, the wall refused to budge, I bounced off it and then lay down on the floor to think things over.

My assailant's face came into view as he bent over me. There was a mighty smell of garlic from his breath. Is this a clue? I asked myself. If so I must note it in my filofax and pore over it while in hospital. I braced myself, but when the blow came it was goodnight, ladies, sleep tight and don't let the bedbugs bite.

I must have dozed a little for, when I opened my eyes again, Marty was bending over me and the two primates had left. He helped me up onto one of the beds, looking as solicitous as a man can who has one ear twice the size of the other. Neither of us appeared to groan, yet there was the echo of one bouncing around the room.

Marty, a good Samaritan if ever there was one, went over to his bedside locker and took out a half full bottle of brandy. He uncorked it and handed it to me. My crushed fingers were giving me trouble but I managed to get it to my mouth and upend a little onto my tongue. It burned its way down my throat and began a knees-up in my stomach. I let it subside, then I took another snort. This one merely did a soft shoe shuffle.

'How're you feeling?' Marty asked me, putting the bed between himself and myself.

'Oh, grand, grand' — this in spite of the fact that my left hand was frozen into a fist and was likely to remain so until I could get to a tin of three-in-one oil and that my head felt as if a jumbo jet had recently taken off from it.

'Who the hell were those two Neanderthal men?' I asked Marty. 'And don't tell me they were your uncles up from Mayo to persuade you to come home and marry your childhood sweetheart.'

'How'd you guess?'

'Don't give me that crock of shit. Unburden yourself or I'll get to work on your other ear with a pliers.'

'Would you believe me if I said I'd never seen them before tonight?'

'No.'

'I didn't think you would.' He sat down on the other bed and cradled his ear. 'It's like this,' he went on, 'about a year ago I met some people in a nightclub in Leeson Street ...'

'What people?'

Marty looked at me. 'Can't you let me tell it? They looked all right to me at the time. Well dressed, quietly spoken, polite. They bought me a drink, let me rumba with one of their girls ...'

'By rumba you're speaking figuratively?'

This time he tried to glare, but only succeeded in looking shifty. 'I got to talking to them,' he continued. 'One of them told me he might have a little money to invest. Turned out it was quite an amount of money.'

'How much?'

'Over the last six months one hundred thousand pounds.'

He had all of my attention now. Outside in the street could be heard the noise of a lorry rumbling by, but inside in the room it was as if the air had been sucked out.

'You took it?' I asked him. 'To invest?'

'What else could I do?'

'Well, you could've politely declined, said you were sorry but you didn't handle that kind of money. Why didn't you tell them you were only small cheese where you worked?' I looked at him, then it dawned on me. 'You boasted about being a wheeler dealer, probably told them you were a broker and up to the hilt in half the millionaires in the country. That's it, isn't it?'

I knew by his face that I was right. 'And I know the kind of people they were too,' I went on. 'Sleazy types, but all done up in expensive clothes like monkey's uncles. Dangerous to be around, so that you were hugging yourself at what a daring young man you were being. You knew they were crooks as soon as you laid eyes on them, didn't you?'

'How could I tell?' he asked, not meeting my eye. 'I've no experience of that kind of thing. They said they were business-men, in scrap metal. Said business was booming and that they had a little money to play with on the stock exchange. I took them at their word ...'

'You also took their money. What'd you do, put it into the wrong management fund?'

'Everything was going fine,' Marty cried. 'Then Black Monday came along and the bottom fell out of the market. You know that ...'

'Oh, I know it all right. And you know it. But your friends didn't. Or didn't care. They only wanted their money back. And obviously you haven't got it to give.'

'It's just a question of time. The market's recovering. In another month or two it'll be back to normal.'

'In another month or two you could be lying some place holding a lily and with your balls in a plastic sack beside you. Or worse, with them stuffed in your mouth.'

'Christ, don't say that.'

I sat up and, with my better right hand, gingerly fingered the bump on my head. 'You're up to your oxters in it now, Marty my man,' I told him. Then a thought struck me and I said, 'Both of us are, come to that.'

'What d'you mean?'

'Figure it out for yourself. You owe these apes money. I interfered in their business. We can both recognise them. Don't you think they'll be back? And with reinforcements this time. Maybe a bazooka or two to raze the bloody house to the ground.'

'I think we'd better call the Guards.'

'That's a no-no,' I told him. 'What'll they do? We'll swear out a warrant, and they'll deliver it. The kind of people we're dealing with here, they wipe their gable ends with police summonses. The Guards are powerless. The villains are so well organised, you wouldn't believe it. There's a web of safe houses, safe alibis, safe methods of disposing of hot money, used shooters and unwanted witnesses. And if the hard men do stumble and are brought to court, there's a posse of over-paid solicitors and barristers just creaming their charcoal grey pinstripes in anticipation of going to bat for them. It's possible to cloud everything nowadays with legal jargon, drag court proceedings out ad infinitum, harass jurors, bribe, corrupt, coerce. These days you could do in an entire chorus line and, if you have enough money and the right connections to back it up, find someone willing to testify that they got caught up in one another's bra strings and strangled to death.'

Marty was looking at me with eyes and mouth open. 'You're exaggerating,' he breathed.

'Only a little.'

I squeezed my head a little more, then beat my left hand on the counterpane to see if it was still numb. It wasn't. 'I don't know about you,' I told him, 'but I'm done in. I'm going to bed. If those two baboons come back will you ask them to knock you about quietly. I've had enough excitement to last me for one night.'

I levered myself up, feeling old and grey and full of tears. Only that morning I had been a carefree private investigator with nothing much to investigate except where to find three months back rent on my kip of an office. Now I had two different problems to resolve, a mummified hand, and a head that felt as if Little Oskar had been using it as his Tin Drum.

I went across the landing, lay down on my bed, and thought deep, dark thoughts.

9

WHEN I WOKE up next morning, my hand had been restored to me. Except for some pins and needles it felt about normal. Unfortunately I couldn't say the same for my head. Some dimwit was playing the bongo drums in behind my frontal lobe, and the reverberations were making my teeth chatter.

I showered and shaved, then patted a little *eau de cologne* into my strategic areas. My beige suit was lying crumpled on the floor, so I bundled it into a plastic sack and made a mental note to drop it in to be cleaned.

I found clean underwear and socks, then I put on a blue shirt, grey slacks and my grey sportscoat with the narrow lapels and the buttoned-down pockets. I went downstairs, opened the front door and looked out at the ten o'clock Tuesday morning. The weather had turned a little colder, the sky was a chilblainy blue, and thin clouds were wisping about in it trying to keep warm.

There was an aroma of coffee wafting from the direction of the kitchen, so I went in there and sat at the table. I pulled a hand-carved mug over to me, looked at Kate, who was standing by the stove, and said, 'Here's looking at you, kid.'

For a change she did the decent thing: asked no questions and poured me some coffee. This morning she was wearing a tan leather jacket, cream silk blouse and co-ordinated tweed trousers. To set it all off her hair was now a burnished brown, a hymn to the dyer's art.

Settling one hip against the dishwasher, she cocked an eyebrow and said, 'A bit of a commotion last night. I didn't stick my nose in in case it was the good ole boys having a bit of a rip up ...'

'There were a couple of good ole boys here sure enough,' I said sourly, 'but it was the carpet they were ripping up. And Marty's ears ...'

'Marty? What'd they want with him?'

'He's been painting graffiti on walls about them and they were out to confiscate his brushes.'

'Funny.'

I glanced at her over the rim of the mug. 'You don't want to know anything about this,' I told her. 'What you don't know, can't hurt you. Marty's got himself in deep with some hard men ... gamblers ... and he's a little short on what he owes them. I found them bouncing him around when I came home last night. They decided to include me in the action.'

'Why didn't you call the cops?'

I lit a cigarette, blew a smoke ring, then stuck my finger through it. 'I'll handle it,' I said, then, feeling that my tone lacked conviction, I went on, 'It's my line of work, isn't it? Marty can put me on a small retainer, I'll make a few phone calls, set up a meeting ... Easy as falling off a log.'

Marty, who had come in quietly while I was talking, sat down at the other end of the table and asked me, 'How big a retainer?'

'That's you all over, Marty,' I told him, 'as close as a well-kept secret. I don't have to get involved in this at all, you know. It's only out of the goodness of my heart that I'm sticking in my oar.'

'How much?'

I sighed. 'Forget it,' I said, 'I'll do it as a freebee. You think those goons'll be up around Leeson Street tonight?'

'They're always there.'

'Okay, we'll go have a talk with them. Maybe make them smoke the pipe of peace.'

'How, may I ask?'

'Look,' I said, 'if the money's as big as you say it is, those guys are not going to take any chances on losing it. They were only putting the frighteners on you last night. They'll take good care to see that nothing bad happens to you, at least until they get their money back. But I take great exception to them coming around here and throwing my belongings in the air. This is my home, my castle. I like to be able to come back here at night, put on my slippers, toast some marshmallows on my antique toasting fork, and conjure up pictures in the fire's flames. I'm old fashioned like that ...'

The two of them were looking at me as if an onion had suddenly sprouted out of my ear. 'It's the truth,' I told them, my hand on my heart. 'You walk in here and do something bad to me in my own house, you do it at your peril. Everyone has to have somewhere to call his own.'

'Good for you,' Kate said. 'I go all the way with you on that. And while you're at it, the roof needs mending, the window in my room is stuck, the radiator's leaking ... If you're so anxious about home sweet home, you'd better get it patched up before it falls down around your ears ... and around my ears too.'

I finished my coffee and stood up. The conversation had taken a turn that made it imperative I be off about my business. 'I'll see you in Kiernan's pub about eleven tonight,' I told Marty. 'We'll take a saunter up the Strip and show the flag ...'

He nodded, looking miserable. His ear had swollen up to the point where it resembled one that kids stick on at Hallowe'en. 'Cheer up,' I told him. 'Maybe you'll meet that floozie you rumbaed with. She'll make you forget your aching lughole.'

I left them, and on the way out stopped and looked at myself in the hall mirror. 'You, me and the cat,' I told my reflection.

10

I DROVE INTO the city. The Gas Company was redecorating the streets again, so my progress was a stop-start affair. Why do their employees always look so happy when they're digging holes? I asked myself — whistling, laughing, jostling one another, picking their noses — digging holes is that jolly?

I parked in my usual spot, bought a paper and confirmed that the Wexford team was due to play against Cork on the following Sunday in Croke Park. My ancient father would be sure to be up for it: thundering into town in his Morris Minor, bedecked in purple and gold favours, a battle-scarred old warrior with the blood lust still in his eye.

I had a kind of bitter-sweet relationship with my father. Ever since my mother died he'd been like a shaggy old dog with a thorn up his bum, running this way and that, bumping into things, wanting company, yet unwilling to admit it. He lived with me for a week, then decided that he could communicate better with me when there was a matter of eighty miles between us. He found it difficult to come to terms with the pace of modern life; he was stuck somewhere back in the forties; his old grey head perplexed, his motivation all screwed up, his sense of morals shredded by a climate that allowed singing priests, dancing nuns, and unescorted women in public bars. He was the kind of man that believed in the efficacy of red flannel, a bath at Easter and Christmas, Brylcreem for the hair, Carbolic soap for the complexion, a Vick rub for the chest, Beechams Pills for the digestion and Liquid Paraffin for the wholesome. In short, he was an anachronism, a throwback to a time that was simpler than ours — not necessarily better, but definitely simpler. He was also my father and I loved him.

I stopped outside Batt's still closed-up emporium and took out my loose-leaf notebook. I opened it and wrote on one of the pages: 'Name the actors who played the Ladykillers'. I shoved the paper under his door. Maybe that would put me one ahead of the posse.

Upstairs, the anteroom was as deserted as a eunuch's jock-strap. I went on through, opened a window to banish the stale air in my office, got a mouthful of the fumes from outside, and closed it again.

There was some post: a brochure advertising thermal underwear, a telephone bill, a reminder from the public library that I still had their copy of John Banville's *The Book of Evidence*, an invitation to the opening of an exhibition of watercolours by a friend of mine, John Daly, and a begging letter from the order of nuns that I'd helped out. Nothing very pressing there, so I threw everything except the invitation into the waste paper basket.

Next I rearranged the few *objets d'art* on my desk: the phone, the in-tray, the out-tray, the wooden paper knife, the framed photograph of Annie and myself glaring at one another. I took the bottle of Bushmills out, stared at it, then put it back again. An iron-willed private investigator like me ought to have no need of such ephemeral stimulants. Says who?

I got up and walked around the office a few times, then I sat down, hooked the phone over closer to me, and dialled Annie. When she answered, I said, 'I've got a hard-on like a cucumber. What d'you suggest I do about it?'

She said something unbelievably foul and hung up. I dialled again, told her I'd behave and asked her to tell me something about the home for down and outs called 'The Star of the Sea'.

'The Star of the Sea?'

'That's it. Surely in your capacity of social worker you know all the best dosshouses?'

'I know it.'

'Then tell me about it.'

'Why?'

I sighed, a long drawn out theatrical one. 'Because I've asked you to,' I said. 'It's not often I ask you for anything. Think of it as a favour to a chum.'

'It's up in Fishamble Street.'

'And?'

'And what?'

'Who runs it? If I went up there would I be allowed to poke around?'

'It's run by the social services and they'd welcome you with open arms.'

'I don't want to stay there, I just want some information about one of their inmates.'

There was a pause, then she said reluctantly. 'As luck would have it — and I'm being sarcastic — I'm going up there this morning. There're a couple of my old ladies that I have to see to.'

'I can tag along?'

'I was afraid you'd ask that.'

'I'll be over right away.'

'No need to strain yourself. It'll be another hour before I'm ready to leave.'

'Annie,' I said, 'you're the top ... You're the smile on the Mona Lisa.'

'Smile?'

'That's it, the enigmatic smile, the smile that makes men mad ...'

'Curious ... I'd always thought she was trying to suppress a fart.'

'Oh my God, how could you ..?'

I held the phone away from my ear out at arm's length, and shook it, then I cautiously put it back again. I was too late, she'd hung up on me.

11

ANNIE IS NOT a beautiful woman, but she'll do until one comes along. She has red hair, but disputes it: 'It's auburn,' she's forever telling anyone who says different.

Her face is oval shaped, her eyes grey with greenish flecks. She has wonderful skin, unblemished except for a shading of freckles across the nose. Her body is tomboyishly healthy; she has big, firm breasts, a small waist, wide hips, a perfect *derrière,* and legs that Fred Astaire would have marked ten out of ten.

On that particular morning she was sitting in a room on the second floor of the Municipal Offices on a wooden kitchen chair. She had it tilted back at a gravity-defying angle, her legs propped on a cluttered table cum desk, and she was talking to a female person in a shapeless woolsack-type dress who had enough hair to stuff a medium size mattress.

'This is Victoria,' Annie introduced me, as I came in and stood looking around for somewhere to sit. The room was chaotic; books, files, sheaves of paper leaned drunkenly against one another, piled on the floor, on chairs, on wooden ledges fitted into the walls. There was a sink in one corner and it too was piled high, only this time with cups, saucers and mugs, all stained brown as though Cowboy Joe had been using them to spit tobacco juice into.

Victoria's mass of hair parted, and I saw glasses glinting at me through the foliage. 'Howdy doo,' she said, with a Liverpool accent you could swat a Beatle with. She swept some papers off a chair and gestured at it. I sat down, crossed my legs and tried not to look too much like a supplicant. Government buildings and public offices always have that effect on me, as though I'd been caught defacing statues or holding out on the Inland Revenue.

I took out a cigarette. 'Is it okay for me to smoke?' I asked, 'or is this place a designated fire hazard?'

Victoria brushed back some more of the candy floss, and I saw that she had a small, round, pale face, with huge butterfly winged glasses perched on a button nose. She grinned at me and said, 'Be my guest, loike.'

I lit up, drew in, exhaled, and fidgeted. Victoria found an incredibly dirty brass ashtray somewhere and handed it to me, and I balanced it on my knee. 'Coffee?' she inquired. I looked across at the crockery in the sink and politely declined.

'Nice day for the time of year,' I said. 'Seasonal. A bit of east wind about, so you'd need to keep well wrapped ...'

Annie had taken up an official typed sheet of A4. She now put this down and stared at me. So did Victoria. Surprised, I said, 'The weather ... It's only an opening gambit. I get better as I go along.'

'Would you like to bet on that?' Annie said.

She stood up, nonchalantly pulling at the tight crotch of her jeans. Above the jeans she had on a brightly patterned, lumpy wool sweater, with a matching scarf tied cravat-style round her neck and tucked into the vee of the jumper. She wore only a suspicion of make-up, her eyes highlighted, her lips outlined in pale pink. Her hair was cut short, tight against her head in a Louise Brooks helmet. She was Annie, as familiar to me as the beat of my heart, and I wondered, not for the first time, how things could have gone so wrong between us, how we could still love one another and yet not be able to sort out the trivial complications that prevented us from living together.

She put on a navy blue pea jacket, with shiny elbows and shoulder insets, and a black knitted tea cosy hat. She saw me staring at her and said, 'Don't say it ...'

'What?'

'Hello, sailor.'

I grinned. 'Hello yourself, cheeky.'

We bade farewell to Victoria and went down two flights of

stairs and out onto the quays. The wind had indeed got up, and the Liffey was high, angry-looking and slapping viciously at its restraining walls. Down on the new Custom House docksite a pile driver was booming like a metronome and a long, thin, yellow crane pointed its finger into the sky and dribbled steel wires from its extension rod. This was to be the regenerated commercial heart of Dublin, a teeming hive of moneyed men, multi-million pound contracts and soaring stocks and shares. A conference centre was due to be built to house armies of expense account conventioneers and an opera house for Pavarotti to come and sing in. And all on the spot where up to recently hordes of soulful emigrants with hope in their hearts and no arses in their trousers had boarded ships to take them to foreign places. Too late for some, but maybe the new young would benefit from all the labour.

Annie insisted on driving her own car, a cream coloured Citroen Dyane that had bicycle wheels and a chassis that a perambulator would have sneered at. I squeezed in beside her, and we took off up the quays to the sound of a bag of cats copulating.

While she waited for the lights to change at O'Connell Bridge, Annie asked me why I was interested in the Star of the Sea. 'I'm looking for someone,' I told her. 'A tramp.'

'Well, it's the place to go. They've got all sizes and shapes up there.'

'This's a guy called Redmond Walsh-Overman. He was high society at one time, but he couldn't cut it and now he finds his dinner in dustbins and sleeps in the doorways of the better class of shop. D'you know him?'

Annie put the Citroen into gear and we hoppity-hopped across the intersection. 'Can't say that I do,' she said, her tongue between her teeth with the effort of piloting the car. 'But then, they don't always provide breed, seed and generation on request. That's why a lot of them are as they are. They're out to forget and be forgotten. Why're you looking for him?'

'His Mumsie asked me to find him.'

'His Mumsie?'

'Mrs Joseph Walsh-Overman. She wants to see him one more time before she goes boating with Charon.'

'Who?'

'His mother.'

'No, the other guy ... Charon?'

'The boatman of the Underworld. He ferries souls across the River Styx and into Hades.'

'You don't say. Did you get that out of a book ..?'

'I'll have you know I was once a classical scholar. That was before I fell into the company of philistines, and auburn-haired women.'

'You lump the two together, do you?'

'Not necessarily, but they both proved to be a distraction.'

'So you're blaming me for your not becoming a university professor, or another James Joyce?'

'Who he?'

'Come off it ...'

Annie ran an amber light, and then cursed as an oncoming car blew at her. I glanced over. 'Did I say something?'

'Forget it.'

'I didn't mean anything.'

'You never do. I said forget it. Tell me more about this Redmond Walsh-Overman.'

I sighed, a small splinter of irritation rubbing at my mood. Where Annie was concerned, I always seemed prone to that one comment too many. Around her I should put my foot in my mouth and suck my big toe.

'Redmond's got the little finger of his left hand missing,' I told her. 'Does that strike a bell?'

'Nope.' She cursed again as a Mercedes passed her out on the inside. It wasn't too difficult, seeing as she was travelling at a flat-out twenty miles per hour. 'A number of tramps have been killed over the last few weeks,' she went on. 'Three, I think. One was found only last Sunday, thrown into a rubbish skip ... up near where we're going, actually.'

'I know, I read about it.'

'Anything to do with your fellow?'

I tried to shift in my seat but I was held as firmly as if someone had put U-hu glue on the seat of my trousers. That car wasn't just made for midgets, it was made for small midgets. 'I don't know,' I said. 'I hope not, but the thought's been nagging at me since I was handed this chore. There's a brother, Charles, who I presume is set to inherit all the lady's loot ...'

'She's loaded?'

'Surely you've heard of the Walsh-Overmans? The department store people ...'

'Oh, those Walsh-Overmans ... You think this Charles is murdering every tramp in Dublin in the hope that one of them is his long lost brother? Seems a bit far fetched to me.'

'Well, you never can tell, as the woman said when the trout sat up and barked at her.'

'You think Charles is the type?'

'No, but he could have hired the type. And that reminds me, the house was visited last night by a couple of toughs ...'

'Toughs?'

'A couple of hard men came around looking for Marty Lynch ... a gambling debt. I sent them packing with their tails between their legs.'

'You did?'

'Yes, I did. Why d'you sound so surprised?'

She ducked that one: 'I hope you didn't break up the furniture. I've still got a stake in that house.'

'I broke an antique hurley stick on one of them. Otherwise everything is still in place. You want to go up there and check? The house misses you.'

'Only the house?'

We were stopped again in a snarl of traffic, and I glanced out at the entrance to the Friary at Merchant's Quay. A couple of vagrants were sitting on the steps and, as I watched, one of them got up, turned away, then came back and clumsily kicked the other in the body. The first one then fell on top of his companion and they rolled down the steps and under the feet of the passersby. It was a sorry sight, and it gave me a queasy feeling about Annie.

'It must be tough for you at times,' I said, watching her profile as she concentrated on manoeuvring her heap of scrap through places where there seemed to be no space at all.

'What, driving this car?'

'No, dealing with the kind of people you meet up with in the course of your work. You must find yourself in some hairy situations at times.'

'We always travel in pairs. Normally Victoria'd be with me.'

'She's always in a hairy situation.' I waited for her to grin, then I said, 'Why're you on your own now?'

'I'm not, you're with me. Anyway, I think Victoria's being tactful. She probably believes that we've got things to talk about.'

'And have we?'

'Well, there're a few financial matters we could discuss.'

Hastily I steered the subject onto another topic: 'I could use a bit of help,' I told her. 'When we arrive at the Star of the Sea I mean. You're known there. Maybe you could introduce me, see me right?'

'Wouldn't you prefer to fare for yourself? After all, if you can handle two tough guys with an antique hurling stick, you shouldn't have too much trouble with the manager of a home for the homeless.'

We went up the hill crowned by Christ Church cathedral, the car protesting and threatening to slide back down as the incline became steeper. We made it, just about, and turned into Fishamble Street, where it wrapped itself round the boundary of the cathedral. Halfway down, on the right, is a bronze plaque reminding all and sundry that the first performance of Handel's *Messiah* was given there at noon on Tuesday, April 13th, 1742.

The Star of the Sea, further down on the left, is a red-brick building, set back from the road behind silver railings with curlicues that told of an earlier time and more personalised workmanship than obtains today.

A pair of modern gates guarded the entrance to this imposing-looking edifice, and Annie drew up before them and blew her horn. The beep-beep brought a decrepit individual in a worn brown duffle coat and a leather headpiece with flaps out of a wooden structure that resembled a coffin standing on its end. He shuffled over and stared at us through the bars of the gate.

Having imprinted us on his memory banks for further reference, he commenced pulling at the gate, first opening one section, then the other, and ushered us in. With great ceremony he closed them behind us, snuffling and hawking, then he went back into his sentry-box and banged the door. There could only have been enough room for him to stand upright in it.

Properly awed by this performance, I extricated myself from the affectionate embrace of the Citroen and followed Annie up a set of concrete steps to the front door. It was big enough to admit a carriage and four. We made our way into an echoing, cavernous hallway, tiled underfoot with old fashioned red tiles and with the walls and ceiling painted a functional grey. It smelled of urine and Jeyes Fluid, an institutionalised odour that reminded me of public toilets. Bolted to the cold, damp-looking walls were a number of wooden benches, and reclining on these, in various stages of disrepair, was as motley a collection of humanity as one could wish to see.

An old dame in a straw hat held her coat together with both hands and munched her gums, her shrunken jaws going ten to the dozen, while a fat old guy in a gabardine mac tried to catch her attention. Probably in a little while he'd flash her — the mac was made for it.

Two more ancient relics sat further on, their chins on their chests, their arms down by their sides, their legs stuck out —

they might have been department store dummies resting between sales.

What appeared to be a bundle of old clothes on one of the benches turned out to be a snoozing gent with muttonchop whiskers. He was playing the tuba from his back passage, and you could slice the air around him, bottle it and sell it as a tincture for killing bluebottles. Holding my nose, I investigated his hands, but both of them had a complete complement of fingers. I shrugged at Annie who was regarding me oddly: 'Just curious to see if he'd had them manicured this morning.'

We went along the hallway and up a flight of metal stairs, our footsteps echoing eerily. At the first landing there was a door marked 'Office', and Annie pushed it open and went in without knocking. I followed.

The room we were in was walled in frosted glass, with a clear pane staggered here and there to break the monotony. The furnishings included a gun-metal steel desk, four matching chairs with fabric seats, a filing cabinet, and a broad-beamed individual in a white coat bent over and staring out through one of the peepholes.

We stood for a moment enjoying the view, then Annie said, 'The coast clear, Steve, or are you just tying your shoelaces?'

The guy turned his head without straightening up and stared at us. He frowned. 'I've told you before not to call me Steve,' he said.

'Then what should I call you?'

'Why don't you try Mr Norton?'

'Try him for what?'

Annie grinned at him, but he didn't return it. He took one more lingering glance out through the glass, then he went over behind his desk and lowered himself into a more sturdy version of the other chairs in his office.

And it needed to be well fortified, for he was immensely fat, with a belly that would soon require two hands to hoist it when he had occasion to point Percy at the porcelain. He was about forty, with nicely-waved chestnut hair, a round soft face with smooth jowls, and the self-satisfied air of a man who had fed well, whose bowels were in good working order, and whose underwear was clean and well aired. On first sight I didn't like him, but, as I've mentioned before, I make judgements like that and often live to regret them.

Annie sat down on one of the steel chairs and opened the briefcase she had brought with her. 'I've some documents here for two of my old ladies to sign,' she informed Mr Norton, alias Steve. She inclined her head in my direction. 'This is Mr Shight — spelled S-h-i-g-h-t — and he's also from social welfare. He's trying to locate a gentleman who's been known to board in this establishment, but he'll tell you all about it himself.' She sniggered and rattled her papers, then stood up. 'I know where my ladies are,' she went on, 'so I'll just go down and get these signed.' Then to me: 'I'll collect you on the way out, Mr ... ah ... Shight. Have a nice visit with Steve. He's a load of laughs when you get to know him.' She went out, leaving both of us glowering.

Norton eyed me uncomfortably. 'Your name is not really ... ah ... what she said it is, is it?' he asked me.

'No, no,' I assured him, 'it's Smythe actually — spelled S-m-y-t-h-e. How d'you do?' I leaned over and took his limp paw and flipped it up and down. 'Walsh-Overman, that's who I'm after. You're the manager of this establishment, of course ..?'

'It's managed by a Trust — The Erasmus Carlisle Trust to give it its full name. I'm its secretary.'

'Yes, quite.' For a moment I wished I had glasses and a snap-brimmed hat like Humphrey Bogart in *The Big Sleep*, but I settled for taking out my notebook and a ballpoint pen and perching myself expectantly on the edge of my chair. 'Perhaps if I described Mr Walsh-Overman?' I said. 'He might not be using his own name.'

'Walsh-Overman ...' Norton said it as though it rang a bell, but then he shook his head and muttered, 'No, never heard of him. Not often we get them with double-barrelled names, though ...'

He took out a tin of cheroots, shook one loose, popped it in his mouth, lit it. He had the fastidiously exact movements of the very fat, a prim economy with hand, arm and shoulder that had a grace all its own. I was tempted to look under the desk to see if he had very small feet.

'Go ahead and describe him,' he told me. 'But I must warn you, if he's not one of the regulars I'll hardly know him.'

I described Redmond, mentioning the missing half finger yet again. While I talked, he took up an official-looking document from the desk and began studying it. I finished and sat back, notebook and pen poised. Norton went on gazing at the paper in his hand.

After a while I coughed, then I shuffled my feet. Norton glanced at me. 'Sounds like Major Moran to me,' he said, but not with any great interest. He flicked some ash from his cheroot.

'Major Moran?' I squeezed out through gritted teeth.

'Well, that's the only one your description puts me in mind of. Comes here on and off when the mood takes him.'

'Does the mood take you to tell me if he's here now?'

That was a mistake. His eyes narrowed and his mouth clamped shut around the little cigar. When he unscrewed it again he said, 'I'm a busy man. I have to deal with a crisis in this place every half hour. I can't keep track of everyone that comes and goes.'

'Then who can?'

He tried to outstare me, but I've won prizes for that kind of thing. When he was in danger of going cross-eyed he gave up and began to fiddle with a console fixed to his desk. He tsk-tsked, spoke into it and cocked his ear to listen. I did the same, but the voice that emerged sounded as if it belonged to a duck and I couldn't make out a word. Norton's ear must have been tuned to the right wavelength, for he turned to me and said, 'Not on the premises. And hasn't been for a week or more.'

'You're sure?'

That was another mistake. This time his eyes got distant, about as distant as snow on a mountain top. This wasn't my day where tact was concerned.

'D'you keep records?' I asked him, gamely battling on. 'Maybe there's somewhere else that he's a habit of visiting? Where I can find him?'

'It's you lot who keep the records,' he said, throwing me for a minute until I remembered that Annie had told him I was from Social Welfare. 'Why can't you look him up yourself?'

'Nothing like that on him there,' I said lamely. 'That's why I came over to see you.'

Now he was suspicious. 'Why're you looking for him anyway? Most of these down and outs get too much done for them. And d'you think they ever show a modicum of gratitude?'

That gave me an idea. 'There's a question of money due,' I said, watching avarice ignite in his hitherto uninterested orbs. 'A small bequest, you understand.'

'How small?'

'Oh, substantial enough really,' I lied. 'Even by today's outrageous standards.'

Norton extracted another cheroot, this time offering me the tin. I declined and instead took out a Dunhill. He lit it for me, leaning across the desk to do so. I was beginning to think that his hair was as false as his manner: it certainly had the same oiled artificiality about it. 'Sometimes the people who frequent this place turn out to be quite well off,' he told me, his right eyebrow quivering excitedly. 'And it's not unknown for them to leave a little something to the Trust. We are, after all, the last to show them a little kindness and understanding.'

'Before they float across to the other side?'

'That's it.' He leaned back complacently and folded his hands across the dome of his stomach. 'Maybe if you spoke to The Hacker,' he suggested. 'No one knows his real name — and I'd advise you not to ask him — but I've seen him a time or two with Major Moran. He's laid up at the moment, but I could send you down to see him.'

'That'd be too, too kind.'

I sat and beamed at him as he once more cranked up the console and sent a summons out into the wild blue yonder. It was soon answered by a young, harassed-looking, moon-faced guy in a white smock and matching trousers. Calling him Pepper, Norton instructed him to take me to St Jude's ward and introduce me to The Hacker. 'We do like to co-operate when we can,' Norton told me smoothly. 'If you do find Major Moran and he is your man, don't forget to remind him that he spent some of his happier moments in our little home from home.'

'I'll do what I can,' I said, standing up. 'But I'm not promising anything. He's been known to have had relations with animals, so it's likely that he'll leave the money to the dogs' and cats' home. They're queer like that, you know.'

His mouth fell open and he stared at me. I raised my eyebrows, put my finger alongside my nose, and left him to his thoughts.

Pepper led me up and down sets of metal stairs until I felt as though I'd become imprisoned in a Joan Miro painting. My headache of the morning returned and played a descant to my feet, clang bang, clang, clang, bang. To pass the time I tried querying my companion as to the history of the Star of the Sea. By the look he gave me I might as well have asked him if his auntie was a prostitute.

Eventually he brought me to a large, barn-like room that echoed dismally to the groans of its inhabitants. Set at intervals, every few yards and along both walls, were curtained alcoves, through the openings of which beds could be spied. Some of them were occupied, some not.

The one Pepper conducted me to was occupied: 'The Hacker,' he announced, sweeping the curtain aside with all the anxious aplomb of a magician not entirely sure that his trick was going to work.

He need not have worried: The Hacker was sitting up looking at us, not with any evidence of welcome, but there nonetheless. He had probably been a big bruiser once, but now the flesh was dropping from his bones and he was all head and eyes. His physical condition didn't stop him from dredging up a very snotty expression, however, as much as to say, 'Whaddya mean coming into my bedroom unannounced?'

I went in, and Pepper dropped the curtain behind me. 'Hi,' I greeted him. 'So how are we today?'

He looked at me, then hawked and spat voluminously into the plastic container he held cradled on his chest. 'You want to know if I've passed a motion?' he asked me in a voice like a rasp at work.

'Huh?'

'The bowels,' he said angrily. 'A bowel movement ...'

'Not particularly.'

'Well, I haven't. As hard as concrete,' he said, with evident satisfaction. 'You'll need a stick of dynamite.'

'What would you say to an enema?'

'I'd say go stick it up your own hole. Hardbound for a month now I am.'

'Congratulations. But that wasn't what I came to talk about.'

'No?'

'No.'

I looked around for a chair but there wasn't one, so I made to sit on the edge of the bed. Immediately The Hacker squared up to me, setting his jaw pugnaciously. 'So what're you,' he growled, 'a fairy?'

'I beg your pardon?'

'You walk in here and try to get into bed with me ...'

'Perish the thought.'

I straightened up and leaned against the wall. It was cold and clammy to the touch and reminded me of a gravestone in early morning mist. I got one of those intimations of galloping mortality and shivered. 'I'm looking for a gent called Redmond Walsh-Overman,' I said quickly. 'May also call himself Major Moran.'

'You expect to find him in here?' the man in the bed asked me sourly. 'Why don't you look under the pillow? He might be hiding in there waiting for the tooth fairy.'

'You've got fairies on the brain.'

'I'd rather have them there than somewhere else.'

'That's a thought.'

We sneered at one another, but he was better at it than me. 'Got a fag?' he eventually asked me. 'I took you for a doctor, but you haven't got the smarmy manner.'

I shook out a cigarette, lit it and handed it to him. He took it shakily and just about managed to get it to his mouth. The first puff made him cough, like paper tearing. After that he settled for causing the window frames to rattle.

'The guy I'm looking for is in his fifties, fat, maybe well spoken, and has the little finger of his left hand, or part of it, missing.' — I'd intoned this so much in the last couple of days that it was beginning to sound like a prayer.

The Hacker stopped coughing long enough to spit. I imagine his lungs probably had the same consistency as a sieve. He was game, though. He dropped the spent cigarette into his spittoon, hauled himself up by grasping the iron bedhead and pulling. I wouldn't have thought he'd have had any moisture in him, yet his face was beaded with sweat and the armpits of his pyjamas were dank with it.

'I fought in the war, you know,' he suddenly told me.

'Oh yeah? Which one?'

'Which one d'you think?'

'I can't really tell ... There's been so many of them.'

'A lot of fellows lost bits and pieces,' he said musingly. 'A little finger is nothing compared to losing an arm or a leg ... or your bollocks ...'

'True. But I don't think my man lost his pinkie in the war ...'

'I knew a Sergeant Nolan ... from Wexford, I think. Or was it Wicklow? No matter. Had his arm blown off by a mortar shell. You know what he did? He picked it up and beat a German colonel to death with it.'

'Never!'

'When the gas blew in you had to piss in your handkerchief

and put it over your face.'

'Wouldn't it have been simpler, not to mention more hygienic, to have worn a gas mask?'

The Hacker was lost in reverie and didn't pick me up on that one. I was beginning to think I'd get nothing from him, when he said out of the blue, 'Major Moran was never in no army. Had no discipline. Didn't know how to salute.'

'That's important, is it?'

'Odd kind of bugger. I only knocked around with him because he had a nice warm doss over on the northside.'

'Was it in the boilerhouse of a school in Fairview?'

'Something like that. There was a furnace that stayed hot at night. Cosy when the wind blew.'

'When did you last see him?'

The Hacker suddenly looked crafty. 'There was a commotion last Sunday so I went a.w.o.l. to see what it was about. The bastards chased me down the hill in their white coats.' He glanced at me proudly. 'Nothing wrong with me,' he said, 'except that the shit backed up and caused a blockage. I fought them off, but there was too many of them ...'

'Sure,' I said, trying to imagine it. 'But you did see Major Moran during your moment of freedom?'

'Yeah. He was sitting in a rubbish skip with his throat cut. Funny sight on a Sunday morning ...'

I experienced a feeling of let-down, as though a chair had abruptly been pulled out from under me. Was this to be the end of my case, finished before it had even started? With poor old Redmond just another piece of human lumber on life's rubbish tip?

'You're sure it was him?'

'Oh, it was him all right. Wasn't he wearing that outfit of his? Bowler hat, natty sportscoat, those half-trousers with the socks up to the knee — no one else dressed like that.'

'Well now,' I said thoughtfully. I took out a cigarette and played with it, and The Hacker's eyes lit up. 'Gimme one,' he said, indicating the cigarette.

'With your chest?'

'What's my chest to you? Nothing wrong with my chest.' He looked down at it, then said with disgust, 'You doctors are all the same, trying to stuff a man into the grave before he's more than half ready ...'

'I'm not a doctor. Don't you remember?'

'Piss off.'

I shrugged, ignited the coffin nail and passed it over to him. Then I set fire to one for myself.

We smoked and thought our own thoughts. I don't know about The Hacker, but mine were as dry as dust. If the murdered tramp in the bin was Redmond, then my job was done and there was nothing more for me to do except go out to Howth and inform his mother. I wondered how I would put it to her: Someone cut your son's throat and dumped him in a waste container? Not a very pleasant message to bring an old lady whose own life expectancy was as tenuous as a butterfly's. Then again, maybe this was what she had feared, with tramps being slaughtered willy-nilly. It could be that she had wanted Redmond back at home for his own protection.

I had one more card to play before I marked the case as closed, and that required me to be elsewhere. Anyway The Hacker appeared to have dozed off, the cigarette still burning between nicotine-stained fingers. I reached for it, and he suddenly opened his eyes and glared at me. I felt foolish leaning in over him like that. 'Why do they call you The Hacker?' I asked him, gazing into his faded old eyes.

He grinned, startling me with teeth that a ghoul would have been ashamed of. 'I knew you'd ask me that,' he said. 'It's what everyone wants to know.'

'Yes?'

'And I'm telling you what I tell them: Bugger off and mind your own fuckin' business.'

There was no comeback on that one, so I gave him the remainder of the cigarettes and left him to cough his way through the rest of the day.

12

I COLLECTED ANNIE, who was waiting for me outside Norton's office. We retraced our steps, down the metal stairs and through the cavern of the hallway. None of the old wrecks seemed to have changed position, but the tuba player had quietened down and was now merely sizzling, in the manner of a pan of frying bacon.

The porter struggled out of his box and released us and we rocketed off back down the quays. Some wicked-looking clouds had trundled into the sky, and the wind was as raw as a crosscut onion. We were in the snarl of traffic at O'Connell Bridge before Annie asked me how I had got on.

'Not so good. It seems Redmond has adopted a new identity — calls himself Major Moran. Or at least he did until last Sunday. Last Sunday terminated things: the candidate for a body bag that was found in the skip ..?'

'It was Redmond?'

'Seems like it. An acquaintance of his told me it was him.'

'So that's that then?'

'Well, this guy recognised Redmond only by the clothes he was wearing. I don't think he got a really good look at him. It might be worthwhile trying for a positive identification. The body should still be down in the city morgue.'

That last remark put a damper on things where conversation was concerned. Annie dropped me in the city centre, after promising faithfully to have dinner with me later in the week. I went into a public telephone kiosk, more in hope than expectation, but by some miracle it was actually working. I rang a friend of mine called Leo Quinn at the College of Surgeons, a bedside manner voice telling me to hold on and he'd see if Leo was present and available.

Leo has been trying to be a doctor now going on for ten years and, although knowing everyone and anyone in the medical line, he is still no nearer his objective. He has an aunt down the country who finances him, so it is possible that he deliberately procrastinates in order to prolong the good life.

He finally came on the phone and I asked him to meet me in half an hour at the morgue. He protested that he was busy, but I told him that it was a matter of life and death, mainly death. When that didn't work I promised to buy him lunch. Although almost skeletal in appearance, Leo has a voracious appetite and is about as fastidious as a goat as to when and what he eats. He said he'd see me at the main door of the morgue, but that he was to do the talking.

I decided to pass the time by walking and I stepped it out, moving briskly to make up for the fact that I wasn't wearing an overcoat. I passed the huge, glass-walled City Bus Terminus. A large tour bus wheeled out through the entrance, then ground to a halt in a hiss of airbrakes. Rows of heads turned in unison to watch me walk across in front of it — old age pensioners, probably, availing of their free travel to visit beauty spots in Cork and Kerry.

I thought of how, when I was young in Wexford and slept high up in an attic room, I used watch the same farm labourer trudge through the fields every morning. How I envied that man his life, which seemed so free and uncluttered, while I was bound up with the necessity of school and the routine of learning by rote. Every time I had an exam, an interview, a demand on my time, I would think of that man, and he has continued to haunt me down the days, my shade, the personification of release in the midst of restraint. The possibility that he was a sheep shagger par excellence makes no difference whatever to my conception of his free wheeling lifestyle.

When I got to the black, double gates of the morgue, Leo was outside stamping his feet. His face was blue from the cold and, if he hadn't been moving about, one could have mistaken him for a candidate for admission.

Leo always reminds me of Oliver St John Gogarty's description of the Abbey playwright Lennox Robinson: 'Poached eyes on ghost'. He is thin to the point of being a brush handle, and has a perennially surprised expression on his face as though he has just been poked in the behind. He walks leaning forward, the upper half of his body inclined at an angle of some thirty degrees. His clothes always look like remnants from a bring and buy sale, the shoulders of the jacket halfway down his arms, his shirt tails sticking out, the legs of his trousers flapping at half mast about his shins.

He also has a sing-song Cork accent that he accentuates on occasions, mainly, I suspect, to annoy. I greeted him, he nodded, we knocked, and a small gate in the bigger one opened. We stepped inside.

The great thing about Leo is that he has friends everywhere, and this character who let us in looked like one of the odder ones. He had a round, countryman's face, a lick of sandy hair, a pale gleam of moustache, and teeth that some dental mechanic must have carved when in the DTs — they appeared so ridiculously false that at first I thought he'd put them in to give us a laugh. He was wearing a kind of blue-grey boiler suit and bright yellow wellington boots. If I had been trying to imagine a morgue attendant, he was it to a tee.

He greeted Leo effusively, drenching him in a shower of spittle in the process. I couldn't believe it when Leo introduced him to me as Sammy Davis.

'Jr. or Sr.?' I asked him, causing him to laugh heartily and me to duck.

In a stage whisper, Leo proposed that I should recompense his friend for the trouble he was about to undertake on my behalf. I fished another of Charles's fivers out of my pocket and watched it disappear into Sammy's bib.

I told him what I wanted, feeling compelled, for some reason, to speak in a whisper. We could have been three conspirators planning a coup here in the house of the dead.

'That'll be lot 39,' Sammy informed me. 'Unidentified male Caucasian ...'

'What happens if he stays like that?'

'Like what?'

'Unidentified.'

'The city will bury him, don't you know.'

'Does the city have to do that very often?'

Sammy looked pensive, the Ken Dodd teeth puckering his mouth into an anus of distress. He looked faintly like a cocker spaniel with an overbite. After a moment he unzipped again and said, 'Not too often. Usually we manage to get hold of some kindly benefactor. Are you interested in doing the necessary for ... ah ...'

'Lot 39? No, not really. I just want to take a look at him.'

'You've an interest in the dearly departed?' Sammy's little piggy eyes glinted. 'Did you hear what the fellow replied when asked if he was a necrophiliac?'

'Huh?'

'No,' he said, 'it's dead boring ...' Sammy again laughed, instituting another spray, then abruptly broke it off and asked, 'Coffee?'

'What?'

'Would you like some coffee? I could share my sandwiches with you, don't you know.'

'That won't be necessary,' I said hastily. 'We're in rather a hurry.' The prospect of eating in a morgue was about as attractive to me as having sex in a graveyard.

Sammy shrugged, then led us through a series of cold, silent rooms, our footsteps bouncing back off the walls and hurrying us along. Conversation would have been superfluous, not to say blasphemous. This was a place for silent running and for getting out of as quickly as possible.

Eventually we came to a larger apartment that contained a number of block wood structures like butchers' tables, some sinks and four huge stainless steel baskets. The tables were occupied by sheeted figures with only their feet on display and

Sammy went into a well-rehearsed spiel to the effect that each corpse had to be tagged as to name, social security number, sex and cause of death — 'Wouldn't do to mix them up, don't you know. Imagine Aunt Polly coming for Uncle Fred and being given Uncle Eustace by mistake. That'd cause a fair bit of consternation ...'

He led us over to one of the tables and unveiled what was on it. A fat old item, scrubbed and shining, his hands joined on his bare chest, grinned up at us with two mouths, one above and one below his chin. Gingerly I reached out and disentangled his arms, to find that the hands had the usual number of fingers and thumbs. Whoever's quarry this was, it wasn't mine. I put the limbs together again, and whatever way I disturbed the corpse's insides it suddenly broke wind noisily. I jumped back as if shot at, which in a manner of speaking I had been.

Both Leo and Sammy thought it very funny, and they kept breaking into giggles as we trundled back to the office to look over Lot 39's clothing. I couldn't see the funny side of it at all.

While I went through the odds and ends that Sammy handed me in a plastic basket, the other two shared the packet of sandwiches. I was not surprised to see that the filling was egg and onion.

The clothes were as The Hacker had described: brogues, long fawn stockings, brown plus fours, and a quilted sports jacket. They were filthy and smelled of the men's locker room on a Saturday night, but when they'd been new they had cost someone plenty.

'Satisfied?' Leo asked me, gazing curiously over my shoulder.

'I guess.' I turned to Sammy, who was still masticating egg and onion sandwich, the teeth churning like the steel masher in the back of a garbage truck. I was reminded of Cedric's piranha fish. 'Anyone else come to ask about Lot 39? Other than the usual set of officials.'

Sammy nodded, swallowed, then said, 'One other. Said he

thought it might be his brother, don't you know.'

'And was it?'

'Regretfully, no.'

'What'd he look like?'

'Fat. Colourfully dressed. Very friendly. Didn't enjoy viewing the remains. I told him he'd have to give his name and address as this particular item had been murdered.'

'And did he give it?'

'Yes. A very ordinary name. George Brown. We get a lot of George Browns.'

'Didn't you ask for identification?'

'Did I ask you?'

I conceded that one to him, and Leo and I said our goodbyes. He seemed sorry to see us go.

Outside again the wind was still blowing, the light bright and hard on the eyes. The traffic was as thick and clotted as curdled cream. Leo had a nose on him like a pointer dog's, and we followed it along Talbot Street until we found a cafe that served mid-afternoon snacks. I had a turkey sandwich that had spent an indefinite period of time in the freezer, while Leo proceeded to load enough junk food into himself to keep an army on the march for a week.

We didn't talk much — Leo and I never do. Apart from asking me who I'd thought the tramp was and being told, 'The Earl of Lucan', he busied himself with the gunge he was eating. He finished off with half a lemon curd pie, tamping it in like Old King Cole filling his pipe. Saluting me, he then left, waddling off about his business — and for a thin man like Leo to waddle, is no mean trick.

I drank some coffee and watched the condensation from the window trickle down into the soup tureen. It was obvious that it had been Charles Walsh-Overman who had visited the morgue before me. Idly I wondered why he had bothered hiring me if he was going to do the legwork himself. Probably hedging his bets — it could happen that he'd stumble onto something that I might miss. At the moment I was a long way behind him and not even showing in the race.

Then there was the business of the latest tramp's clothes. Had he stolen them from Redmond? Had Redmond given them to him? Maybe Redmond was already dead, one of the first two to be murdered, the others being killed to hide the fact. Then again maybe the tramps being knocked off had nothing whatever to do with Redmond. 'Fuck it,' I told myself, 'no point getting yourself into a knot about it.'

The turkey sandwich was lodged somewhere about the point of no return in my gullet, so I cursed that too. Then I cursed the bill which took away another of Charles's fivers.

I went out of that cafe cursing like a docker whose bailing hook had got caught in the overhead power line, but God's judgement was waiting around the corner for me: a parking ticket adorned the windscreen of my car. The traffic warden knew quite well that no doctor would be driving a motor as disreputable-looking as mine.

This new blast of outrage when I saw the ticket had one positive effect, however, for it dislodged the remains of the turkey sandwich with the explosive force of a depth charge.

13

IT WAS FIVE o'clock and the shops in O'Connell Street were closing down for the day. The traffic was worse than ever. I dodged in and out, moving diagonally across the road. Most of the drivers looked murderous, especially one grim-faced female who jumped her car forward as I hesitated until it was bumper to bumper with the one in front. I left her to savour her small triumph and went around behind her.

The Roxy video shop was all lit up, the punters jostling and shoving to get the latest Clint Eastwood or Charles Bronson vigilante movie to take home with them to suburbia. With their feet up and the television on, they could watch the villains falling in droves and experience a vicarious sense of safety.

There was a time when the centre of Dublin would be crowded at night, with long cinema queues, people going dancing, people strolling about. There were no steel meshes across the shop windows then, no alarm boxes pimpling their fronts. You could look at people without getting punched out for doing so. Now, at night, the streets are full of menace. Many of the doorways hold the huddled shapes of homeless men and women; children sit begging all along the neon-lit facades of O'Connell Street; in the public toilets young boys barely into their teens sell themselves with the fatalistic cynicism of those for whom nothing better looms on the horizon. And more affluent young people express their sense of futility in rough-house behaviour, filthy language, cider parties, acid parties, and shooting up on whatever coke, crack or nose candy they can lay their hands on.

Dear old dirty Dublin, I thought, as I pushed my way into the Roxy looking for its proprietor, what a pass you've come to: riddled and moth-eaten and down on your knees. It is said that James Joyce, in exile, knew Dublin so well that, if it were to be destroyed, it could be rebuilt from the descriptions in his books. Maybe it wouldn't be such a bad thing if that were now to come to pass.

I found Batt and asked him if I had had any visitors. He answered in the negative, then told me he was missing one of the Ladykillers. 'Try Danny Green,' I told him, and left him scratching his head. Everyone got Alec Guinness, Herbert Lom, Peter Sellers and Cecil Parker; it was Danny Green who stumped them.

I went through the anteroom into my office and sat at my desk. After a moment I picked up the phone and called Leo. When he came on I asked him to check out the records of the other two murdered tramps to find out if either of them had a missing little finger on his left hand. He asked me no questions, I told him no lies.

The light was beginning to fade and I watched darkness, my old friend, creep into the room like a promise of forgetfulness. I didn't feel anything in particular; I wasn't cheerful, but neither was I depressed. I was in a kind of neutral state, waiting for something to happen. For want of anything better to do, I pushed the button on the answering machine. A woman's voice came on to tell me that she was Mrs Ada Mulloy and that her husband had done a runner owing her a tidy sum in child maintenance and would I contact her so that I could get some of it back. For a minute I wondered if it was Annie doing a funny voice.

There was a message from Tom Saddler, who was with an insurance company, to tell me that he had some work that I might be interested in. My father then came on to confirm that he would be up on Saturday for the big match, and there was a rather apoplectic piece from my landlord to the effect that I had one more week to pay up or else.

I rewound the machine so that I could listen to the messages again at another time. I took out my bottle of Bushmills and treated myself to a shot to ward off the evening chill. I lit a cigarette. I got up and switched on the light. Sitting at the desk again I looked around for something else to do. Other than teetering back in my chair and falling out the window, I could think of nothing exciting enough to cause me to break into a jig.

I toasted the office at large one more time from the Bushmills bottle, then I got up, went downstairs and walked to my car. The streetlights were on, and a wind thin and chill enough to do the work of an icepick stabbed at me. I put on the fan heater and drove down Gardiner Street, with its rows of bed and breakfast emporiums similar to the one I'd visited that morning, then around by Amiens Street station and out towards the North Strand. During the Second World War some off course German bombers had dropped their loads along here, mistaking it for the Liverpool docks, and for years afterwards hordes of old doxies had cadged free drinks on the strength of having been there and living to tell the tale.

I drove into Fairview, passing the park on my right. Just before the metal overhang of the pedestrian bridge I pulled in. I shut off the motor and the lights and sat for a time, watching the world go by. The school was directly facing me, a dark bulk against the lighter shading of the sky. There would be an alarm, but I wasn't interested in getting into the main building. It was the boiler house I was after.

I smoked a cigarette and drummed my fingers on the steering wheel. A tall number all wrapped up against the weather walked past and looked in at me. There was something familiar about him, but then, Dublin being such a small place, there was something familiar about most people. Deciding that if I didn't move soon I'd start attracting a crowd, I stripped off my sportscoat and hid it under the rug on the back seat. I got out, went around to the boot and took out a black leather jacket that I kept there. I put it on, snuggling my shoulders comfortably into it. I also donned a pair of black pigskin driving gloves. Maybe I looked like James Bond, and then again maybe I didn't.

To get into the school grounds I had to climb over a metal gate, but that didn't pose any problems for an athletic type like me. What did delay me was finding the furnace house. I finally came across what I presumed was it at the end of a strip of tar macadam walkway guarded by a stand of particularly thorny rose bushes. There was a fume extractor with a little tin hat on it sticking out of the roof, and the brick wall was warm to my touch when I leaned against it.

I felt my way around until I came to the door. It was securely bolted and padlocked. Moving again, I went round the other way. For some reason the back wall was not built of brick; instead it was a badly made structure of ill-fitting planks, and at least three of them had been removed to reveal an opening that would admit one fat man, or two thin ones moving side by side.

I paused to listen, but the night was as quiet as a stalking cat. A hunter's moon played tic-tac-toe with some scudding clouds. I was in the heart of Dublin, that thousand-year-old city, yet I was as alone as Proust in his cork-lined room.

I shrugged and went in, the planks groaning as I brushed against them. I stopped again to listen, but all I could hear was my heart thumping. When it subsided, I ventured in further, and walked straight into something that clanged like a manhole covering falling into place. I chanced switching on the pencil flash I'd brought with me and saw the furnace cover swinging back at me.

It wasn't the only thing that was swinging at me. Something hit me on the side of the head with enough force to drive me forward onto my knees. In the darkness I put out my hands to protect my face, but they encountered empty space, and then I was really falling: falling into that bottomless pit that I'd also encountered the night before at the hands of thug number one. Familiarity definitely breeds contempt. For me, the lights went out all over Dublin.

14

SOMEONE WAS singing, nice and low, no strain, one of those old tunes remembered from childhood:

'The sun has got his hat on,
Too rah loo rah lay,
The sun has got his hat on,
And is coming out to play.'

I lay and listened to it, and after a time discovered the singer was me. I had woken myself up, but it was a slow and painful process, so much so that a couple of times I nearly decided it wasn't worth the effort. There was a hot metal bar encircling the front of my head and a steel claw tearing away at the back of it. Further down, small people in hobnailed boots were trampling on me, obviously intent on enjoying their work.

I remained in the same position for a while and let pain wash over me like liquid fire. Then I began to fight back. I groaned. I lifted my head a little, tentatively, just by way of trying to discover if it was still in one piece. It was hard to judge in the pitch darkness.

After a number of fits and starts I managed to lift myself so that I was sitting. Whatever I was leaning against was nice and soft and pliable. I reached out and touched warm flesh.

My first instinct was to scream, but I argued myself out of that. Best to maintain a dignified silence. Instead I took a rest, like my comatose companion. Perhaps after a suitable interval, and if we felt up to it, we might try a duet.

Time went by. Then I noticed a tiny shaft of light below and to my right. I scrabbled for it and found that it was my pencil torch, still glowing. Oh goody, I thought, and I picked it up and shone it on my silent friend and beheld Charles Walsh-Overman staring fixedly at me as though blaming me for some indiscretion or other. I snapped off the light, then switched it on again. He was still there, glaring just as accusingly at me.

I waved my hand in front of his face, but he didn't blink. Curious ... I put my ear against his lips but couldn't feel or hear anything. The fact was inescapable: he wasn't breathing. Which fact led me to conclude that he had passed out of this vale of tears and was now testing out his infant wings in a newer and, I hoped, better place.

In spite of my pain — or maybe because of it — I experienced a riffle of sorrow. Only the day before I had spent a pleasant hour in his company. He had been nice to me. He had given me ten new five pound notes to spend. He hadn't demanded much in return, merely for me to find his long lost brother and return him to the fold. And now, here he was himself, as dead as mutton in a dusty, dirty boiler house and with only myself and the cockroaches to keep him company. It was enough to bring tears to the eyes of a dressmaker's dummy.

I switched off the torch and took a number of deep breaths. It was beginning to dawn on me that I might soon be in an amount of trouble if I didn't make myself scarce. Whoever had done in Charles and whacked me — and there was no reason to believe that it wasn't the same person — had probably called the police by now, and they could be here at any moment, stomping their way in, pushing their hats back in the way they had, gazing at me quizzically, and not believing a word out of my mouth.

I took one more look at Charles, and at the red bib of blood that half-mooned across his chest. His throat had been cut much in the manner of the three tramps. Had he been mistaken for his brother? It seemed a reasonable assumption. It wouldn't have been too difficult for him to find out about this hidey hole. The assassin was probably lying in wait. One swish of cold steel, a gurgle, and it was all over.

Deciding to shelve my thoughts for the moment, I scooted backwards on all fours and arse-over-elbowed my way out of there. The cold night air attacked my poor battered head like a douse of ice water, but it did serve to remove the muzziness and helped to clear my senses. I crawled back over the gate and made it to my car just as the first sirens started up. My reading of the situation had been right.

With a certain amount of difficulty I backed the car out onto the main road, but instead of heading into the city I drove on towards Clontarf, taking it nice and easy in the inside lane.

Out near the wooden bridge that leads to the Bull Island is the Seagull Inn. When I came to it, I drove into the parking lot and knocked off the engine. I got out, doing a fair imitation of the 1,000 year old man, went in to the men only bar and straight through to the toilet. An old gent pissing exuberantly into the steel urinal turned to look at me. Obviously not liking what he saw, he hurriedly shook himself off and made tracks. I leaned over the sink and bathed the back of my head in cold water. In the stained mirror my eyes were bloodshot and had the look of someone who had seen the Second Coming before the first one had ended. Otherwise I was as good as could be expected.

I dried myself off with toilet paper, combed my hair and lit a cigarette. Aside from a slight cindery smell from my trousers, I might never have been lying in a dirty boiler house holding hands with a corpse.

I went out and stood at the bar and ordered a double Bushmills. I threw it back, then chased it down with a hearty draught from a pint of Guinness. The barman paid no more attention to me than if I were the invisible man. He had enough on his mind doling out gargle to his thirsty customers. Down from me the old guy from the urinal was wiping froth off his whiskers. I nodded companionably at him, as one who had shared with him one of life's more intimate moments.

The room was large and echoey, with a low ceiling that caught the rolls of smoke from the many pipes and cigarettes before pushing them back down on the perpetrators. Pipes were in the ascendancy, the clientele being old, well-weathered and loud in one another's company.

I knew the scene well, for when I visited my father in Wexford I was invariably brought out to a pub such as this, full of retired men who knew each other, and each other's business. The older men get, it seems to me, the more insensitive they become. They share a crudity of manner and expression that exhibits itself in them blowing their noses in their fingers, pissing suddenly and unexpectedly in public places, being earthy at the expense of one another or of anyone who comes within their orbit. It seems to be a shared belief among them that their age and the fact that they may soon be taking off for parts truly unknown allow them an excess in their way of life not given to others coming up behind them. Possibly it's a way of thumbing their noses at convention, of shedding the skin of civilised living, of doubling back towards the outrageous behaviour of childhood in the hope of being overlooked for the chopper.

Jesus Christ, I suddenly thought, what am I doing here with this collection of old farts? I could soon be arrested on an accessory to murder charge. It was time for me to mount up and gallop on out of there.

I inquired from the barman as to where the phone might be and he pointed wordlessly towards the door, where a stand holding coats hid whatever was behind it.

I went over, burrowed in and found what I was looking for. Inserting some coins, I rang Annie's new address. A man's voice answered. Taking my nose between two fingers, I spoke in a falsetto voice and as near an approximation of a Liverpool accent as I could manage: 'This is Victoria,' I piped. 'Kin I speke to Annie?'

Harold, for undoubtedly it was he, gave credence to my estimation of his level of intelligence by saying, without equivocation, 'Sure, hold on a minute. I'll get her.'

I listened to him clump away, breathing in the muggy odour

of old coats. The pain in the back of my head was doing its best to kick its way out towards the front, and the front was resisting stoutly.

I thought I had been listening for Annie's footsteps, but she crept up on me, and when her voice suddenly spoke in my ear it made me jump.

'Hi, Vicky, everything all right?'

I took a deep breath, then said quickly, 'It's not Vicky, it's me. Don't hang up. I'm in trouble and I need you to come and get me. I'm in the Seagull Inn on the Clontarf Road. You know where it is?'

I had expected a blast of indignation, but as always she served to surprise me, putting the ball over in the corner of the court so that I had to stretch for it. 'You want me to come and collect you,' she said matter-of-factly. 'Right. I do know where the Seagull Inn is and that's me coming in the door. Throw a peanut in the air and by the time you catch it, I'll be at your elbow.'

'Annie ...' I started to say, but there was a click in my ear and the buzz of a disconnection. One of thesee days I'll hang up on her, but first I'll have to learn to be as quick as a striking snake.

Another pint of Guinness, an elbow on the counter, and I was back scrutinising the wall behind the bar. There was a poster advertising a pub quiz, a few pin-ups, a number of pitch and putt trophies, and a blown-up, colour photograph of a very fat female in a bikini eating an ice cream cone. Not the most edifying of collages for a man of my taste and sophistication.

I was pretty sure that Annie would come and collect me, but it was still a relief when she came swinging in the door about a quarter of an hour later. She stopped just inside, halted by the blast of sound and the rumble of male conversation. She was wearing her navy pea jacket, dark slacks, and a red scarf tied loosely round her hair. Unusually for a woman, she didn't carry any handbag.

There was a lull in the conversation as heads turned to look at her. I straightened up and she saw me and came over, her hands deep in her pockets and her unconcern at her intrusion into this male-dominated bastion as provocative as a spit in the eye.

She looked at the barman and told him to pull her a half of stout. Turning her shoulder to him, she leaned on the bar, hunched her head, winked at me and said, 'Well, howdy, stranger. Fancy meeting you in this neck of the woods.' Elaborately she gazed about her, facing down the stares until most of the faces turned away. Conversation murmured, then began to grow again in volume.

'Nice performance,' I said, acknowledging her little act. 'Ten out of ten for content, style and poise.'

'Attack, they say, is always the best form of defence.'

'You feel defensive?'

'Merely a figure of speech.' She bent her head and looked at me from under her lashes. 'What d'you think?'

'Not you,' I said admiringly. 'You could gather up this collection of granddads and blow them out in bubbles ...'

'Mass fellatio?'

'Me speaking figuratively, commending you on your calmness under fire. Some great self-possession, the way you cock a snook at convention.'

'Don't you mean snook a cock?'

'Nice one, Cecil. Another ten marker.' I wet my finger and drew it along the bar. 'Chalk that one up to you.'

The barman brought over her half of Guinness, put a coaster down and settled the dripping glass on it. While I fumbled for money, he set his hands wide apart on the counter and leaned in towards Annie. 'It's a men only, Miss,' he whispered. 'You'd be more comfortable in the lounge.'

Instead of looking at him, she gazed about her slowly, squinting her eyes. Then she turned to him. 'Call any of them up,' she offered, 'and I'll take them on at anything you propose: arm wrestling, back flips, the ten pound hammer ... you name it, I'll win it.'

The barman frowned, then looked at me. I gave him no help, merely raising an eyebrow and shrugging. He was obviously in a quandary, not wanting to cause a scene, yet not wishing to lose face either. It was Annie who eventually came to his rescue. 'Don't worry,' she told him, 'I'm only going to drink up and move out. Watch,' and she took up the glass, put it to her mouth and shifted the contents in one swallow.

We went outside and stood under a sky overcrowded with stars. A swipe of wind made contact with the lump on the back of my head and froze a grimace into my face. 'You showed some rare understanding in there,' I told Annie.

'You're implying ..?'

'What?'

She shuffled her feet. 'Maybe that I'm not always as understanding where you're concerned.'

'Could be.'

'Didn't I drop everything to come and get you?'

'What'd you drop?'

'Harold's essentials. What else?'

I looked at her. 'I'm sorry,' I said, 'I really do appreciate this. And you haven't even asked for an explanation.'

'I reckon you'll tell me in your own good time. I thought I'd cheer you up first. Have I cheered you up?'

'A kiss'd be a help in that direction.'

She duly obliged. Our lips were cold at first, but we worked on it and by the time we broke apart we had generated an amount of steam. A kiss on the hand may be quite continental, but one on the lips from Annie is a whole wide world experience.

We stood and breathed cold air at one another, then she punched me on the shoulder, not hard. 'So what's it all about, Alfie?' she asked. 'Not just your car breaking down surely?'

'No, the car's okay. It's me that's having the engine failure.' I looked at my watch. In fifteen minutes I was due to meet Marty up in Leeson Street. I would much sooner have gone home to bed, preferably with Annie, but a promise is a promise. 'Look,' I said, 'maybe you'd drive me over to Kiernan's pub on the southside? I'll leave my car here and explain all to you on the way.'

She shrugged. 'If docility is not my middle name, what is?'

We squeezed into the Citroen and after a few false starts got going. I closed my eyes and the racket the car made turned my eyeballs into ping pong balls. The pain in my head was the bat knocking them to and fro.

We had travelled for a time in silence — that is to say, we were not talking; silence in that car would have been as miraculous as crossing an elephant with a duck — when Annie turned to me and said, 'So?'

'You remember how I told you I was looking for a guy called Redmond Walsh-Overman ..?'

'I thought you found him in a skip up in Fishamble Street?'

'Not him. Someone else done up in his clothes. I went and had a look at him in the morgue. Fitted the general description in all but one particular, no missing little finger. I found out the real Redmond had a doss in the boiler house of a school in Fairview. That one there,' I told her, for we were indeed passing it at that moment. There were lights on in the main building, but the yard was at the back and I couldn't see if there was much activity abroad in it. Annie slowed and I quickly cautioned her to drive on: 'I went there earlier tonight. Just to have a look around, you understand. I'd only got into the boiler house when someone gave me a goodnight thump with a sack of wet sand. When I came to I was playing ring-a-rosy with a dead man ...'

'What? I mean, who?'

'Charles Walsh-Overman, Redmond's brother. His throat had been cut. It may have been a case of mistaken identity. The two of them look somewhat alike.'

'How come the same hadn't been done to you?'

'You mean?'

'Why hadn't your throat been cut too, you dummy?'

I looked at her, but she was staring fixedly ahead. 'Do I detect a note of concern?' I asked her. 'A crack in the hard-boiled veneer?'

'I was merely thinking of the trouble and expense of a funeral. And I don't fancy widow's weeds ...'

'On you they'd be flowers.'

'Be that as it may ...'

We pondered my escape from death, burial and a joust with the after-life for a minute, then I said, 'I figure I wasn't sliced up because whoever killed Charles felt that if I were implicated it'd take the heat off him — or her. In some quarters private detecting smells as sweet as pig slurry ...'

'By the law, you mean?'

'Indubitably.'

'So you fled the scene of the crime?'

'I did. I drove out to the Seagull Inn, bathed my poor head, bolstered my flagging spirits with some liquid refreshment, and waited for you to arrive like the United States cavalry.'

'Why did you need me?'

'Why d'you think?'

'Well, other than for the obvious reason of wanting mouth to mouth resuscitation.'

'I was afraid someone had seen me loitering around the school and could furnish a description of me and my car to the minions of the law. There was one character who looked vaguely familiar' — I tried to bring back into focus the tall character in the long black coat who'd looked in at me, but he stayed tantalisingly at the edge of my vision. 'This way, with the two of us driving in state in this tin can, we could be Darby and Joan on their way home from a meeting of the Friends of the Earth ...'

'Thanks a lot.'

I reached over and squeezed her thigh. 'You're not surprised, shocked, put off at the fact that I've just told you I found the body of a murdered man a matter of hours ago?' I asked her. 'Violent death doesn't give you the colly-wobbles?'

She was concentrating on her driving. 'You know the kind of work I do,' she said after a pause. 'I see some form of violence every day in the week. Arguments, fights, some awful injuries at times. You may say, so what, aren't those people the dregs, the also-rans, little better than animals. But they're not. No matter how ill, or scarred, or far gone they are, they're still human. When you see the body of an old woman that's lain for weeks in a basement cellar and been gnawed at by rats, your stomach still heaves. At least in your case, you can make an effort to find out who killed this Charles. With me, who do I blame? Who do I take my anger out on? The social services? Dublin Corporation? The politicians? The unheeding mass of the public? I have to swallow my anger and regurgitate it the next time I come across injustice, or the appalling inability of people to take care of themselves or be taken care of by inadequate resources or uncaring administrators. At the best of times it's a vicious circle, you pick and you poke and you patch up, knowing that tomorrow you'll have to do the same thing again ... and again ... and again ...'

'I'm sorry.'

Once more I gingerly laid my head back against the seat and closed my eyes. I had no answers for Annie, and she knew it. She was merely letting off steam. That's one in the eye for you, Harold, I thought: she might have set up house with you, but it's to me she brings her troubles for an airing.

We were driving along by the canal when Annie asked if I had any idea who might have punched Charles's ticket. 'I suppose it could've been Redmond.' I told her. 'He's a likely candidate. Reading between the lines, I don't imagine they got on all that well. Maybe Redmond was reclining on his couch looking over his collection of Meissen porcelain when Charles blundered in and broke one. You know how awkward situations like that can be ...'

'You find it funny?'

'No, not really.'

'But if that's the case, then it must be Redmond who's been

killing those other tramps.'

I thought about that one, but I didn't like it very much. It didn't make sense, unless of course Redmond was a homicidal maniac. Then again, there was a case to be made for that. His wife Bernadette had told me that he had a ferocious temper. Maybe that was why his mother wanted him found. She'd have read about the murders and thought it likely that her son was involved. I remembered how his sister had drowned in mysterious circumstances while out boating with him. More and more I was beginning to think that I'd got myself into something that I should be running away from as fast as my legs could take me.

'Maybe you should go to the police after all?' Annie said. 'Tell them what you know. Wash your hands of the whole affair.'

'You must've been reading my thoughts. But I don't really think I can do that, especially after leaving the scene of a major crime and not staying to give my account of it in triplicate.'

'You could write to them anonymously.'

'I could spit in my fist and wish I was Paul Newman.'

'You should be so lucky.'

I fished in my pockets for a cigarette, but couldn't find one. I chewed my lip instead and gazed out at the streetlamp lit canal bank. A skinny woman was being pulled along by a huge black dog — she could have got up on his back and ridden him home. I thought of Mrs Walsh-Overman, how she had sent me out to find one son, and now how she'd lost the other one. What was she thinking about, in her vast house by the sea and surrounded by the appurtenances of wealth? Was she thinking that maybe if she'd had less money she'd have had more of her family circle about her to keep her company now that Old Father Time was calling in his debt? Loneliness is not something you can make a pact with, fob off or shove in behind the wainscoting. I knew that only too well. Since my split with Annie I had spent many a night in our old house listening to the walls whisper of past times, good times. At least I could get up, go out, and get drunk. The old lady up on the hill of Howth was immured in her solitude, held as securely as a fly in amber.

15

A PALE SICKLE of moon had given itself a leg up among the stars by the time we arrived outside Kiernan's pub. There was a lot of activity, so Annie had to double park. I rolled down the window to test the air temperature and the wind blew in and gave my nose a tweak.

'So what now?' Annie asked me. 'Don't you think you've had enough excitement for one night? What're you doing here anyway? You were never much for a night on the town.'

'I'm meeting someone,' I told her. 'A business confab.'

'Business, eh? When I was sharing your life you were at a loose end so often you'd become frayed.'

'I've pulled up my socks since then,' I assured her. 'Now they're falling over themselves to avail of my services ...'

'Some of them are falling down dead.'

'True.' To get off that subject, I mentioned Marty: 'Our first paying guest,' I reminded her.

'When he did pay, that is. Which wasn't often.'

'Well, he's in a bit of trouble ...'

'How much trouble?'

'He's being leaned on by some villains ... It's to do with laundering dirty money.'

'I thought you told me it was a gambling debt?'

I rolled the window back up to prevent my face from getting frost bite. 'He's hired me to talk to these people,' I told her patiently. 'Just to talk to them,' I hurriedly went on when I saw her face darken.

She sniffed. 'Don't come calling me up again if you get into more trouble,' she said. 'I'm signing off for the night.'

'Going home to Harold?'

'At least he's able to handle his own trouble himself ...'

'My dear woman ...'

'Don't call me your dear woman' — this through gritted teeth.

I looked at her, but I could see that she was really mad this time. I considered a chaste kiss on the cheek, then settled for tipping her on the shoulder. I opened the door and got out, and she took the car away like a cat with mustard under its tail. I pitied any pedestrians who might foolishly stray into her path.

Kiernan's was jam packed, the punters endeavouring to get enough of a load on to prevent them having to buy bottles of sparkling wine done up to look like champagne in the various nightspots. The Leeson Street scene is a relatively new phenomenon in Dublin, a kind of tawdry boulevard of dreams, without any of the authentic ruthlessness to make it truly wicked. For all their much publicised wildness, the Irish have a conservative streak where debauchery is concerned. Put some Irish down in a real red light district like that of Hamburg, or Marseilles, or Amsterdam, and their toes will curl and their lips pucker as though given a lemon to suck instead of something more succulent. There's a certain ingrained naiveté always present, almost a fear of finding that the missionary position can be improved upon or even dispensed with entirely. To most Irish people 69 is merely the number that comes before 70 and after 68.

This is not to say that the newer generation is not willing to give it a go, hang in there and try to be as bad as any old Leroy Brown. French kissing is fun, but a kiss further down can serve to get the lady of your choice hyperventilating, and a blow job is not just inflating a balloon anymore. The Irish are learning where explicitness is concerned, while still not being fully conditioned to go all out for the shit or bust effort of flaunting it whether you have it or not.

There is a certain air of gaucherie about the Leeson Street scene as it is at present constituted. The clubs themselves are in basements, below ground, hidden away. There is no ostentation, no opportunity for any real loss of innocence, no joy in daring to be different. Instead there are dim lights that leave swathes of darkness where uneasy revellers can lurk, booths to hide in, curtained recesses in which to hold hands and breathe the musky scents of tumescent yearnings too long pent up.

The clientele of these clubs can vary. Among the males there are the jolly sportsmen, who stick together, indulge in horseplay, and usually end the night by defiantly vomiting on the floor. Then there are the executive classes, quite often pale young men in long coats like Philip Larkin's priest and doctor: they sit quietly fingering their filofaxes, and treating any female they might chance upon as some form of computer software they would like to programme.

Now and then bunches of hard-eyed men come in, hunch over tables, drink a little, and converse animatedly in whispers. They may be villains planning a robbery, or policemen hoping to forestall it. They all know one another; they even laugh and joke together on occasions, but if they are offered the chance to do each other down, they'll take it avidly.

The women are equally recognisable: secretaries who appear timid but can be as shrill as Myna birds when provoked; aging housewives who fear they are over the hill and want one last night out before galloping stagnation sets in; would-be models who might condescend to turn a trick providing the client may be useful and is willing to be a hand held boy; prostitutes who aspire to hotel beds rather than plastic macs in public parks or perfunctory jig-jigs on the back seats of company cars.

On the Leeson Street strip pretence is the reality: there is nothing more to it than what your mind can conjure up for itself. You can dress up and go there, but you have to convince yourself that you've been anywhere. It's like drinking tap water from an old boot while a gaudily-dressed ugly sister screams in your ear that it's champagne from Cinderella's slipper. That's the way it always is with the hard sell: you pay your money, you're handed the air gun, but it's up to you to win the fluffy toy. But it is still where the life is, if you count life as being motion, noise, and a glitter of light to push back the night sky.

I stood in Kiernan's and sucked at a pint of lager, and all around me the brave young cannibals — and a few not so young — pushed and shoved and brayed into one another's faces. Of Marty, however, there was nary a sign.

Eventually I spotted a mutual acquaintance, an actuary who had made his pile and was now sitting on it waiting for it to hatch. A small brandy would see him through the night; he was one of those who only came to stand and stare. I knew him as well as a fist knows a pound note, but a nod is as good as a wink to a blind man, so I elbowed my way over to him and asked if he had seen Marty.

'Marty?'

'Marty Lynch. Small, round, and a pillar of the stock market. A supporting pillar ...'

'Oh, that Marty.'

'Yeah, that Marty. Have you seen him?'

'As a matter of fact, I have.You are Blaine?'

'That's me.'

'He said if you came round he'd see you in the Green Parrot.'

'Green? Surely you mean blue?'

'Blue?'

'As in the film *Casablanca*. Sidney Greenstreet. Owner of.'

'I haven't the faintest idea what you're talking about.'

'A mis-spent youth. You were probably playing with your calculator. Where is this Green Parrot?'

'Halfway down the street, on the opposite side. Look for the flashing bird.'

'A bird exposing himself? It's a funny old world.'

I left him and went out into the wind. It was whistling down the tunnel of high Georgian buildings not caring whose feathers it ruffled. A taxi drew up and disgorged a well-known television chat show host. He was in evening wear with a white scarf looped round his elegant neck. The girl with him was tall and smooth in ringleted hair, a fur jacket and a long dress slit to the waist. Her legs were the kind you'd like to follow to find where they ended. She wasn't his wife, but then, who is nowadays?

I found the green bird. It was down a flight of steps and its wickedly winking eye was the bell one pressed to be admitted. I speared it and after a reasonable interval — or unreasonable if you were eager to get in, which I wasn't — a metal grill was pushed back and two eyes, a nose and a mouth stared out at me.

I stared back, then I said, 'I've a message for the parrot's sister. She's to put the kettle on so that we can all have tea.'

The eyes blinked, then the mouth opened and said, 'Are you a member? Only members allowed in.'

'My member's attached. You want it, you'll have to take me as well.'

'Huh?'

Resignedly I took out one of Charles's remaining fivers and smeared it across the grill. When I took it away again the eyes looked much friendlier. The grill snapped shut, there was a rattling of locks and bolts and the door was opened just wide enough for me to squeeze through.

I was standing in a postage stamp sized foyer confronting a little guy in a tight, striped, three-piece suit. He had both thumbs stuck in the watch pockets of his waistcoat and his dainty rump jutted out as though inviting either a kick or a caress. I was certainly the man for him if it was the former.

'Three pounds cover charge and two to become a temporary member,' he said, moving his lips at least a millimetre in the process.

'How temporary?'

'Temporary enough to get you in for the night.'

'Oh, that temporary.'

I gave him the five pound note and watched him tuck it away in an inside pocket. I fancied I could hear a prehensile sucking sound as he did it. Over his shoulder I could see a beaded curtain and behind it strobe lights flickered and I could make out the jerky movements of people dancing. The disco music was carrying out a searching examination of the tension capacity of the building's foundations.

'Why's the music always so loud?' I shouted at Flypaper Lips.

He cupped his ear. 'Wha?'

'See what I mean?' I told him. I stepped around him, then pushed my way in through the curtain. The beads were difficult to brush off: maybe they were trained to pick your pocket and then pass the contents out to be ingested by the doorman's suit.

Inside, there was a raised circle of dancing space where a number of people were gyrating like zombies; I had chanced on a slow number, Frank Sinatra having dislodged the disco beat to praise the delights of 'New York, New York'. To my left were some tables covered in red and white striped oilcloth, and a waiter got up to look like an Apache dancer, complete with beret and pencil moustache, was oozing his way between them, empty tray held aloft and a supercilious look on his face.

Marty was sitting at one of the tables talking earnestly to a cool-looking character in a white Miami Vice style linen jacket with the sleeves rolled back, an open-necked purple shirt, and a medallion nestling in a chestful of designer hair. He had a narrow head with a lot of blond curls and an unblemished jawline that no fist had dented, certainly not recently. Two reasons for that were propped on either side of him, over-dressed, over manicured and overweight: the two thugs from the night before, the smaller one, I was glad to see, sporting an ear as swollen as Marty's.

There was a small bar in the corner where the disc jockey cum barman held sway; he was a coloured man with big teeth and double jointed body movements who kept throwing bottles in the air and looking anxious until he caught them again. The walls of the cavern were white-washed brick, the ceiling smoke-grimed, and the air as damp as a crypt. If a couple of potholers had crawled by I wouldn't have been in the least bit surprised.

I stood there, probably with my mouth open, until Marty and his companions spotted me. None of them looked particularly pleased to see me. I waved, then went on over. 'Hi, guys,' I greeted the two thugs, 'still out canvassing for the Legion?'

No flicker of life crossed their maps, but the guy between them smiled broadly, letting me admire his expensively capped teeth. 'There was something?' he asked me. He opened his mouth to say it, unlike the doorman who closed his.

I pointed at Marty, then held my hand over my heart and tried out a soulful expression. The guy's eyes were sharp, but devoid of any particular animosity as yet. Obviously he felt I didn't pose any threat to him. He measured me up and down, then he spread his hands and gestured for me to sit down.

The thug with the ear hooked a chair from an adjoining table with his foot and half kicked it, half dragged it over. The people sitting there looked at him in surprise and, so help me, he growled at them.

I sat down, took out a cigarette, and the bigger heavy this time reached out an expensive lighter and set fire to it for me. I blew smoke in his face by way of thanks but it didn't even cause him to blink.

'Where's your manners, Marty?' the guy in the white linen jacket asked. 'Introduce us.'

Marty came to life as though stuck by a pin. 'Certainly, certainly,' he said, rubbing his hands. 'Wilson, this is John Blaine. John, this is Wilson Whelan ...' He gazed at the other two but was obviously at a loss to put names to them.

Dutifully I stuck out my paw and Whelan took it and squeezed. I was expecting it and had tensed a few sinews, but we still only came out about even in the hand pressing stakes. We disengaged, neither of us willing to show pain.

'Wilson?' I said, furrowing my brow.

'Yeah?'

'Unusual first name. Seems to me there used to be a character called Wilson in the Wizard comic some years ago. He was a hundred years old, but could still run, jump and swim as well as a man of thirty.'

'Is that so?' Whelan was all teeth and interested. 'A hundred years old, eh? And didn't look a day over thirty. How'd he manage that then?'

'Lived on herbs and wild flowers. Stayed up in the mountains and sat naked in the snow. Took a bath in icy rivers ...'

'Whooo,' Whelan said, looking pained. 'I wouldn't fancy that. No, I wouldn't fancy that at all, wha? Didn't he get piles? Or frostbite of the goolies? No way would you get me into that scene.' He glanced slyly at the bigger of his companions. 'What about you, Humphrey? You ever sit out in the nip on a heap of snow? Ever eat a wild flower?'

'Not me,' Humphrey demurred, shaking his head from side to side to reinforce his words. 'Catch me larkin' about in the snow in me birthday suit. And give me steak an' onions any day of the week ...'

'And you Sid?' Whelan inquired, turning to his other side.

Sid frowned, clearly having trouble with his bad ear. Cradling it in contemplative fingers, he offered: 'Tha's a load a' bollocks. Nobody lives tha' be a hunnert except old grannies with pusses like dried prunes.'

Whelan shrugged. 'Well, you heard our friend,' he said. 'He read it in a comic, so it must be right.'

Sid gazed at me with an expression of scorn, then he growled again, deep in his chest.

We sat and listened to Sinatra who had now moved on to Chicago, that toddling town. I'd heard of Whelan, but knew him as Eddie 'The Whacker' Whelan — the Wilson was a new one on me. Obviously he had come up in the world. Since I stopped playing hurling I'd taken an interest in hunting, and through the gun club I joined I'd made a number of contacts with individual policemen. They talked, as men will when they share long and lonely vigils together. Whelan was an associate of one of the more influential gang leaders, a real beauty known as The Waster — presumably not for wasting time but rather for wasting people.

Once he too had been a run of the mill villain, mainly into extortion down in the docks. With the opening up of the drug market, business had bloomed and he now had most of the inner city tied up and dancing to his tune. Whelan was one of his men for all seasons, a tough cookie who wasn't averse to doling out abrupt and extreme prejudice to competitors. I was beginning to feel that I was a little out of my league in this company.

The music stopped as old Frank went for a breather, and two women detached themselves from the heaving mass of dancers and came over and joined us. They were pretty in a brittle, cheap kind of way, one being a brunette, the other a blonde. The dark-haired one wore a flash of mini-skirted red, while her companion was poured into a black trousers suit with bolero top that had white painted skeleton hands supporting her pear-like breasts. Their make-up looked as if it had been put on with a six inch paint brush.

Whelan introduced them as Cindy and Ruth, without specifying which was which. The blonde nodded at me, but the brunette might have been looking at an empty chair. Only Marty perked up at their arrival. Humphrey and Sid wore the inscrutable expressions of a pair of stone pillars.

Whelan was the first to resume conversation. He gazed around at us and said, 'So, here we all are. Nice and friendly and having a chat and a laugh. Your pal hasn't a drink, Marty. Why don't one of you girls pour him some of this plonk that we're payin' an arm and a leg for?' He gestured, and the blonde upended one of the fake bottles of champagne into a glass, and then offered it to me. I took it and toasted the table before drinking. The wine was dry and resinated and did as much for my palate as a rub of sandpaper. 'Enjoy it in good health,'

Whelan said. 'It's all on my bill. No need for any of you gentlemen to put your hands in your pockets unless it's to ease your boners now that the girls are with us, wha? What d'you say, Cindy and Ruth? You think they fancy you?'

They looked us over, but didn't appear impressed. The brunette had slightly irregular teeth and some of her lipstick had come off onto them. She saw me looking at her and ran her tongue in and out a few times. I've been more excited watching someone peel a banana.

'Marty tells me you're a private detective,' Whelan said. 'Pretty classy that. Also you're the one socked Sid on the ear. Sid didn't like that, did you Sid?'

Sid didn't. He scowled to show me, then did his chest rumble to show me some more.

'Marty's been a bad boy,' Whelan added. 'We wanted to tell him that and to make sure he'd be a good one from now on. Then you had to come along and stick your hooter in. You shouldn't've done that. That's another strike against you.'

I shrugged. 'May as well go for that hat trick then, I suppose,' I said. 'He's hired me to explain some things to you. To see if he can be accommodated until his ship comes in and he's able to unload the cargo and hand it over to your boss.'

'Boss? What Boss?'

I grinned at him. 'You're not trying to tell me you're the kingpin? The chief tutti-frutti?'

His eyes got mean and he began twisting the chunky gold ring on the third finger of his left hand. Glancing at the two women, he said, 'Take a hike. Go on over to the little girl's room and replaster your pusses.' He waited until they'd gone, then he said to Marty, 'Why'd you tell this gazebo about our little deal? That should've stayed between you, me and the lamp post. No third party. You're fixin' to have more than your ear pulled.'

'Let him alone,' I said, surprising myself and causing Marty to wince. 'It makes sense to lay off him,' I went on more placatingly. 'If the money's as sizable as he says it is, then he's your best hope of recovering it. The market takes turns like that, one day up, the next down. Get yourself a second opinion if you don't believe me ...'

'I don't need nobody to tell me my business ...'

'Watch it, Whacker, that's a double negative.'

That puzzled him for a minute, and in the pause Marty stuck in his tuppence worth: 'I only asked him to come along because he's a friend of mine. We live in the same house, for God's sake. That's how he came to be there last night. I had to tell him ...'

Whelan frowned — guys like him always had a nice line in frowning, as though they practised it in front of a mirror. 'You hired him as a minder?' he said. He measured me with his eyes. 'How tough are you? Can you crack a walnut between the cheeks of your arse?'

It would have been easier to have backed down, but I didn't. 'No,' I told him, 'but I could sit on your face and give you a squeeze to remember.'

Marty and the two goons eased back in their chairs, their mouths open to enable them to breathe quietly and evenly. Whelan's sun ray lamp tan got even more tan. He clamped his mouth shut so tightly that his jaw muscles creaked and when he tried to swallow it was as if a lump of coke had got stuck in his gullet. When he finally got his vocal chords working he told me that I was a dickhead and a slime ball. Then he got to work on my parentage, my fetishes, and my relationships with the lower animals. He went on and on until he saw me grinning at him, then he shut down like a door closing. I preferred him mouthing obscenities.

But, like Macbeth, I was in so far now that going back would be a pain in the rump. 'That's what I like to hear,' I told him, 'the real you. Dress a turd up in pink ribbon, it's still a turd. Designer clothes, a gumball hairdo, a diamond stud in your ear, a Boucheron watch on your wrist ... put it all together and what've you got? You're still Eddie the Apeman with a shiny pink fundament and blue balls. You're just a cheapie, imitating the American gangsters you see on the silver screen, and that's all you'll ever be ...'

This time he caught hold of the table, and I tensed, waiting for the boom to fall. A full minute went by and nothing happened. Whelan looked quick-frozen, his hands stuck to the table. The other three were also immobilised for some reason, their faces blank, their eyes wary. The whole place had become locked into a frieze of paralysis, as though a hiccup had occurred in the space-time continuum. Then I followed Whelan's gaze over my left shoulder, and saw two heavily built characters in dark suits standing just inside the curtained archway. They were grinning over at us, but not in a particularly friendly manner: they reminded me more of how wolves might have eyed poor old bare-arsed Wilson from the Wizard comic as he sat out in the snow.

I didn't need to go over and measure their feet to know that they were flat. One of them I knew slightly: he was a Sergeant in the Special Task Force. I had had a run-in with him once when we were both looking into an insurance fraud; there was a question of a reward which both of us had claimed, but his being in the official police prevented him from getting any of it. I hadn't seen him since, but now I would have kissed his foot in welcome. In this case the devil I knew was eminently preferable to the devil I didn't know.

The two of them came over to our table in a hush so palpable you could have worn it to keep out the cold. The disc jockey had disappeared, maybe to answer a call of nature, maybe responding to a call of expediency now that the law had arrived. I could see the two ladies, Cindy and Ruth, hovering about in the background, clearly poised for flight also.

'Well, what've we here?' the one I knew said in his best Dixon of Dock Green baritone. Suddenly I remembered his name: it was Hanley. He went on, 'Is it a gaggle of villains I see before me? Plotting a dastardly crime no doubt ...' He winked at his companion, who laughed dutifully.

We held our positions and said nothing. Marty tenderly

scratched his ear; Sid, possibly prompted, did likewise. Humphrey shuffled his feet and did his imitation of a plank, Whelan relaxed his grip on the table, and I started breathing again.

'Not talking, eh?' Hanley said. Once more he turned to his companion, a slightly less bulky version of himself, with red hair, freckles, and a beautiful shiner of a black eye. 'Why is it, Bill, that we always have this effect on scrogs?' he asked him. 'Instant dumbness, instant loss of memory. It's like a miracle in reverse.'

Bill shook his head. 'Beats me.'

'I suppose we could try a laying-on of hands.' Hanley held his up for our contemplation. They were large, thick-fingered, nicotine-stained. 'Maybe we're some kind of faith healers without knowing it. If we can strike them dumb, we can strike them into speech.'

'Strike being the operative word,' I said, as usual rushing in where angels fear to tread.

'Aha,' Hanley said, 'one of them's come alive. And the very one we're after too. I can't say it's nice to see you, Blaine, but in the line of duty it's necessary that you spend some time in our company. You don't mind that, do you? Simple Simon says nod your head if you agree. A visit to Swift Street. A cordon bleu meal. A view of Thunder Alley. If you're good we might even give you a used condom to play with ...'

'Not one of yours, I hope. It'd be so small it'd drop through the crack in the floorboards.'

'Sticks and stones may break my bones ...'

'... but names will never hurt me,' Bill, the partner, supplied.

'Great double act,' I acknowledged. 'You should be on the stage. But what about this guy here?' I flapped my hand in Whelan's direction. 'Surely he's more worthy of a visit to Swift Street than I am? Or has he paid for his visit already without taking it?'

Hanley scratched his head and looked quizzically at the ceiling. 'What d'you think he's getting at now?' he asked no one in particular. 'Is he hinting that we'd take a bribe? That we'd pocket this gentleman's money and not provide him with his time in the sun? Surely not ..?' He came closer and stood behind me. 'Because if you are,' he went on, 'I'd have to tweak your little ear like these gents' — he nodded at Sid and Marty — 'have had theirs tweaked. Or maybe even slap your wrist ...'

Moving fast for a big man, he suddenly brought his fist down on my left hand where it was resting on the table. The pain was a bright flash of fire in my mind, and I reared back. Bouncing off Hanley's solid bulk I went forward again into the edge of the table. This time my ribs felt the force of the blow, the breath soughing out of my open mouth with a whoosh.

When the tears cleared from my eyes, I saw that Whelan was laughing, showing off those brighter than bright teeth. There was even a hint of emotion etched into Humphrey and Sid's stonework. I looked quickly at Marty, but at least he had the grace to look anxious.

Now Hanley and Bill were all business: 'I'll have to ask you, Mr Blaine, sir, to accompany us to Swift Street Garda Station on foot of a request by my superior, Superintendent Quinlan,' Hanley recited, 'in order that you help us with an enquiry into a highly confidential matter ...'

At the same time Bill put his hand under my elbow and helped me gently but firmly to my feet.

'Aren't you going to read me my rights?' I asked them mock seriously.

Hanley looked at me with feigned surprise. 'Now, now,' he said, 'don't be like that. We're not arresting you. Just an invitation to partake of a little late supper and maybe a chat about this, that and the other. Especially the other. Why, the Super is already carving the duck, and the duty sergeant is mixing up a batch of orange sauce. I can almost smell it from here ...'

Now they were both flanking me, a hand under each arm. I could feel the warmth of their bodies, the hard rolls of muscle under their trendy suits. They might not be the United States

Cavalry, but they were the next best thing.

I surveyed the table, then said, 'Sorry I have to rush off, gents. As you can see, matters of state are pending. Be nice to Marty, he's the only one knows where the treasure map is, and the boss'll give you the black spot if anything happens to him. Say goodbye to Cindy and Ruth for me, and tell them the earth definitely moved ...'

We marched out, through the beaded curtain, past the toothpick doorman, up the cement steps and into a Leeson Street that was slick with recent rain. Now the rain had cleared off and the stars were once more winking out from behind scraps of cloud. I was in no mood to wink back at them: my head was aching, my hand was aching, my ego was aching. If I had a blood-stained bandage round my head and a tin whistle, I'd have put one foot in the gutter, limped along and tootled 'Dixie'.

16

SWIFT STREET GARDA Station is an imposing cut stone building with parapeted windows and cantilevered cornices that some wit once upon a time suggested were used as gallows. It had been a DMP barracks, had been attacked and gutted during the War of Independence because it was believed to have housed 'G Division', the intelligence gathering unit, had been refurbished to a model of its nineteenth century self, and was now rapidly being reduced to a dump under the tender ministrations of the present lot of guardians of the law.

At one a.m. the street outside it was deserted and windblown. The wrecks of crashed cars in the compound beside it gave melancholy counterpoint to the operative ones parked outside. Most of the lower storey windows had pull-down blinds on them, but the ones further up were bare of any covering, probably because if you wanted to see into them you'd have to climb up the sandstone face of the building.

We had travelled over there in an unmarked Volvo car, with Bill at the wheel and myself and Hanley in the back. There had been no conversation, the three of us preoccupied with our own thoughts. I felt only a mild curiosity as to why I'd been sent for; I knew Quinlan, we were both members of the same gun club, we'd gone hunting a number of times together. He was a career man, not much older than myself, but he had risen quickly through the ranks. Slow and plodding, he liked to give the impression of kindly incomprehension, a pained disinclination to believe that the awful events he had to deal with, and the horror stories he had to listen to, could ever really have happened. He had fooled many an aspiring criminal into trusting him, and then put in the boot when the time was right.

I liked him, respected his integrity, but would in no way ever presume on his good offices if I happened to do anything even mildly questionable. He went by the book and, if his grandmother was brought in for pinching someone else's granddad, he would throw the book at her.

We got out of the car. A Black Maria was at the kerb and, as we watched, a couple of uniformed constables erupted from the back of it doing their best to hold onto a struggling youth in a denim jacket and jeans and with a head that would have no trouble substituting for a cannonball. They dragged him across the pavement, the three of them weaving and staggering as though engaged in some intricate dance.

We went along slowly behind them, up the slate steps and into a wide entrance hall. The gouger suddenly began to yell, his shouts bouncing off the yellow-tiled walls as though he had been groped in a church.

Hanley had been muttering since he first spied the threesome; now he took off with a skip and a jump and landed a mighty kick on the youth, right up between his jean-clad legs. The unfortunate transgressor went up in the air on the restraining arms of his captors, then came back down again like a swing that had been given a hefty push. His shouts stifled, he gazed with wild eyes back over his shoulder.

'Put a sock in it, Amby,' Hanley told him, still looking mad. 'Otherwise I'll rip your head right off your shoulders and shit in the hole.'

'Yes, sir, Mr Hanley,' a chastened Amby said, and he walked off docilely between the two grinning constables.

Hanley looked at Bill and myself, spread his hands and shrugged. 'An old friend,' he said. 'Just a love lump ....'

'You've given him a new meaning to "They also serve who only stand and wait",' I said. 'Old Amby won't sit down for a week.'

'Don't you believe it. Amby'll bounce back. He always does. He'll be back on the streets tomorrow. He knows that. I know that. It's like a merry-go-round ....'

'So you belt him, to give him something to remember you by. Just like me ....'

'That's it.' Hanley scowled, but behind it his eyes were wary. 'You going to tell Quinlan about my over-familiar handshake?'

'You think he'd be interested?'

'Probably not.'

'Then why're you uneasy?'

'Uneasy! Me uneasy!' He turned to his partner. 'Do I look uneasy? Are those my knees knocking together or what?'

'Naw, you're not uneasy, Clarence,' Bill said, trying to look serious but being let down by his black eye. 'Last time I saw you worried was when you ate that suspect's foot. You were afraid it'd give you food poisoning ....'

Hanley flapped a hand at me. 'You see?'

I raised my eyebrows. 'Clarence, eh?'

We walked further along the corridor and stopped outside the duty sergeant's glassed-in office. There was no one at the counter, but from behind a half-open door came the murmur of conversation. 'You know where to go?' Hanley asked me, then without waiting for a reply he continued, 'Up the stairs, turn left, two doors down. Child's play unless you have to do pee-pees along the way ....'

I looked at him, then at Bill. 'So what do I say? That an hour in your company is worth two in a threshing machine ...?'

They exchanged glances. 'I think you should cut your losses and get up them steps,' Hanley said. He licked his lips as though still savouring the suspect's foot. 'Don't worry anyway, we'll be seeing each other again. You can bet your sweet bippy on it.'

'Is that a threat or a promise?'

Hanley shrugged. 'Take it which way you like and go piss up your leg.' He went on into the office behind the counter, a smirking Bill following on behind.

I climbed the stairs as instructed, taking them one at a time. I was suddenly very, very weary. My head still hurt, my hand was throbbing, my brain was a stranger that had become clogged with bits of debris that had no business being there in the first place. As I dragged along I entertained the charming thought of what it would be like to have my throat cut. Seemed reasonable to suppose that it was next on the list. Just about everything else had been done to me. I also wondered what kind of person would get his or her kicks by performing such surgery. Redmond was still the chief candidate. It was funny — though not falling down, laughing funny — but I knew all his vital statistics, had been thinking about him on and off for the past forty-eight hours, and yet he was as hidden in shadow as a short-taken pisser behind a tree. How come I couldn't find him in a city as small and personalised as Dublin? He was as elusive as the Scarlet Pimpernel. Was he the kind of man who would commit four murders? And for what? Maybe there didn't have to be a reason. Maybe he just felt persecuted. Maybe he felt compelled to strike out at any encroachment, whether real or imaginary, on his territory. In the kind of world he now inhabited, life was cheap and the leaving of it random and undistinguished. Annie had confirmed that to me. With one part of me, however, I hoped I was wrong about Redmond. Old Mrs. Walsh-Overman might not be the most lovable, but she didn't deserve that on top of Charles's death, especially if it was proved that it was her own flesh and blood that had done it.

I finally came to the second door on the first floor landing. It was closed. A radiator beside the door gurgled, but when I put my hand on it I found it was as cold as a fish's belly. Down at the end of the corridor and facing me was a large framed likeness of Eoin O'Duffy, the first Commissioner of the Guards. He didn't look very happy. Maybe his feet were cold. I'd just have to have a word with the furnaceman on the way out. Then again, maybe I should stay away from furnaces for a while.

I knocked softly, turned the knob and went in. Superintendent George Quinlan was sitting at a paper-cluttered desk in a pool of light shed by an angle-poise lamp. He looked up as I came in, nodded, indicated an armless steel chair, then went on reading the document he had been perusing.

I sat down and crossed my legs. Except for the light from the angle-poise, the room was in darkness. Quinlan was an L.S. Lowry matchstick man, all bones and stretched white skin. His hair was wiry and stood up on his head with all the colour and brittleness of a thatch of steel wool. A bony forehead formed an outcrop for deepset, haggard eyes. There were sharp wrinkles etched vertically down each side of a rather thin-lipped mouth. This evening he was wearing a floppy cardigan over a check shirt with a button-down collar and a loosely knotted maroon tie. The bottom part of him was hidden behind the desk, but I guessed that he was probably wearing trousers of some kind. He looked bothered and tired and irritable enough to chew staples.

I took out a cigarette and put it in my mouth. Leaning over, I picked up his lighter from beside a cut glass ashtray. The lighter was the cheap variety you can buy for fifty pence from any street stall. So was the ashtray. 'Pretty class furnishings you've got here, George,' I said. 'Makes me feel humble.'

He looked across the desk at me, then resumed his reading. I lit the cigarette and put the lighter back on the desk. I crossed my legs, then crossed them the other way. I blew a smoke ring, yawned, grimaced when a twinge from the back of my head elbowed its way to the front. I was becoming slightly impatient.

'Why does a donkey eat thistles, George?'

'Huh?'

'Because he's an ass.'

Still without looking up, Quinlan said, 'Don't get smart with me. I've work to do. Here it is past one and I'm attending to paperwork that someone else should have done.' Now he was looking at me. 'You think I'm sitting here writing my memoirs? Or waiting till the last man is in so that I can lock up, tuck them in and kiss them goodnight?'

'Don't get shirty.' I threw the package of cigarettes on the desk in front of him. 'Have a smoke. Relax. Think of moonlight tip-toeing across the Liffey ....'

He stared at me, his eyes hooded under those beetling brows. On the wall behind him his shadow was a monster, shape without definition. Then after a moment, as though coming to some agreement with himself, he reached out and took up the remains of a cigar from the ashtray. His fingers were thick and spatulate, out of proportion with the thin boniness of the rest of him. He put the cigar in his mouth, pushing it in and out until he had it moistened. With great care he then lit it, rolling it about and puffing out clouds of blue-grey smoke. When he had it going to his satisfaction he leaned back. He replaced the lighter on the desk. He sighed. For all the attention he paid me, I might have been in Ballyjamesduff looking for Paddy Reilly.

'You're not going to fart, George, are you?' I asked him. 'Or pick your nose?'

'Don't be disgusting.' He took another puff at the frayed end of the cigar. 'What're you doing here anyway? Have you no home to go to?'

'I was brought here,' I said indignantly. 'By two of your finest and roughest. There I was, minding my business, having a drink and a chat with some of my friends in the Green Parrot ....'

'The Green Parrot?'

'Come on, George, stop messin' about. You wanted to see me. Here I am. Either piss in the pot or get off it.'

He put the cigar down again in the ashtray. Then he made a steeple of his hands. Almost tenderly he said, 'There was a murder committed tonight.'

'So?'

'Out in Fairview. One Charles Walsh-Overman had his throat cut. He was found in the boiler house of a school. You know him?'

'I'm doing a little work for his mother.'

'You're not surprised he's been found dead?'

'I'm overcome, George. But I'm doing my best to suppress my feelings. I wouldn't like to cry all over your carpet.'

'Murder isn't funny.'

'Neither is your carpet.'

I retrieved my cigarettes and lit another one. George watched me sourly. 'You smoke a lot,' he said.

'Is that a question or are you warning me off them?'

'Why don't you try a cigar? Or a pipe, maybe?'

'Cigars remind me of turds. And I haven't got the face for a pipe.'

He took up his half-smoked cheroot and looked at it. I must have tickled a nerve because he put it down again without giving it any further business. Instead he picked up a thin letter opener in the shape of a miniature sword and began fiddling with it.

'Look, George,' I told him, 'I saw the guy twice. Once to wave to, and the second time in my office. He knew that his mother had hired me. He was fishing around to find out why.'

'He didn't know?'

'Obviously.'

'But you told him?'

'And renege on the oath I took when I got my tin star and my Sam Spade face mask?'

'But you're going to tell me ...?'

I had got tired crossing my legs, so now I stretched them out in front of me. The chair I was sitting on was balanced on a steel frame and it rocked gently each time I moved. I took my time about making up my mind, showing George how painful it was for me. Then I said, 'She wanted me to find her other son, Redmond. He's become an elderly drop-out. She's old and she'd like to have all her family about her again. It seemed like no big deal. Anyway, that's my business, finding people.'

'And did you?'

'Did I what?'

'Find him.'

'Not so far. I've fished around a bit. He has a wife and I went to see her. She told me about a home for dossers called the Star of the Sea that Redmond frequents. I went up there and poked around. I didn't get anywhere.'

'They didn't tell you about this furnace house in Fairview?'

'Well, now that you mention it, an old relic I met did sort of refer to it.'

I knew George was no fool, so I gazed steadily into his eyes, or at least into what I could see of them under the cliff of bone that was his forehead. I wanted to appear helpful and sincere without giving him the impression that I was ready to leap over the desk and lick his face.

'So you knew that Walsh-Overman used the furnace house as a temporary resting place?'

'Which of them?'

'Which of the brothers?' George was getting mad now, I could tell by the way he was bending the letter opener. 'You know bloody well which one. Maybe you went out there too to do a bit of poking around. Someone was seen loitering about the school earlier tonight. Then we got a call telling us about the body. A man's body. It wasn't you by any chance, putting a little business our way?'

'So help me, it wasn't. Me, I mean. I'd have got around to it eventually, going out there, but I had some other business to attend to first.'

'My, you are the busy private detective. How come you've so much on your plate all of a sudden?'

'I'm doing a special all-in price, and I'm giving tokens. You save a thousand of them and you're eligible to go into the hat for a draw to win the hat.'

'Very funny.'

George began to pick at the top of the desk with the letter opener. It was obvious this was not the first time he'd gone prospecting there: the wood was scarred and pitted as though a troop of woodworm had held a picnic on it. 'So what'd he do when you refused to tell him what his mother had hired you for? And before you say 'Who?', I'm talking about the late, and for all I know, the great, Charles Walsh-Overman.'

'He thanked me politely and went away.'

'Just like that?'

'Yep.'

Giving his full attention to the desktop and without raising his head, George said, 'We found a receipt for fifty pounds in his pocket. It was very like the one you gave me the time you sold me the Ruger twelve gauge shotgun ....'

'It was signed by me?'

'No.'

'The kind of receipt book I use, you can buy one in any cutprice shop. Just like your lighter.' Deciding to act the outraged citizen a little, I went on, 'What're you trying to hang on me here, George? I met the fellow briefly. I've admitted that. I'm doing a chore for his mother. I've admitted that too. Otherwise I don't know him from a hole in the ground.'

'A rather unfortunate choice of words,' George said drily. He paused in his excavations, the little sword poised in the air. 'It's just one avenue of the investigation that I either want to close off or develop.'

'And?'

'Let's say that I'm keeping an open mind.'

'Shame on you, George, doubting the word of a friend.'

'This is the fourth incident of throat-cutting in the space of a month. You can't be unaware of that. The first three were vagrants, but this is a different matter.'

'You mean because Charles was a more valued member of the community?'

'No, I don't mean that. It's different because the pattern's been broken. But now that you tell me the other brother's a down and out ....'

He let the sentence hang in the air, probably waiting for me to grab hold of it. I let it dangle. I lit another cigarette and blew smoke so that it curled into the tunnel of light shed by the lamp. 'Have you seen the old lady, the mother?' I asked him.

'She's under the doctor's care. I won't be able to interview her until the morning.'

I leaned forward and dumped some ash. George stayed in the same position, the little blade poking out incongruously from between his thick fingers. He looked as if he were prepared to stay like that for hours. When out hunting he showed infinite patience, stalking his prey whether it be snipe, grouse or the humble rabbit with an inevitability of intent that brooked no fear of failure. When after human prey he was just as intense, just as single minded. Not for George the brilliant hunch, the one-off moment of insight. Going through the motions, investigating every detail, tying off all loose ends, exhausting the various possibilities until he came to the right one, those were the ways in which he worked, and he was so good that he had the highest arrest record of any Super on the force. What matter that the way he worked would have bored the pants off most of his peers; it suited him and he stuck to it.

I was getting rather tired looking at him, the strain giving me a tic under my left eye. I decided to open up another avenue myself: 'Charles was gay,' I said carefully. 'Did you know that?' He made no sign to signify yes or no, so I went on, 'He could've been done in by queer bashers. It's not unheard of, out in that neck of the woods.'

George stayed gazing at me for a little while longer, then he said, 'That possibility's being looked into. A fellow called Saunders who works for Mrs Walsh-Overman has given us some names. We're also looking for the brother Redmond now of course ....'

'Is that a warning for me to keep off?'

He considered that one before he replied. 'I suppose you have to earn a crust,' he said grudgingly. 'If you do find him, though ....'

'I'll let you know first off.'

'I'm sure you will.'

We sat in silence, listening to the building creak and groan. We might have been the only two people awake in a city of over a million souls. But that wasn't true either. Out there in the darkness men, and some women too, were going about their nefarious business. They were thieves, who stole for a living. Some of them were born to it, their moral outlook twisted and dented by the uncaring attitude of society at large. More came to it out of what they deemed necessity: the absence of a job, the strain of a gambling debt, the wish to keep up with the Joneses. These were the amateurs, a surprising number of them killers. Envy, lust, the beguiling blandishments of notoriety, these were some of the motivating forces. How can you know a murderer, recognise someone who is capable of killing? Criminologists maintain that the urge to kill can be strong and, in accomplishment, as cathartic as the sex act. In my profession, it was not beyond the bounds of possibility that I might have to kill; violence was endemic in many of the things I had to do.

I watched George carefully taking the cellophane wrapping from another of his vile cigars. His working at it was as precise and studied as everything he did.

'Did you ever kill anyone, George?' I asked him, curious to break through his patina of calmness.

He paused in what he was doing and looked at me. The blade of shadow cut his face in two and I couldn't see what was in his eyes, if anything. After a moment he gave his attention back to the cigar. He rolled it about in his fingers as though testing its pliability. Then he put it in his mouth and sucked it. When he had it moist enough to stick to the wall if he cared to throw it, he took up the lighter and held it to the flame, rotating the lighter this way and that. Clouds of evil-smelling smoke plumed out and roiled in the already fuzzy light.

'Yes, I did have occasion to ... to terminate someone once. It wasn't the most pleasant of experiences. Why d'you ask?'

'Oh, I don't know.' I brushed smoke away from my eyes. 'It's the dog hours of the night .... Maybe I've heard the mermaids singing. Tell me about it.'

I thought for a moment he wasn't going to reply, then he said, 'It happened when I was a young detective. I chased a fellow across some rooftops. I caught him and we fell through a glass skylight onto a cement floor, and I landed on top of him. I walked away. He didn't. It was just one of those things ....'

'One of those things.'

'For Christ's sake, he was fifteen years old ....' George stopped abruptly as though he'd given away a secret. In a more even tone he said, 'Why don't you go home and stop bothering me? I'm fed up looking at you.'

'In a minute, George, in a minute.'

I lit yet another cigarette, mainly as a defence against George's noisome emanations. It tasted flat and dry as though I'd stuck my head into an airing cupboard. 'I met Eddie "The Whacker" Whelan tonight,' I said. 'Except that now he's adopted the christian name of Wilson.'

'And did you enjoy the experience?'

'The pleasure was all his, I can assure you.'

'Hmmm.'

'A nasty bit of goods ....' I prompted.

'He is that. Works for one of the big crime bosses. Billy Clanton, known as The Waster.'

'Clanton?'

'You've heard of him?'

'Well, I've heard of him as The Waster. Didn't know his real name was Clanton.'

'Every constable on the beat knows that.'

'Then why don't you do something about him?'

George made a face, but it might have been the cigar. 'We are doing something. We lean on him every chance we get. He's under twenty-four-hour surveillance. But he's a cute hoor. Covers his tracks like a cat does his shit.' George picked up the sword paper opener again and stabbed it into the desk as though by wish fulfilment he could turn it into The Waster's backside. With a harder edge to his voice he said, 'What were you doing talking to a low life like that?'

I stubbed out the cigarette before it burned a hole through the back of my throat. 'He's doing a bit of leaning himself,' I said. 'On a friend of mine. A gambling debt,' I lied. 'My friend thought I might be street wise enough to do something for him.'

'And were you?'

'Well, I'll put it like this: If your bully boys hadn't arrived, the next time I took a crap I'd've had to throw my leg over the roll of toilet paper, hold the end in my mouth and pull it through to wipe my gable end. That's because my arms would've been broken.'

'There you are, you see,' George said, 'we are good for something. I hope you thanked Hanley and Bishop nicely ....'

'I promised them my undying admiration. Then I rang up the change and found myself a little short. Hanley and I have done a round or two before. We called it a draw, but the melody lingers on. He'd as soon do me a favour as stick his John Thomas into a bully beef tin.'

'They got you out of a fix, didn't they?'

'Yes, without knowing it. If they'd known what a plop-doodle I was in, they'd've stood on the sidelines and clapped.'

'Oh, dear,' George said, mock seriously, 'ingratitude sharper than a serpent's tooth.'

He stood up slowly, all six foot two of him. Carefully he put out the cigar, and then laid its remains reverently on the flange of the ashtray. 'He who stubs and puts away,' he intoned, 'will have a smoke another day.'

I got up too, like a spring that needed oiling. I felt about as lively as a stepped-on bug. While I held the door open, George switched off the lamp and fumbled his way out from behind the desk. Then we went down the corridor together, in step like two weary but battle-hardened warriors.

Before we parted at the front entrance, George put his hand on my arm and looked me in the eye. 'All things come to those who wait,' he told me. 'But sometimes they need to be hurried along. I could get quite well disposed towards anyone who might aid me in putting the Waster where he belongs ....'

'In the doghouse, you mean? Up to his neck in dogshit?'

'Yes, that. Or behind bars would do too.'

He gazed at me. I gazed at him. He nodded. I nodded. That was to show that we understood each other, that we were buddies and pals. He trusted me. I trusted him. We always told one another our little secrets. In a pig's eye!

17

THE CLOCK IN the Central Fire Station tower stood at a quarter to two. I paused to look at it, then transferred my gaze to the sky. The clouds had scooted off and the night was clear.

I walked along by the wall that bordered Trinity College, my footfalls echoing hollowly and making me sound like a platoon. A figure moved in the shadows of the ornate public toilet, and when I came level with it a whisper redolent of licentiousness swirled across the street and tried to crawl up the leg of my trousers.

I caught a taxi at the rank in Dame Street and told the driver to take me home. Then I changed my mind and asked him to drive me to Clontarf. I'd need my car and it was best to collect it before it was stripped down and arrested for indecent exposure.

The driver played at being a Dublin character; then again, maybe he was running true to form. He started talking as I got into the taxi and he kept it up while he drove, turning his head and throwing spit-impregnated verbiage back at me, interspersing it with repeated doses of 'Am I righ' or am I righ'?'

He told me about the long shifts he worked. He told me that his feet ached, his back ached, and that his gut was a mess from all the junk food he had to consume because he always seemed to be in a hurry and couldn't linger over his meals like an ordinary nine to fiver. He asked me if I did shift work myself, didn't wait for an answer and included me in his plea to God to have mercy on such as us.

I let him drone on while I gazed out at the empty, paper-littered streets. We passed Fairview Park and then the reclaimed land further on. Out across the finger of water the deep sea docks site was a hive of activity. Lights blazed and I could hear the muffled tremble of heavy machinery.

I dozed a little and was chased through empty, echoing streets by a huge set of chattering false teeth. Every time I glanced back they were just behind me, and I had to hop along pretty smartly to save myself from being chewed ragged. Eventually they grabbed hold of me, but in struggling to free myself I woke up to find the driver shaking me to tell me we had arrived at our destination.

I paid him off and made my way into the parking lot behind the now dark and shuttered Seagull Inn. The Renault was still there, alone in silent majesty. I got in, and the engine started on the first turn as if the old car was glad to see me. Grateful for small mercies, I lit a cigarette, then nosed out onto the main road and headed back towards the city.

Without the taxi driver's monologue to distract me, I had to entertain my thoughts. I first of all welcomed Billy Clanton, otherwise known as The Waster. Then I introduced him to the Clanton who owned the lodging house in Gardinia Place where Bernadette had her penthouse. Father, brother, cousin, uncle? I'd bet a pound to a penny that they were one and the same.

It's funny how things have a habit of fitting together. I thought that between Mrs. Walsh-Overman and Marty I was dealing with two distinct bits of business, but now they were beginning to blur into one another. The long arm of coincidence? Maybe. Then again, perhaps it wouldn't do any harm to snoop around a little more.

I wasn't too far from Gardinia Street, so I turned off and headed in that direction. Who cared that it was three o'clock in the morning? To the kind of people who frequented this neighbourhood, three o'clock in the morning was the middle of the afternoon. The Place itself was all battened down and stowed away, not a light showing, not a footstep slithering. A cat paused on its tentative prowl and looked back over its shoulder at me as I got out of the car. Get lost, puss, I said out loud, and it twisted its moustache and scowled at me as cats will, before it flicked away into a puddle of shadow.

I stood for a while and let the silence all about reassure me. The buildings were faceless, the windows blind eyes. I was the only watcher, tensed up, a coiled spring, but there was nothing to see except an empty street, two parked cars, and a tilted-over dustbin.

I went up the familiar steps to 19A and tried the door. It opened inwards with its usual creak. I peered around it, expecting to see Milly with his twin-barrelled nose at the ready, but there was no sign of him. Everything was the same as the evening before: the Argentinian writer Borges has said that you can never go down to the same river twice, but he could never have said it about the vestibule of 19A, Gardinia Place. It was still steeped in a silence as deep as despair, the hanging bulb only played at emitting light, and the smell of dust and decay hung in the fetid air like a pall.

I shuffled across the floor and looked in over the counter at Milly's hidey hole. All was present and correct; the curtain was drawn and the red fluffy mules were coyly keeping guard. The thought of another conversation with Milly made me wince, so I passed on rousting him out and instead went carefully up the stairs, keeping close to the wall in case the banisters suddenly chose to give way and deposit me down in the cellar.

I made it to the second floor landing without bringing out the fire brigade. The moon had risen and it was giving me the eye through the big window to my left — I gave it right back, I wasn't going to be outstared by a big ball of cheese.

Still, I was grateful for its light as I fumbled my way along the corridor. I came to room 23 and stood against the door, breathing like a voyeur at a keyhole. What I was doing there at that time of night I had not the faintest idea. Instead of sitting outside and keeping tabs on whoever went in and out like any normal private investigator, here I was doing what amounted to breaking and entering in the wee small hours. Call it intuition, I encouraged myself, but myself only sneered back at me.

Whatever way I looked at it, and that meant from all sides, it was a pretty dumb show.

How dumb it was I found out when I went inside. Opening the door, ducking through, and closing it behind me took only the work of a moment. Then time seemed to slow down. The room wasn't as bright as earlier in the day because someone had knocked over two of the three lamps, but the hanging bulb still shed enough light to show me more than I cared to see.

Bernadette was sitting in her usual spot in the middle of the sofa. Her head was leaning to one side in the same sleeping position, but there was no snore this time and her dark glasses were askew on her nose. Seeping through the blond hair above her right temple was what looked like an amount of bubbly raspberry jam, and when I bent down I saw that her open mouth was full of thick oily blood.

I knew it was useless, but I went through the motions anyway: I felt for a pulse in her wrist, then I held my finger against the big artery in her neck. Nothing for either of us there. I gazed at her well-endowed chest, but I'd have to question my motives about that one, so I left it. It was obvious that Bernadette had danced off to that insubstantial, fairy place where time, tide nor the seasons could touch her ever again.

I stood for a moment to collect my thoughts. The first thing I did was to take out my handkerchief and wipe the inside knob that I had just handled. I glanced at the door to her bedroom. It was ajar. A little tickle of fear ran up and down my spine. Her killer might be standing in there, holding his breath like me. The hanging curtain in the other corner then caught my eye. He could be in there either, thinking dark thoughts and fingering the carving knife.

My wisest course of action would have been to scram, scoot, take it on the lam out of there. But there was something I had to do first. Reluctantly I approached the sofa. This was the second dead body I had come across in the space of one night, but familiarity wasn't making it any easier for me.

In spite of my exaggerated care, I suddenly stepped on

something that rolled beneath my foot. I looked down. It was a Pernod bottle, on its side and with the heavy bottom part painted a sticky red. The weapon that had stove in Bernadette's head? I didn't need to be Sherlock Holmes to come to that conclusion.

I left it where it was. Instead I examined the glass-topped table with my eyes. There was no sign of the card I had given Bernadette the evening before. What a long time ago that now seemed. Carefully I put my hand in the pocket of her dressing gown but, instead of pulling out a plum, I extricated an empty cigarette packet, a box of matches and, to my relief, the little rectangle of pasteboard with my vital statistics on it.

I straightened up, thought about investigating the inner room and what I took to be the cooking annex, threw that thought aside and moved on to the next one. Namely that it was time for me to be long gone. I might have partially satisfied George Quinlan about my involvement with the late Charles Walsh-Overman, but if I were to add the late Bernadette Walsh-Overman, nee Mordaunt, to the list, then galloping dubiousness might set in.

I took one more look at her before I left. She had certainly been dealt a stacked hand. Here she was, a Liberties girl who had hit the big time and then had it snatched away as though she'd spat in the eye of the deity that doled it out. What'd you do to deserve to end up like this, Bernadette? I asked her, but she merely looked at me through those impishly tilted sunglasses and kept her own counsel.

I backed out, wiped off the outside knob and made my way back down the stairs. In the foyer I had a thought: maybe someone has done a Polonius on Milly and stabbed him behind the arras? Carefully I went in behind the desk and drew aside the curtain. His slippers were there all right, but either the living, breathing Milly had been assumed into heaven or he had taken himself off somewhere to kip down for the night. Either way, I wasn't going to put myself out looking for him.

I went outside, eased into my car and drove it off in a

westerly direction. The second public phone box I tried was working, so I dialled 999 and informed a disinterested voice that if the Gardai were to call to 19A, Gardinia Place, they might find something in room 23 to interest them. I felt I owed it to Bernadette not to leave her alone and unlamented.

18

THE HOUSE WAS as quiet as a suppressed sneeze. I went upstairs and had a shower. Then I had a bath. I lay in the scented water and tried to conjure up something pleasant to think about. The fragrance logo on the bath salts had said 'Pine', so I endeavoured to imagine the kind of woods that Robert Frost tells us are 'lovely, dark and deep'. The only problem there was that after a time I began to discern the flash of tooth and claw, and the shriek of some small animal dying violently brought me out of a warmth-induced snooze with an alacrity that caused my headache to come back.

I climbed out and dried myself. Condensation had blotted out the mirror, so I rubbed at it with the towel. Slowly my face came up in its surface. The haunted visage that appeared made me quickly back off: I looked like Hamlet's father's ghost.

I put on a dressing gown and went downstairs. In the sitting room, my favourite place in the whole house, I switched on a lamp. My rocking chair — medicinal for the back injury that had put an end to my hurling career — was waiting, so I sat into it. I had always liked to do this late at night, the time when the ghosts of the house's former inhabitants came out to play. They were friendly spirits. The old couple who had sold us the house told us it was a happy place. They had raised their family there, and nothing very awful had happened to any of them.

Annie and I had made love on the rug in front of the fire in this very room. We were so easy with one another then, no effort involved, taking for granted something that needed to be nurtured. My fame as a hurler had involved us in a social whirl, but as injuries and the frustration of losing began to take their toll I had grown morose and difficult to live with. Annie had shown patience above and beyond the call of duty, but in the end found the strain of living with me too much even for her sunny personality. I behaved like a shit, I knew it, and I tried to use drink to flush myself away.

But in the beginning, things had been so different. Sometimes my father came to visit, and he and I would attend to the necessary things that an old house demands of its owners. We refastened slates, replaced drainpipes, screwed down floorboards so that they wouldn't creak. We installed an alarm system that had a mind of its own: it went off when it felt like it. Annie and my father had some strange affinity between them; there seemed no need to talk, yet there was a warmth of communication that went way deeper than words or gestures. Whereas he and I would fight, shout, laugh and tease, they would raise an eyebrow at one another, wink, walk away and never fail to look back over their shoulders.

Rocking backwards and forwards, I let my memories wash over me as a balm to present hurt. And once again I must have dropped off, for suddenly Bernadette appeared brandishing the blood-stained Pernod bottle and prancing about in a grotesque dance of death. In the background Charles Walsh-Overman sat perched on a crimson throne. He was laughing gleefully and, every so often as he threw his head back, a little bird would spring from the gaping wound in his neck and give a little whistle.

With a jerk I came awake, the cold chill of fear an echo in my mind. Why had Bernadette's throat not been cut like the others? It broke the pattern. It presupposed that another hand was at work, another murderer whose method of operation was different from the first. I had been in the private detective business a little over a year, and the worst atrocity I had come across was a woman who methodically cut up all her husband's clothes, his suits, shirts, ties, underwear, socks, all scissored neatly into narrow strips that must have taken her a full day to get through — and all because she believed, falsely as it turned out, that he was cheating on her with his secretary.

Now in the space of two days I was up to my neck in murder and mayhem. Was I a Daniel come to judgement? I wondered, or had some evil in the Walsh-Overman family resurfaced to suck in me, Bernadette, and a trio of wandering tramps?

It was cold in the room, and colder in my mind. I did have a theory as to what was going on, but as to how I might prove it to myself and, more importantly, to others, I had very little notion. My client was due a report, but what had I to tell her? Some hit and miss guesswork, maybe, but I was still no nearer to finding Redmond. And George Quinlan would be after my hide. He knew I'd been to visit Bernadette. Now she was dead. The same had happened to Charles. What new story could I concoct? The truth might provide the simplest and straightest path, but so did a plank and not everyone was willing to walk it.

I got out of the rocking chair, not without difficulty, and creaked over to the hi-fi. There was a tape in it, so I pushed the play button. Janis Ian eased her voice into the room, accompanying it with a riffle of piano music. She sounded sad, and so did her songs: she was telling me that she needed to live alone again. I don't need it, Janis, I told her, but I'm stuck with it. I thought of Annie, and wondered if she was lying safely folded in Harold's tree trunk arms. At least with him life was simple; there were no tests to be faced, no obstacle course to be negotiated.

I needed no one to tell me that the root of my problem lay in being unable to comprehend that someone as vital and good as Annie could love me utterly and completely. I couldn't see myself as being worthy of that kind of love. Therefore I set traps to test her each day, until eventually she grew tired of trying to justify something as unexplainable as the heart of a rose. You can love someone too much as well as too little.

I leaned back into my rocker again, settling into the pool of sadness that Janis Ian was creating. It seemed right for the time and the mood:

'The evening sun it paints the sky,
And who will love me when I die?
The stars that fell tonight,
Do not appear as bright,
My love, I fear the morning light.'

19

I FEARED THE morning light so much that I slept until long past noon. I woke up a couple of times when the telephone rang and someone came to summon me, but I stayed quiet and refused to be summoned.

When I did get up and came downstairs, the house was empty. I went into the kitchen and there was a note to tell me Leo had rung and that I was to ring him back. I complied, and he informed me that he had checked out the other two tramps and that neither of them had had a finger missing. This did not surprise me: I had good reason to believe that Redmond was very much alive, possibly even taking on the characteristics of Supertramp, his underpants over his plus fours and flying around the city on a bottle of VP wine.

I dressed, got in the car and drove down to the office. The day was fine, a blue sky, sunshine doing its best to generate some heat, a light ripple of breeze. Good hunting weather.

On my way after parking the car I picked up the evening paper, which I took with me up to the office. Happily I made it without getting hit over the head or being arrested.

The newspaper didn't connect up the deaths of Charles and Bernadette. There were separate accounts of their murders, but only Charles was named. Over the piece about the killing in Gardinia Place was a photograph of Milly, a head and shoulders shot, his mouth open, nostrils flaring. He was described as being the manager of a boarding house. In his statement to the Fourth Estate he said that he had been indisposed and had only learned of the unfortunate woman's death when roused by the police. Obviously none of the reporters had lit a match in his presence, otherwise they'd have been beating flames out of their eyebrows.

I thought about ringing George Quinlan before he rang me, but then decided against it. Let him find me. Instead I put through a call to Mrs Ada Mulloy, she of the absconding and non-paying husband. If I didn't attend to my other cases, I'd lose my standing in the Yellow Pages.

A child's voice answered and told me to hang on for his or her Mammy. The Mammy, when she came on, had a yelp like a Pekinese. Yes, her husband was behind in his payments. He was so far behind he was out of sight. Sure she had tried to contact him. He might as well have been in Philadelphia. He worked as a long distance lorry driver and spent most of his time in the cab of his sixteen ton lorry. That was of course when he wasn't shacking up with a biddy from Cabra, who'd piss in your eye and say it was raining.

There was a lot more of this claptrap, but I finally got her to give me the address he stayed at between shuttles. It was a Joyce Road in West Cabra, not too far away from where I lived myself. She let me know I was in for a percentage of the takings, advised me to kick him in the goolies for her, and rang off. If her husband was half as tough as she sounded, I was in for a trying time.

I then tried Tom Saddler of the Mutual Trust Insurance Co. His secretary told me he was out, but she took my message and said she'd get him to ring back. I read the paper, disagreed with the Wexford hurling team for the following Sunday's match against Cork, wondered where next I could look for Redmond Walsh-Overman, and tried not to think about the Bushmills in my bottom drawer. No call came.

I left the office at two and drove up into Cabra and hunted around for the address that Mrs Ada Mulloy had given me. Every so often there were little enclaves of shops and small businesses, barricaded, their frontages gaudy with slogans, rude, obscene, and rudely obscene. Around here graffiti defaced anything that couldn't get up and walk away.

I stopped and asked a youth with pimply skin and a sneer

you could hang your hat on if he could tell me where Joyce Road was. He gave me directions reluctantly, talking out of the corner of his mouth and edging away nervously. He was probably afraid his pals might see him talking to me and accuse him of collaborating with the work force.

I drove into an estate of council houses with wine coloured, pebble-dashed walls and windows iced with lace curtains. This was one of the older areas where the people had undergone a rash of respectability. Gardens were neat and nicely manicured, motor cars were relatively new and had all their wheels, and there was no junk or burned-out wrecks strewn about the roads.

Number 42 let down the rest of the street. Most of the pebble-dash had fallen off the front wall into the wilderness of scutch grass that masqueraded as the garden. The windows were dirty, the curtains that cloaked them as threadbare as a politician's promises. A banger in the driveway had collapsed from exhaustion and old age, the splattered comments of playful birds insulting its well-earned retirement.

I parked and sat for a moment, thinking. Then I reached down and found the reinforced woollen sock that I kept under the passenger seat. The foot was packed full of ten pence pieces. I put it in my pocket, got out and locked the car. The weather had turned cold again, and a sprinkle of rain shook itself out of the sky as I sidled along between the dividing block wall and the battered remains of the Fiat 127. From the twitching of the downstairs curtain, I knew that I was being watched, but I pretended not to notice.

The front door was so thirsty for paint that I fancied I could hear it gasping. There were two pimpled glass panels, but no bell or knocker. I rattled the letterbox and immediately a face was pressed against one of the glass insets. It appeared so suddenly that I took a step back, my hands closing around the sock in my pocket.

The face withdrew, then the door opened a fraction and an eye was applied to the crack. I exerted a little pressure by leaning forward and was rewarded by the sight of a youngish woman with long, greasy-looking brown hair. She had pale, suety cheeks, dull eyes, a button nose that had been badly sewn on, and a mouth that drooped sulkily. I tried a smile on her, but elicited only a frown.

'Feldstein's my name,' I told her breezily, 'and money lending's my game. You wanna buy a new video, a second TV, a curling tongs,'—I paused and grinned lecherously—'an up to date vibrator encompassing a nine inch dildo with rubber corrugated surface and feather tickler ...?'

The sulky mouth straightened out, then dropped open.

'Wha?'

I tried again. 'I'm attempting to build up a little business,' I coaxed. 'New at it but willing to learn. Very good terms I'm giving. Three months interest free and lotsa time to pay. A nice girl like you. Maybe a new wardrobe? Clothes to put in it, the latest fashions ....'

She frowned again, her assimilation threshold obviously not too high. Then I noticed her eyes, which were vague, the pupils dilated and shiny. She was on something, either alcohol or something that packed more of a wallop. Raising a hand, she put it against her face, the fingers curled. Then she giggled.

I giggled along with her. 'Can I come in for a minute?' I cajoled. 'Maybe the man of the house might like to hear my proposition? Crisp new fivers I bring, all hot and steaming from the printing room.'

I moved forward carefully, not being too pushy, and she retreated before me. Then she suddenly turned and ran off back down the hallway, leaving the door open. I stepped inside. The walls were sweating with damp and what wall-paper there was sagged in dispirited tatters. My feet scraped on the uncarpeted hall floor. There was a smell of cabbage and stale grease, and the fetid odour of unwashed bodies and air too long pent up formed a miasma that I had to wade through.

I looked into a room on my right. Two dilapidated chairs, a packing case containing the remnants of a meal, a soot-stained fireplace. There was a pool of something in one corner and the wall was stained as though someone had pissed against it. How the other half lives ..?

Moving on, I gazed into what might once have been a kitchen — now it seemed to serve as the municipal dump spillover. Nothing to be gained by venturing in there. Both my stomach and my nose told me that.

Resignedly I climbed the stairs. The steps were clothed in a strip of frayed matting that was suffering from a terminal dose of the mange. The tiny landing gave me a choice of three open doorways. I choose the middle one and peered in. What looked like a large and lumpy bear was laid out full length on the sagging double bed that was the room's main furnishing. Items of clothing were scattered about, both male and female, discarded and left lying as though in the wake of a carefree game of strip poker.

There was another packing case, this one bearing an advertisement for oranges from Spain: the multi-hued picture on the side showed Spanish senoritas with their skirts held high and roses in their hair and gave a touch of colour to the room that it hardly deserved. The top of the crate held a wallet, a bunch of keys, a packet of Rothman's cigarettes and a one third filled gin bottle. Also littering the floor were a number of other bottles, dead men by the look of them.

I approached the bed, cautious on ballet dancer's feet. The hirsute thing on the bed was in reality some species of naked human male — he had a dong big enough to beat an elephant to death. I could have said stark naked, but with that amount of hair, stark he could never be. It grew from between his toes, up over his trunk, crawled across his chest and nudged itself over his chin and into his ears. Strangely enough, it ended there. He was as bald as a cue ball. Didn't seem fair, somehow, to be encased in so much fluff and still have the poor old skull vulnerable and bare.

But it wouldn't do to start feeling sorry for him. Mentally I conjured up a picture of Ada Mulloy in a Mother Courage posture, surrounded by a posse of woebegone children. All of them with imploring eyes, their hands held out, and chorusing, 'Kick him in the goolies.'

I looked around, but there was no sign of the girl. Bigfoot on the bed blew some air through fluttering lips, raised a hand and scratched himself — I won't say where. He appeared to be a pretty powerful specimen; I guessed it would take no great effort on his part to pick me up and throw me through the wall.

Tentatively I poked at his wallet, then flipped it open. It contained a plastic identity card, complete with photo, proclaiming that Hugh Francis Mulloy was registered as a driver with Trans European Freight. The photograph had probably scared the pants off many an unsuspecting customs official.

There was also a blood donor's card — whoever got Hugh Francis's blood would want to watch out each time there was a full moon — an advertisement cut from a newspaper for a preparation to cure baldness, and two twenty pound notes, both of them showing the signs of much manhandling.

I began to experience that sinking feeling you get when you realise you're flogging a dead horse. There was no treasure trove to be plundered here, unless Ada was willing to settle for the deposits on the bottles decorating the floor. I extracted the notes and was about to transfer them into my keeping when a great hairy hand suddenly rose up in the air and clamped itself like a handcuff round my wrist — Hugh Francis had woken up and was ready for his dinner.

Instinctively I stepped back, hauling King Kong with me. Luckily he stepped on one of the night before's leftovers and the bottle rolled under his foot, causing him to lose his balance. To save himself he had to release his grip on my arm and throw his hands out wide. It was to no avail. He went over backwards onto the bed which, with a discordant jangle of springs, collapsed under him, the middle giving way and the mattress closing around him with the greedy embrace of a carnivorous plant. He was held fast, like the jam in a jamroll.

Feeling pretty good, I stood and watched until he calmed

down a little. 'I come bearing greetings from your wife Ada,' I told him. 'She's a little short of cash and the kiddies are demanding food and drink. She was wondering if you'd cough up a little something to help her over the hump.'

'Cough up' was an unfortunate choice of words, for he suddenly spat a wad at me that if it had landed would have left me being called jelly head for the rest of the year. It went past my ear like a guided missile and knocked plaster off the wall behind my head.

It gave me pause for thought: if he could do that with a spit, what could he do with the rest of him? Still, I wasn't to be found wanting for lack of trying. 'I'm taking this forty quid on account,' I told him, 'and I'm trusting you to send on the rest. Scout's honour ...?'

His eyes, which had been in danger of popping out of his head, had now retracted and were staring over my shoulder. I turned, just in time to behold the girl who had opened the door about to brain me with what looked like a cast iron poker. I got my arm in the way, and then flinched when it made contact, but it turned out merely to be a child's rubber toy. The girl's look of bafflement turned my fright into a wobbly kind of laugh that staggered out of my mouth and rebounded off the wall.

Hugh Francis was well on the way to releasing himself by now, so I decided to take my leave. As I pushed past her, the girl clawed herself onto my back, and I went down the stairs like the favourite heading for the final jump in the Grand National. I had a vision of being left like that, a Sisyphus with her as my boulder; but when I got as far as the hall she gave up, let go and fell over onto the cement floor. I glanced back at her. Her mud coloured shift had ridden up around her waist. She wasn't wearing any pants, but then neither does a bramble bush and it would have looked just as inviting.

Hearing a heavy foot on the stairs, I got out of there as fast as an Indian Holy Man travels across a bed of live coals. My car was still at the kerb, the engine started on the second twist of the ignition, and in the twitch of a fly's eyebrow I was bowling merrily down Joyce Road.

There are a thousand stories in the naked city, I told myself as I went, and you have to settle on a no-no. Then the funny side of it hit me, and I started to laugh.

20

BACK AT THE office, I phoned Ada and gave her the bad news. She didn't like it much. As a matter of a fact, she didn't like it a lot. I asked for her address and, after she had given it to me, I hung up on her while she was still in the middle of telling me what a ball's up I'd made of the whole affair. I was tired of Ada, and Hugh Francis, and all who sailed in them.

I sat for a while, but somewhere in the back of my mind I heard the Mulloy children calling to me, so I hunted around and found an envelope and stuck the two twenties into it. That didn't seem to satisfy them, but when I added three more from my own private stock their faces lit up and they began to purr.

I licked the flap, affixed a stamp and put it aside for my secretary to post — not just the stamp, the envelope too. Hold on there a minute, I then reminded myself, you haven't got a secretary. What's the harm in a little wishful thinking? myself replied. I gave up after that, took out the Bushmills and had a snort. Tea might be the cup that cheers, *à la* Sean O'Casey, but whiskey is your only man when the cheering dies down.

Back out in the street again, I posted the letter in the postbox at the corner and then hurried to my car. The rain had found its rhythm and was tap dancing on every available surface. The heavy, steam-coloured sky was supporting itself on the tops of the higher buildings, and a number of the shops had their lights on.

I pulled into the turgid, slow motion flow of traffic and turned on the radio. Ronan Collins was talking to a guy who played the harmonica; he did little trills and warbles like a feline floozie answering her tomcat lover. Then another guy came on who made a trumpet sound with his mouth: now, if it had been the other end then it would really have been something. Anyway, give me a sweet plucking banjo player any old day of the week.

It was past five when I finally got onto the Clontarf Road. The traffic was moving a little faster now, so I opened up the Renault in spite of its protests. Two cars back from me a silvery grey Bluebird pulled out and began to overtake. I had been watching it since I'd turned onto the front road. It could have passed me a number of times, but it had held back on each occasion.

It pulled in behind me, staying within a nice respectable braking distance. There were two people in the front and one in the back, but I couldn't see them clearly to put name and rank on them. Three businessmen on their way home to suburbia? Clubbing together and using only one car to save expenses? Maybe ....

I went past Sutton, up the incline by the cemetery and then into the series of curves that lead to the summit. The Bluebird stayed on my tail. Out over the bay the rain was swishing down, a numinous evening light splayed through it like twilight's last gleaming. Along the path that bordered the sea wall two boys in bright yellow raincoats raced their dog, their heads down, knees pumping.

When the gates of the Walsh-Overman estate loomed up I turned in and then stopped. I got out and went back quickly to the entrance. The Bluebird was parked on the hard shoulder a little way from me, its rear lights misty in the rain. It could be the Gardai. George Quinlan could have sent them to pick me up. But why the cat and mouse act? I decided to find out.

I began walking towards the car, but I was still some distance from it when it revved up and moved off. I didn't even get the registration number. I stayed and watched it out of sight, getting wet and angry in equal amounts. Maybe it was time I started making things happen, instead of sitting back and letting them happen to me. You can say that again in spades, I told myself, and this time myself concurred.

I went back to the car and drove on, past the gloom-enshrouded golf course and up to the main entrance of the house. The night-time appearance of the Cottage was spectacular. Floodlights set at ground level bathed the turrets in white light, the rain tiny silver daggers falling through the beams. It looked like a medieval castle waiting patiently for its lord and master to return home from the Crusades. A few sentries in chain mail peering over the battlements would have finished the scene off nicely.

A severe looking middle-aged woman in sober black answered my ring. She looked me up and down, pursed her lips and surprised me by not banging the door in my face.

'Mrs Danvers, I presume?'

She frowned.

'No Mrs Danvers here.'

'A fictional creation, I assure you. *Rebecca*. Book by Daphne Du Maurier, film by Hitchcock. House Manderley. Housekeeper Mrs Danvers. And by a process of circumlocution we are back to you-whoo ...'

'Huh?'

'Sorry, I got carried away there. It's Mrs Walsh-Overman I'm after. The name is Blaine. I work for the lady.'

'Mrs Walsh-Overman is grieving over the death of her son. She cannot be disturbed.'

I moved aside as a rope of rainwater from a damaged chute did its best to drown me. I was tired. I was wet. I hadn't had my tea. Now this ogre was trying to keep me from carrying out my duties as a well-behaved and polite employee. It was enough to ruffle the patience of an anchorite.

I took a deep breath, then said, reasonably considering the circumstances, 'Perhaps you'd go and inquire from the lady herself? If she did wish to see me and you sent me away ..? You get my meaning?'

Indecision poked its way into the rigidity of her expression — if I hadn't been watching her closely she might have nibbled on a fingernail. 'I'll try,' she said, relenting. 'You can wait out here till I get back.'

This time she did bang the door in my face, leaving me cold, shivering and muttering little aspirations under my breath. I huddled in as close to the portals as I could, but the rain turned contrary and blew in on me as though I had done it a dirty trick.

It seemed like an age before the Danvers clone returned and let me in. She told me that Mrs Walsh-Overman would spare me a few minutes, but the information didn't appear to afford her any particular pleasure.

I marched along behind her, barely suppressing the urge to whistle the dwarves song from Snow White. We went down the hall and through a door to our right. Immediately the lady in black stopped dead, and I almost bumped into her.

On a catafalque in the middle of the room Charles Walsh-Overman was lying in state in an ornamental casket. The head of the coffin had been raised, and Charles had the arrested in flight appearance of someone who had been in a hurry to go somewhere. It was probably to a ball, for his mouth was lip-sticked, his cheeks rouged, his hair sleeked down. If the mortician had only raised one of his arms in a rigor mortis gesture of farewell, the tableau would have been complete.

There was a spotlight shining on Charles, but the rest of the room was in semi-darkness. A large mahogany dining table with hand-carved legs and a spawn of six matching chairs had been pushed into a corner to accommodate the arrangement in the middle of the floor. On a small raised dais, and sitting in what looked like a commode, Mrs Walsh-Overman suited ideally the role of bereaved mother — then again, she could equally have doubled as the corpse.

It was as far from the usual kind of Irish wake as a caress is from a slap in the face. Normally there would be a slew of people, young and old, talking, drinking, laughing fit to burst a gut. Here there was a silence so intense that it thrummed in my eardrums.

The lady in black sniffed, then left us to our own devices. I never did find out her name, her serial number, or her taste in underwear. Slowly I moved across the parquet floor and stood gazing at Charles. His head was sunk on his chest, mercifully hiding the gaping maw of his throat. He was attired in a nice pearl grey suit and white shirt; he had on a red tie and an equally natty red handkerchief flounced out of his top pocket. Wherever he was going, he was in with a chance of being voted best-dressed corpse of the week.

His mother's voice broke in on my reverie, whispering across the distance between us like the rustle of dry leaves:

'You have something to report?'

I bowed my head and tic-tac-toed over to her. Looking up at her I felt like a courtier at the court of Good Queen Bess, about to explain away some misdemeanour that would mean my head if I failed.

'I'm sorry for your sad loss,' I told her, my words sounding unctuous enough to slide across the floor and out under the door.

'Are you really?'

'Of course.'

'Isn't that something that one says on occasions like this?'

'I suppose so. You think custom has staled its efficacy?'

She did a lizard blink, the rest of her face immobile. On her, it was probably the equivalent of a shrug. 'There's no need to keep up a front with me, young man. Very few, if any, will grieve for Charles. He did not inspire warmth or friendliness.'

'What d'you feel, Mrs Walsh-Overman?' I asked her, genuinely wishing to know.

She looked down at me, but her eyes were remote. 'It is an impertinence for you to ask. He was my son. Isn't that enough?'

'Maybe.'

I let it lie. It was none of my business whether her old heart was pierced by sorrow or not. My relationship with her was of the merely perfunctory; I had come to make my report, and that was lame enough in its way.

'I haven't found Redmond yet,' I told her. 'I've visited a number of places where he's been, but he always manages to keep ahead of me.'

'He knows you're looking for him?'

'I've no reason to believe that he does. It's just that he keeps on the move. I feel I'm breathing down the back of his neck, but when I reach out there's nothing there. He appears to have learned discretion as to where he should be at any given time or place.'

'I wonder why.'

'So do I. I think he's in a certain amount of danger. I think you also believe that ...'

'Danger?'

I watched her carefully. 'Mrs Walsh-Overman,' I said, 'have you given any thought as to who might have killed Charles?'

The question hung in the air between us, as significant or otherwise as a sudden intake of breath. The old lady decided to juggle with it for a bit: 'Is it not the business of the police to find that out?'

'Certainly it is,' I answered her, 'and I'm sure they're investigating it night and day. But the forces of the law are inclined to have a very pragmatic turn of mind. They see straight lines where perhaps curved ones exist. Not for them the pretty nuance or the impacted wisdom tooth of doubt. They like everything to be neatly tied and filed away. Cause, motive and effect, that's what they pray for when they get down on their knees at night. But you and I, Mrs Walsh-Overman, we know better. In human terms, and especially where extremes of behaviour are concerned, nothing is ever cut and dried. There are always snags and snarls, the hanging bits that refuse to conform to a pattern unless the formula is truly known.' I paused, then decided to go for it: 'Tell me about Redmond and his sister,' I said. 'It's one of the things that keeps coming up, like a body floating to the surface of a lake.'

'Very graphic,' the old lady said drily, but she didn't seem overly concerned or upset by my question. Then again, she had lived a lot of years and had fair practice at disguising her feelings. 'Someone said that the past is a different country,' she went on. 'Things happen there that have no relevance to the present time.'

I surprised myself by snorting. 'You know that's not true,' I told her. 'The very opposite in fact.' I spread my hands. 'Look, you brought me into this affair by hiring me to find your son. You must look upon me as a confidante. I'm like the priest in his role of confessor; I'm bound to respect the confidentiality of whatever you tell me. The only way I'll find Redmond is to get inside his skin and think like he does. And it's very important that I find him before someone else does. If the episode of himself and his sister has any bearing on why he's behaving as he is, then you must tell me. You can rest assured that it'll go no further.'

'A very pretty speech ...'

'To test the conscience of the queen, you mean?'

She made a little sipping sound with her lips — it might have been her way of registering disapproval, then again it could have been a spasm of pain, the kind that old people are prone to. 'Redmond is in no way devious,' she said. 'As a matter of fact, it's the very opposite. He was always credulous to the point of believing practically everything he was told. And where emotions were concerned, he was a most simple man. He lacked the power of dissimulation ...'

'You talk about him in the past tense. D'you not believe you'll see him again?'

She attempted to sit up straight in the old-fashioned wooden chair. She owned no substance, she was as fragile as a butterfly. It was as if the real person had long departed and only a shell remained. If blood coursed through her veins, it was as thin and cold as winter sunlight. Only the eyes, and the strength of will behind them, retained the spark of life, the rest had long since faded towards dissolution. She engendered no positive feeling in me, merely the prickle of curiosity and the sense of a duty that had to be discharged.

'You will remember that I told you of how my husband and I built up our business to the detriment of our family life,' she said. 'We had three children. Charles was always solitary. He had his own interests, and there's no need to go into them now — or ever again, for that matter. Redmond and Celia were close, obsessively so. I'm not imputing a physical relationship, but there was an intensity about their feelings for one another that is not normally the case between a brother and a sister. They went everywhere together, they shared the same likes and dislikes. At the time I paid very little heed, but in retrospect I can see that there was something not quite right about the closeness and fixity of their intimacy. To make a long story short, in her eighteenth year Celia became interested in another boy, a distant cousin.' Surprisingly Mrs Walsh-Overman did shrug, a mere shifting of her shoulders but a shrug nonetheless. 'What could be more natural?' she went on, the whisper of her voice a susurration in the stillness of the room. 'She was a healthy, passionate girl. And it was said that she was quite beautiful. Redmond became more and more agitated as the liaison blossomed. He succumbed to uncharacteristic bouts of anger. He made a nuisance of himself. In an ordinary household, things would most probably have been smoothed over, a solution of sorts found. But we were no ordinary family, perhaps Joseph and I should never have been granted the gift of children. We were certainly punished for our lack of judgement.' Again she made the sound with her lips, half sigh, half painful intake of breath. 'On a balmy June day, Redmond and Celia went boating on our private lake. There was no wind, the water was still and motionless. Yet for some reason the boat overturned, and Celia, who was a strong swimmer, drowned, while Redmond, who was only adequate in that respect, survived.'

I stared at her with my mouth open. Then I shifted my feet, longing for a cigarette. The silence was like a pall around us, uniting us in the remembrance of the event that her words had projected out of the past. I cleared my throat, a startled wingbeat in the room's hush, and said, 'There was an investigation?'

'Not really. But the canker of suspicion is not easily laid to rest. Redmond underwent a change in personality. He became withdrawn, distant, unable to articulate. He took to wearing ill-assorted clothes, espousing odd causes ...'

'But surely you must have got him specialist attention?'

'Oh, yes, he attended a number of therapists. But I fear the cure was as irretrievable as the sin that brought on the disease.'

'You blame yourself?'

For the first time she looked at me as though really seeing me. 'Blame? There is no blame. There is merely a course of events that happened as they were meant to happen. When old people say they have regrets about the past, they are lying. What they really mean is that they regret not being able to have the past back. As to its content, they couldn't care less.'

'So you don't care that your son quite possibly murdered your daughter?'

'It is not for you to ask me that.'

'Who then? God?'

This time her eyes flickered, and I knew that I had got through to her, but her words still sought to deny the fact:

'I lived my life as I saw fit. If I could have it back, I would take it.'

'Just as it was?'

'Of course.'

'Mrs Walsh-Overman,' I said, 'you're a monster.'

She smiled, although if I hadn't been watching her so closely I'd have missed it. 'And monsters beget monsters ..?'

'You believe that Redmond killed Charles, don't you?'

'Not did, but could have.'

'And his ex-wife, did he kill her too?'

'She's dead?'

'As a doornail. Her head smashed in by a Pernod bottle.'

'How suitable.'

Suddenly I needed to get out of there. I was beginning to get the feeling that Charles had climbed out of his coffin and was creeping up behind me. His mother looked like a witch, her eyes glinting in the chalk-white ruin of her face. I was too naive, too innocent for this sort of scene. I couldn't even dredge up a wisecrack to sustain me.

'You want me to keep looking for Redmond?' I asked her, half hoping that she would say no.

It was a moment before she answered, probably still enjoying the thought of Bernadette and the Pernod bottle. Finally she said, 'I paid you for a week's work ... and I need a written report for my files ...'

'For your files ...'

She shifted in her seat again. The hard wood must have been painful for her old bones — at least, I hoped it was.

'You don't like me very much, do you?' she said.

I shrugged. 'I don't have any feelings about you, one way or the other.'

'You think I'm cold and hard and emotionless?'

I said nothing.

But she wouldn't let it lie: 'Like most, you have the usual misconception of old people. You see them entering into their second childhoods. Incapable of thinking or taking care of themselves. Unable to control their bodily functions. I find the whole thing so distasteful. I've always been a fighter, Mr Blaine, and I'll go out like that, fighting. Is that so reprehensible?'

'I try not to make judgements on things like that,' I said, not completely truthfully. 'You're the one who hired me, and I'll continue to do my best for you as long as I'm in your employ. Liking you or not liking you doesn't enter into it.'

There was a silence which afforded me an opportunity to leave, but I lingered. After a moment she said, her voice barely audible: 'Why do you think I want Redmond found?'

I thought about that one, then I said, 'You're a manipulator, Mrs Walsh-Overman. All your life you've succeeded in pigeon-holing people ... your husband, your son Charles, the many who've worked for you in one capacity or another. But Redmond was different — mad, but different. He refused to conform. He circled around outside your sphere of influence. The fact that he may be capable of committing violent acts doesn't trouble you as much as that he's his own man. I think you want to make one last try at lassoing him and bringing him into some kind of submission. Maybe what you'd really like is to have him and Charles lying in twin coffins here before you. Then you could really feel that they're yours, all yours ...'

She surprised me by nodding. 'Perhaps that would be for the best,' she said. She wasn't looking at me anymore, she was gazing instead into a bleakness that I had no wish to see into with her. 'You can leave me now,' she whispered. 'I'd like to be alone with my dead.'

I got out of there, closed the door, leaned against it, and thought about a wash of pastel sunlight in a green glade. Then I threw in some mountains, purple in the distance, and air cold and bracing, and a vista of space and emptiness that dwarfed to triviality the worries of a more mundane world. I needed a fix like that to prevent me from going off the deep end.

21

IN A WHILE I straightened up and inclined my head to listen. There was no sign of the sombre female who had let me in. The hall was empty, just as the rest of the house probably was. If Saunders had been around, he'd have put in an appearance by now.

I went to the foot of the stairs and looked up. It was as wide as a two lane highway, a strip of deep blue carpet waterfalling down the centre of it. Its lush pile muffled my footsteps as I went up the steps, cautiously and with the odd glance over my shoulder. I was curious about Saunders, and maybe a peek into his boudoir would help to satisfy my interest.

The landing was split level. On the lower part there were four doors, all closed. They opened easily to my touch and I found three bedrooms and a huge, old-fashioned bathroom with a tub big enough to accommodate a football team.

As I was there I decided to take a leak, but when I pulled the hanging chain there was a clanking and banging as though all the pipes in the house had come alive and were wishing one another happy flushing.

I got out of there and did a hurried tour of the bedrooms. They contained a lot of heavy antique furniture, stolid, even a little smug in their burnished brown benignity. The beds were all kingsize, with canopies. I tested each of them in turn, wondering on which one Bernadette had done her duty. Or, more to the point, on which of them she'd performed her off-duty rollicking. The beds kept their thoughts to themselves, hidden behind their flowered silk valances.

I went on up the other four steps and found three more doors. Two of them yielded a smaller bedroom and another bathroom, this one with a tub just big enough for the team coach and his best boy.

The third door was locked. Quietly I knocked, a mere tintinnabulation of the finger tips. Nothing happened. I put my ear to the wood and held my breath. Still nothing. Getting down on one knee, I applied an eye to the keyhole. No eye gazed back at me.

What to do? The door didn't look all that sturdy. When I pushed against it, it gave slightly. It was a question, really, of how much I wanted to get in. I was presuming that it was Saunders' bedroom. Then again Mrs. Danvers might be in there, sipping a discreet gin and tonic, smoking a joint and sitting in front of the mirror asking it who was the fairest of them all.

I decided to chance it. Standing back, I lifted my leg and kicked hard beside the knob with the sole of my shoe. The door flew inwards, met an obstruction and came trundling back. I caught it, ducked inside and left it open a crack so that I could see the landing and the stairs. No one came rushing up to see what had happened. I was alone with my thumping heart and my breath tight as a drum in my chest.

A minute went by, then another. Satisfied, I closed the door and turned to look about me. The floodlights outside muted the interior darkness and lent it a greyish pallor. I waited until my eyes had grown accustomed to it, then I went over and drew the drapes over the narrow window. I switched on a bedside lamp.

Unlike the others, this room was sparsely furnished: a single bed, a cheap-looking chest of drawers with a heart-shaped mirror screwed into two slats projecting from it, a built-in wardrobe with its doors gaping open, a fireplace surmounted by a cluttered mantlepiece. The carpet was thin enough to read a magazine through. On the floor under the window was a steel contraption, with 'Flab Blaster' stencilled on the side — it was the kind you sit into, pull on a stout rope and never get anywhere. There were also some dumb-bells.

I wrinkled my nose at the sickly sweet smell of body odour. It was slight but pervasive, and when I lifted the lid of a cane laundry basket in one corner I found that it was coming from there. It was half full of soiled underwear and was one area that I definitely was not going to investigate.

I poked around in the chest of drawers. In a bottom compartment I found a pile of pornographic magazines. It was the usual stuff, but with one difference. All the women featured were well past the first bloom of youth. Maybe Saunders had an Oedipus complex.

Then again, I cautioned myself, it could be that this is not Saunders' room at all — but then, in another drawer, I found a brand new leather writing case with the name Laurence V. Saunders engraved on it in gold lettering. It contained a pristine block of stationery, an unopened packet of envelopes, a Cross pen in its own individual chamois tube, and a full page of stamps. Obviously a present that Laurence V. hadn't made much use of.

The mantlepiece gave up its secrets painlessly: it had no secrets. Merely a collection of junk. I picked up a glass jar in the form of a boot. It was full of foreign coins. A small globe held a Christmas scene, and when it was turned upside down and then righted again snowflakes quaintly whirled. There was also a trophy in the shape of a harp, but the brass plate had become tarnished and I couldn't read the motto. Probably Saunders' prize for measuring up to the reform school director's worst fears.

I looked in the wardrobe and found a whole row of expensive-looking suits and sports coats. Turning out the pockets, I was rewarded with enough fluff to stuff a million bellybuttons. In the top pocket of a classy Donegal tweed I found something that arrested my attention, but not for very long. When I unwrapped the bundle of cotton wool I found a pink plastic dental plate with two forlorn looking teeth attached. I wore one almost exactly like it. My God, was Saunders my evil twin or was the dentist who had rented my office before me playing a trick on me?

I gave up, stood in the middle of the room and wondered what I should do next. Search under the bed? Dismantle the lamp? Look up the chimney? To hell with it.

I was rather disappointed with Saunders for having such an ordinary dwelling place. I'd half expected to find human remains, a warlock's hat, a steaming cauldron containing newt's brains and gnat's balls. Instead I was confronted by a faceless anonymity that bordered on nothingness.

It was time for me to take off. In line with my new policy of getting my retaliation in first, I took out one of my cards and propped it against the glass boot, by way of letting Saunders know who had visited him.

I need not have bothered. As I was about to steal away I heard the sound of a car's wheels crunching in the gravel outside. I switched off the lamp and took a peek out from behind a discreetly tilted curtain. A small, dark coloured saloon had driven up and the man himself was in the process of getting out of it. In the hard white light of the arc lamps he threw a mighty big shadow.

It was then that I cursed myself for not making sure I had an avenue of escape. It would also have been useful if I had parked my car out of sight behind a mulberry bush.

Should I try to brazen it out? Tell Saunders I had been looking for the john and blundered into his room by mistake? I could easily piss on the floor to lend credence to my story.

Or I could simply stand my ground. However, being an avid exponent of the maxim: He who turns and runs away will live to fight another day, I suddenly moved across to the door, slid out and closed it behind me. It sagged accusingly against the broken lock.

I looked up and down the corridor, then decided to go left. That brought me up against an end wall nicely decorated in satin finish wallpaper, but as solid as government gilts.

I retraced my steps. This end looked much more hopeful. A

short flight of stairs had been built into an alcove and they led to a trapdoor in the ceiling. Praying that it wasn't locked, I went up two at a time. It was bolted on my side, but when I heaved back the bolt the door opened as easily as a greedy boy's mouth to a slice of strawberry cheesecake.

A gust of wind accompanied by some rain blew in on me and when I stepped out I saw that I was on the roof. The arc lights reflecting off the face of the building gave only a little illumination, but there seemed to be a number of outcrops and a sizable copper dome that would keep a scrap metal dealer in business for a year.

Picking my way carefully I made it to the side of the roof. This time I'd chosen wisely because when I leaned out I could see the first few rungs of a metal fire escape embedded in the cement. I swung myself over and began to descend. The iron flanges of the steps were slick with rain, and my rubber-soled shoes caused me palpitations as they slid and slithered. Near the bottom one of the steps had rusted through and it gave under me, and I ended up on one knee in the gravel, a penitent, alone, grieving and wet through.

Cautiously I edged my head around the side of the house. Drops of rain plink-plonked from leaf to leaf of a laurel bush, and further back the trees stood impassively in the murk. My car looked as vulnerable as I felt, but from where I was it appeared to be standing upright on four inflated tyres. Of Saunders there was no sign.

Taking a deep breath, I whipped around the corner and crunched through the gravel. The car rocked gently when I leaned against it — at least I'd had the foresight to face it in the right direction, its snout pointing down the drive.

Fumbling the keys into the lock seemed to take an eternity, but I eventually got the door open. The relief was as cathartic as a good evacuation of the bowels. I got in and started the engine, and once again it came to life almost immediately. Fondly I thought of Roy Rogers, the singing cowboy, and his horse Trigger, and of how he had got his four-footed friend stuffed when he finally kicked off. I would have to do something similar for my Renault 9 when its big end gave up the ghost.

Now that my trusty mode of conveyance was primed and ready to go, I felt in no particular hurry. The blare of light didn't bother me, the rain was only a minor irritation. I got out and stood in the drive. Then I went over to the car Saunders had driven up in and let the air out of the tyres. For some reason the hissing sound gave me a hard-on.

A movement on the roof caught my attention, and I looked up. A figure was standing up there, motionless, gazing down at me. Squinting against the rain, which had eased to no more than a chill caress, I could just make out the pale face and the white hair. Even at that distance I suddenly felt a sense of dread: there was the clarity of an oft repeated nightmare about the scene, the beast atop a high building, his victim puny and defenceless below. My spirits drooped along with my erection, and I got into the car and took it out of there with an abruptness that startled the engine, the gravel, and the soft dampness of the night.

22

THERE WAS NO sign of the silver grey Bluebird as I cruised back in towards town. Sitting upright, I kept my hands at ten to two on the steering wheel. I drove at a steady thirty miles per hour, observing the rules of the road, pausing to allow other motorists out of side roads. The wipers half mooned a view of slick, light-reflecting asphalt and the houses I passed had that folks at home and dinner on the table air about them.

I felt calm and unruffled, which was usually my reaction when something difficult or unpleasant had to be done. It was a form of lethargy, really, that indemnified my procrastination against blame or rebuke. The trick was to find a little capsule of present time that I could climb into and use as a hammock spanning the past and the future. It enabled me to swing low, like the chariot, and watch the cruel old world go by, with people doing things, decisions being made, and plans being put into action.

I knew now why the tramps were being murdered and who was doing the murdering. I could also make a pretty fair guess as to the circumstances of Bernadette's killing. The question now was, what was I going to do about it? I could ring George Quinlan and tell him of my suspicions, fan them out in front of him like a pack of cards. The money on the table in the form of hard evidence was missing, however.

Then again, I was the one who had been hired to do a job, the one to seek out Redmond and bring him safely home. What matter if the maternal instinct in his mother's breast had dissolved into hemlock years ago? Like a knight of old I had been entrusted with a quest, and no matter how tarnished or dented my armour, I was still honour-bound to venture forth in search of dragons.

But for the moment the dragons could wait. I had a dinner date with my true love Annie, and as an antidote for sitting somewhere in a lonesome place thinking lonesome thoughts I couldn't come up with a better.

I was already late, but luckily Harold's health and fitness studio wasn't too far away, so it was only a little after eight when I drove up and parked in one of the numbered slots in front of it. It had been converted from a shop, and the large, plate glass window was still intact. Someone — I liked to think it was Harold — had had the bright idea of spray painting it green, a particularly virulent shade that turned people's complexions the colour of the walking dead. Up to a height of about four feet this shellac was pitted and partly scraped away, probably by small boys in the hope of catching a glimpse of a taut female breast or a straining backside.

I went in and found myself in an aquamarine world that lacked only Neptune and his seaweed-encrusted trident to make it look like the bed of the ocean. The sweat slick humans present wore only the bare minimum of raiment and most of them moved in the slow motion configurations of under-water swimmers. There was a smell of liniment and athletic effort, and the clank and whirr of machines reminded me of Fritz Lang's film *Metropolis*.

A white painted staircase to my left led to the living quarters. I was making for that when Harold himself came up off the floor in front of me, holding in the air what appeared to me to be half a ton of massed concrete.

Harold was about five foot eight — in width, that is. Lengthwise he was my own height. His body was constructed in slabs, all tucked neatly in beside one another and held together by a grouting of smooth brown flesh. If you can imagine a whale in a suit and tie then you have some idea of what he looked like in clothes. He had a square, Teutonic head, the hair cut short to heighten the effect. His features were heavy but in proportion, giving him a handsome, surly look that was completely misleading: I had never seen Harold in bad form; his personality was as light and airy as a summer's day and he was invariably and disgustingly cheerful.

'Howdy, Harold,' I greeted him. 'Don't you think you'd better put down the foundations before the whole building comes down on top of us like a house of cards?'

He looked at the concrete beam he was holding, then gently lowered it to the floor. He flexed his couple of acres of biceps. Rolls of vein criss-crossed tissue stretched and tightened alarmingly. One rent in it and the opposite wall would be peppered with his heaving frontage. Hastily I got out of the way.

'You'd want to watch that,' I cautioned him. 'Let one go and it'd be like fireworks night in a Chinese factory.'

He frowned. 'Say again?'

'You know, sometimes I dream of finding a zipper,' I told him. 'I pull it and the real seven stone you steps out. All the rest collapses about you like a rubber pantomime suit.'

'Not a chance.'

'You never can tell.'

He grinned. He was like that, impossible to feel antagonistic towards. He was the hefty big friendly bear with his snout caught in the honey pot. The fact that the honey pot was my ever loving ex-wife did serve to madden, but trying to knock spots off his imposing carcass, even if it were possible, would solve nothing. Harold was the antithesis of me, he posed no agonies or anguishes of the heart. Life with him would be uncomplicated, an evening sea with little twinkling waves, soft sand, and music quietly tiptoeing in over the water. My hope was that Annie's volatile nature would eventually grow tired of such a calm concerto and begin to yearn for the mind-scratching wail of the midnight clarinet, hopefully with me tootling it.

I was almost standing nose to nose with Harold, and if he didn't give soon I'd have to climb him like a living breathing

Kilimanjaro. 'I've come to take Annie out to dinner,' I explained, grinning inanely.

'Yeah, she's upstairs dickying herself out. Top of the stairs and knock.'

'What if she's left the door open?'

'Then you wheel yourself in.'

'She might be in her underwear.'

'Come on, you've seen her in her undies before.'

'I don't think we should be talking about her in such a disrespectful manner, do you?'

'Huh?'

'After all, she's a married woman. How would you like to hear someone talking about your wife like that?'

'What wife?'

'You haven't got a wife?' I did a mock doubletake. 'Then don't you think it's about time you procured one and stopped stealing other people's? I think a statuesque blonde'd suit you, one with a prow like a battleship's and a backside you could play handball against.'

He frowned, a little tic starting up under his left eye. 'You're having me on, aren't you?' he said. 'You're pulling my leg.'

'What does it take to join this club anyway?' I asked him. 'Did you know that Groucho Marx said he'd never join a club that would have him as a member? D'you stamp name, date and serial number on the wrists of all these characters?'

I looked about me, Harold's worried gaze following mine. If it was my objective to get him confused, I'd achieved that aim. But I didn't feel like going any further. In spite of the fact that he was playing footsie with the woman I loved, I couldn't help but have a spark of real affection for him— like you'd have for Dumbo the elephant.

'Think abut it, Harold.' I told him, then I sidled around him, the perfume of his wintergreen goose-stepping beside me. I went up the stairs and found the door at the top ajar. I drummed a light tattoo on it and called Annie's name. There was no reason for me to believe that the muffled response was anything other than an invitation to come in, so I did just that.

I was in a living room that was furnished in the modern style: tubular steel table, tubular steel chairs, his and her bean bags, a living flame gas fire with artificial ashes that fell through the grate and had to be resprinkled each morning — what would they come up with next? Maybe a wakey-wakey clock that simultaneously played 'If You're Irish', scratched your crotch, sprayed deodorant under your arms, and wiped your bum-bums after your first motion of the day? Or was that already old hat?

Annie looked out at me from an inner room. She was wearing a one piece cream coloured chemise and her hair was caught up in a pink towel. The sight of her caused my old heart to flip over on its back and start to whimper.

'Oh, God,' I said, theatrically putting my hand to my brow and falling back a step, 'It's an underwear party and I'm not wearing any.'

She grinned at me. 'You like it?' She flexed a leg and put her hand on her hip, and her breasts trembled joyfully under the silky material.

I started across the room, and she immediately skipped back out of sight and banged the door. I waited, standing on the Arabian rug in the middle of the floor and breathing hard. Slowly she opened the door again and stuck her head out. 'I won't be long,' she told me. 'Five more minutes and we're on our way.'

'In five more minutes I'll have the rug eaten.'

'You're hungry?'

'Hungry? I'm hungry enough to eat a madman's arse through a hedge.'

Annie wrinkled her nose. 'Such crudity. Why don't you have a drink? I think there's whiskey. Or maybe a sherry?'

She disappeared back inside the room and I padded over to the drinks cabinet. There was a bottle of Irish whiskey, but the only Irish I drink is Bushmills, so I passed on that. Instead I poured myself a generous bumper of Bristol Cream sherry.

It was viscous and sweet to my tongue, pleasant on the first sip but cloying thereafter. Manfully I lowered half the contents of the glass and let the grimace take care of itself.

I tried one of the tubular steel chairs and found it suprisingly comfortable. It maintained its independence and didn't give like most chairs. I sat back and thought about Annie in the other room. I didn't have to use my imagination to conjure up her movements and gestures, I knew them too well. She was probably fighting with her hair, wrestling it this way and that, and eventually giving up and leaving it to its own devices. I had always been partial to spying on the intimacies of her toilette, the flinching from the tweezers, the buffing and polishing of the nails, the little oohs and aahs as she put on her make-up.

Moodily I had another go at the sherry, then I put the glass down, got up and moved across to the open door. Putting my eye to the crack between the door and wall, I could see her sitting at the dressing table applying her warpaint.

After a time, and without turning her head, she said, 'You're watching me, aren't you?'

I unglued my eye and stepped back. 'How'd you know?' I asked her, standing in the doorway. 'Woman's intuition? Eye in the back of your head? Heavy breathing to starboard?'

'It's the kind of thing you do, isn't it?'

'Is it?'

'I wasn't complaining. Just letting you know I knew.'

'There was a time you liked me watching you.'

'I still do.'

'There were other things you liked too. Maybe I should just come in and remind you ...?'

She put the finishing touches to her face, turned and stood up. She was wearing a beige and white, knee-length dress, with a pleated skirt, deep side pockets and epaulettes on the shoulders. It had a wide, turned-back neckline and in the depth of the vee a tiny ruck of lace peeped out coyly. The lace, the chunky jade bracelet on her arm, and the gypsy hoops in her ears, served to offset the severe lines of the dress and boosted the glint of mischief in green eyes.

We stood up and looked at each other, and it seemed the most natural thing in the world for me to take her in my arms and seek out her lips. She kissed hungrily, her mouth open and hard against mine. It was like a contest, my head forcing hers back, hers resisting, until suddenly all resistance ceased and we were familiar and comfortable in one another's arms.

After a time we came up for air, then did a couple of reprises to thunderous applause. Annie squirmed, then pulled away. She grinned at me, and patted the front of my trousers. 'Funny place to carry your gun,' she said.

'Cheeky.'

I reached for her again, but she fended me off. 'Another bout like that and I'd need oxygen.'

'Think of it as mouth to mouth resuscitation.'

She went away and got an off-white, swing coat and put it on. I took up the glass and demolished the rest of the sherry. For no particular reason we were suddenly awkward in one another's company, shy, afraid to touch the mood we had created in case it might crumple and dissolve. For a moment we could have been a boy and girl on a first date.

23

DUBLIN IS LIKE most cities where restaurants are concerned. It has a number of tried and true establishments, shabbily genteel, with real silver cutlery, linen napkins, and waiters who shuffle about with the bone-aching tiredness of extreme old age.

Then there are the new in-spots where the *noveau riche* like to be seen. Many of these are rip-off joints, where you are insulted as soon as you step inside the door by a head waiter named Luigi who most certainly was born within spitting distance of the Liffey. They serve you up minuscule portions of undercooked food, whip your plate away before you are half finished, and present you with a bill that empties your wallet quicker than a pickpocket.

At the bottom of the scale, and sometimes undeservedly so, there's a proliferation of belly-timber parlours, Italian, Indian, Cantonese, Chinese, Mexican and so on, some of them rising phoenix-like from the ashes of others that failed to last the course.

I took Annie to a small and intimate place that had been recommended to me by an accountant friend of mine. It was situated in the Temple Bar area, behind the juggernaut of the Central Bank building in Dame Street, and it was so exclusive that you had to speak into a voice box set into a panel beside the door in order to get in.

We climbed a narrow flight of stairs, Annie in front, me behind admiring her trim ankles. At the top there was a tiny horseshoe of bar, and a craggy old hermaphrodite behind the cash register bore ominous witness to the kind of curse that would be put on you if you tried to get out without paying your bill.

To our right the stair banister had been left, stripped down to the original wood and showing a fine grain of warm old timber. The seating area was split level, with the tables set just close enough together so that you could overhear your neighbour's conversation without having to incline your head too noticeably.

The head waiter greeted us, a tall, mustard complexioned man with a bushy black moustache, bushy black eyebrows and bushy black hair. Turn him upside down and you could sweep the place out with him in two seconds flat.

I had booked under my usual *nom de plume* of G.B. Shaw, but our man made no comment as I murmured it at him. He merely nodded understandingly and indicated that we should follow him. He conducted us to a table on the upper level, pulled out chairs, lit a stub of red candle in its special glazed jar, pushed a menu under each of our noses, plumb lined a fork that had strayed slightly off course — he only stopped short of tucking our napkins down our fronts and patting us on the heads.

He went away and we occupied ourselves with reading the menus. After a while a character in a funny, three-cornered hat and wearing a black and white striped apron came over and inquired if we would like some wine. I gave the list a cursory glance, then ordered a Rioja, Marques de Caceres, 1984. Annie nodded approvingly, as I knew she would. Like myself she liked a full bodied red, both of us believing that white wine is only suitable for quenching the thirst on summer evenings when the Mayfly is rising.

'So,' I said, when Alphonsus the wine waiter had taken himself and his corkscrew away to the cellar, 'what'll we talk about? What'd be a nice safe topic? The weather? The state of the nation? Your favourite colour?'

'The last one is easy. Green.'

'Not much room to manoeuvre there.'

I put down the menu and gazed at her across the candle flame. She gazed back at me. 'Why did you come out with me?' I asked her. 'After three months of asking ....'

She shrugged. 'You were looking a bit down. Slightly crumpled round the edges.'

'This is your give a dog a bone week?'

Her lips tightened. 'You can be a right bastard, you know,' she said. 'I know you don't mean it a lot of the time, but it comes over as if you do.'

'Sometimes people bring out the worst in me.'

'Are we going to fight? Can't we mark this one down to old times and imagine that the bell has rung? I'll concede a ten count if you agree to take off the boxing gloves.'

'Right on.'

I reached across and put my fist under her chin. She rolled her eyes, put her tongue in the corner of her mouth and made like someone who was punch drunk.

We ordered: scampi for me, rack of lamb for her. Alphonse came back with the wine and opened it with a flourish. I took a mouthful, rolled it about on my tongue, considered spitting it out on his shoe, relented and told him it was fine.

The restaurant began to fill up, the swell of sound rising with each new arrival. Annie gave me some of her rack of lamb, I reciprocated with the scampi. The food was good, the wine even better. I was beginning to feel a warm glow of something or other. Whatever it was, it was causing the cares of the last few days to fall away like the leaves from an artichoke heart. Mentally I observed their slow descent, she loves me, she loves me not, then I decided I'd better stop in case I finished counting on the wrong one.

'Hey,' Annie said, 'come back to me. You haven't heard a word I've been saying.'

'Maybe you'd consider trotting them past me again?'

'What's the point? You're a million miles away.'

'No, I'm not. I'm relaxing. I've found a promontory and I'm sitting on it looking out to sea.'

'And what'm I supposed to do while you're out there? Knit an Aran sweater?'

'I'm sorry.'

I pushed my plate away and leaned on the table. 'How come we can be so natural with each other?' I asked her. 'No sweat, no strain. Why can't it be like this all the time?'

'Are you trying to crank it up again?'

'No, listen ....' I paused, then I said, 'I think about you first thing when I wake up in the morning, and the last thing before I go to sleep at night. At least once a day I fall in love with you all over again. I can't help it ....'

She raised her eyebrows. 'So, I'm a very lovable person ....'

'Don't be glib.'

She sat back, her eyes in shadow. In its cave of glass the candle flame wriggled as though striving to get out. 'Why don't you pour me some more wine?' she suggested, but offhandedly, like someone who was carefully weighing up what she was about to say next.

'Don't think about it,' I urged her. 'If you've got something to say, then say it ....'

She put her elbows on the table and leaned her face in the vee of her open hands. 'I feel the same about you,' she said. 'And it's fine as long as I take it one day at a time. It's when I try to put all those days together that the trouble starts. You know what I mean? When it was good between us, it was nearly too good. Because if you bounce that high, then you have to go down mighty low before you get up there again. Maybe I'm cursed with too sunny a disposition .... I just couldn't take those in-between bits.'

'What you lose on the swings ....'

'You think so? Yes, you do .... You were always able to take the difficult times, nail them to the backyard wall and throw smart remarks at them. You could stand back, get them in perspective ....'

'You don't think they tore at my guts?'

She sat back and waved a hand aimlessly. 'I suppose they

did. But you always seemed able to distance yourself somehow. As though watching yourself suffer and maybe even, in an odd way, enjoying it ....'

'Oh boy, now we're getting in deep. What are you, my analyst?'

She ignored that one and went on, 'Sometimes it was as if you were playing a part. Even when you said you loved me, it was as if you were playing a part. It was as if you were trying to get the right feel to the words. You could never leave well enough alone. You just had to go on and on ....'

'Like the guy who followed his own footprints and disappeared up his own backside?'

'There, you see,' once again she sat back in her chair and put her hands almost defensively in front of her — 'you can't resist making the glib remark.'

'It's a defence mechanism, Annie, can't you see that? I do it to cover up my own confusion ....' I was about to go on when I felt someone staring at me. I looked around and a middle-aged party in a dinner jacket at the next table pursed his lips disapprovingly at me. The well-upholstered female with him was also staring in our direction. I lowered my voice: 'That's my way. If I didn't do that I'd probably go around kicking children and old grannies. If you haven't a sense of humour, what've you got?'

'There's humour and there's humour. Yours always had a cut to it. I often felt you were using it to get back at me ....'

'You felt that?'

'Yes, I did.' She took up her wine glass and drank roughly from it. 'You also thought out moves and motivations for me that weren't true. Judging me by the way you'd react yourself. It got so that I was afraid to do or say anything in case you'd misinterpret it. God knows I tried to tell you often enough ....'

'No, you didn't.'

'Obviously I didn't succeed. Maybe I felt you should be able to work it out for yourself. Why couldn't you? I asked myself. Were we too close, our relationship too intense? That's when

I began to think about going .... I always felt you wanted more than I was ever able to give.'

'I'd be happy to settle for a lot less now.'

'Would you?'

I looked down at the table. There was a wine stain imprinted on the cloth in the shape of a rose — well, maybe you would need a little imagination to see it, but it could have been a rose. 'No, I don't suppose I would,' I said, answering her truthfully. 'Where you're concerned, I want everything. Not just coming first, I want to be the only one. I suppose I need your whole life to revolve around me ....'

There was a silence, a melodramatic import hovering over my last words like an echo that I never meant to be there. Cautiously I glanced across the table at Annie, and slowly, slyly, she gave me an impish look and said, 'Like a fly round a cowpat?'

The remark broke the mood, as it was meant to do. 'If you can't beat them, join 'em,' I said, grinning at her, and in a moment we were easy and happy once more in each other's company.

We sat on, chatting about this and that, carefully keeping away from anything that might prove to be touchy. The guy at the next table also gave up listening to our conversation and busied himself trying to feel up his girlfriend under the table. Shame on him, I thought.

The waiter came by again on one of his visits and asked us if we would like dessert—or pudding, as he called it. I fingered the menu and raised my eyes inquiringly at Annie.

Again contriving to look innocently sly, she said, 'Why don't we go back to your place and have our afters there? Something soft and sweet and slow ....' Brazenly she put her tongue in the corner of her mouth again and looked at me under her eyebrows.

I glanced at the waiter. He was thin faced, with a blond crewcut and high, narrow shoulders. He had been attentive to us during the meal without oozing all over us. He had also managed to get the food to us before it congealed on the plate. 'Can you top that offer?' I asked him.

'Not without compromising myself, sir, no.'

'Even then?'

Openly he gave Annie the eye, taking his time about it, then he said, 'Hardly.'

I added my admiring gaze to his, and she sat there, loving it. Then, to prevent our little tableau from entering into freeze frame, I told him to bring the bill.

'Will you be paying cash or credit card, sir?'

'Which'll get us out of here soonest?'

'Cash.'

'Let it be so then,' I said. I looked across at the bar. 'What about the lady at the register?' I asked him. 'What does it take to make her go into overdrive?'

'It's a gentleman, sir.'

'You don't say?'

'Well, it's never been proved conclusively to me, you understand,' — one of his eyelids drooped a fraction — 'but it's generally held to be so.'

'Held by whom?'

The waiter's eyes swivelled, mine following, until we were both gazing at the *maitre d'*. After a moment we looked knowingly at one another. For a small space of time we were men of the world together, united in a weary recognition that it takes all sorts ....

Annie sensed it and did not like it one bit. 'Why don't you go and get the bill?' she suddenly asked the waiter. 'The soufflé won't stay up indefinitely.'

There was a slight tightening of the lips, but all he said was, 'Certainly ... ah ... Miss.'

'Mrs.'

'That's nice to know, madame. So few married couples work at keeping the romance in their lives.'

'I didn't say we were married to one another.'

'Yes, well ....'

He moved away looking vaguely disappointed, another one of his ideals destroyed. When he brought me back the bill I gave him a sizable tip, which he hurriedly pocketed. Then he thanked me and told me his name was Timothy. I assured him that I would look himself and the restaurant up again. For a moment I thought he was going to take out a whisk like a barber and brush me down.

While I presented the bill Annie ducked into the Ladies. The citizen behind the desk had a long, sallow face, lank hair, and hands like a hen's claws. His formal dark suit was going green round the edges, and he exuded the stale odour of someone who was only put out for an airing when the wind was north-north-east. He handled my money as though considering the possibility that it might be radioactive.

'You the owner?' I asked him.

He put the receipt on the counter in front of him, keeping his claw on it. 'You've a complaint, sir?' he croaked, the 'sir' delayed just long enough to show me that he wasn't overawed by my tone or bearing.

'There's a man over there with his hand up a lady's leg,' I told him. 'Quite put me off my dinner, he did.'

'Really?'

He eased himself off his stool, like someone who was about to break wind, but he still could not see over my shoulder. I moved aside and he gazed at the room at large. I helped him out. 'The table in the far corner? Can you see? It's the one with the woman with that look on her face. And the fellow is eating steak. Rare,' I told him, with a meaningful look.

Annie had come out of the Ladies and was waiting for me at the head of the stairs. I made my way over and joined her. Before we descended, I looked back. Hen's Claws had called over the head waiter and they were engaged in animated discussion. Quite a delicate situation to be left with. I would have loved to have stayed to see how they sorted it out, but time, tide and Annie were waiting.

24

THE RAIN HAD got its second wind and was coming down in earnest, falling straight and hard through the streetlights and clicking against the pavement. We made a run for it, but by being a gentleman and holding the door for Annie I was soaked by the time I got into shelter.

Instead of driving away immediately, I lit two cigarettes and handed her one. I watched as she rolled down her window to let the smoke out. 'There's something I want you to do for me,' I told her.

'Can't you wait till we get home? I've never thought carrying on in a car's all it's cracked up to be.'

'I didn't mean that.'

'What, then?'

'I want you to help me look for Redmond Walsh-Overman.'

'Oh?'

'You know the woman who was found this morning with her head bashed in? She was his ex-wife. And I was the one that found her.'

'You did?'

'Yep.'

'I didn't notice any mention of your name in the papers.'

'You know me and my natural modesty. I took cover in an anonymous telephone call.'

'But why?'

I tried rolling down my window but, when I did, the rain blew in on me. I stubbed out the cigarette in the car ashtray, poking at the hot ashes until they were completely extinguished. 'I didn't want to have to answer any more awkward questions, I suppose,' I said. 'I'd already done one interview with George Quinlan. Maybe I shouldn't involve you, though.'

'Is Redmond in danger?'

'Yes, he's been in danger from the start. Now even more so. Before, it was business, but since last night an element of revenge has crept in. He's been lucky so far, but it can't hold forever. I could stand aside and let him sink — he probably deserves no better — but I was hired to find him ....'

'A sacred trust?'

'If you like.'

A car inched down the narrow street towards us, its head-lights an eye-squinting glare through the windscreen. There was a shiver of dampness trying to get into my shirt so that it could run up and down my back. I was also suffering from cold feet, both literally and figuratively.

'What d'you want me to do?' Annie asked.

'Put aside whatever you've got on hand for the next day or two and give finding Redmond your best shot. Do a trawl through all the dosshouses — sorry, places of refuge — and see what you can turn up. Or is that a bad way of phrasing it?'

'Sort of ... but I get your meaning.'

I could feel her watching me. 'If you find him, all I want you to do is call me right away. Don't try to talk to him or get involved with him in any way.'

'He's not dangerous, is he?'

'He may well have killed, not once but twice.'

'Cripes ....'

I felt her shiver, so I reached out and she slid along the seat and into the curve of my arm. I was about to kiss her when she said, 'How could anyone do that?'

'Do what?'

'Cut someone's throat.'

'I didn't say Redmond was responsible for that,' I said, giving her a squeeze and hoping the reassurance I meant to convey proved more effective than what I actually felt. I had a sudden vision of Charles in the furnace house with his mouth and throat gaping open. 'It would take someone with a special kink of evil to do that,' I went on. 'Someone who gets his kicks that way ....'

I switched on the ignition, then took my arm from around Annie and used it to put the car into gear. The rain was heavier than ever. Carefully I nosed the Renault out. My line of vision was non-existent because of the fogged-up windows, but I made it out okay. So did another car, a wide vehicle that filled the narrow space of the street behind us.

In spite of the downpour, I lowered my window and stuck my head out. Immediately the other driver put on his full lights, but not before I had seen the silvery grey bodywork of the Bluebird.

My dart of alarm made me step on the accelerator and the Renault shot forward.

'What's the matter?' Annie asked me.

'Nothing, someone walked over my grave.'

I put my arm around her again and guided the car up the lane and out into Dame Street. I turned left towards Trinity College, cut along by the Bank of Ireland, through the wide thoroughfare of Westmoreland Street and across O'Connell Bridge. There was a taxi rank beside the statue of Big Jim Larkin and I pulled in beside the cab at the top of the line.

I held the steering wheel tightly and breathed deeply. The rain was so heavy the windscreen wipers groaned with the effort of pushing it aside. 'Listen,' I said, 'you're not going to like this, but I want you to get out, take a taxi up to the New Cabra Road and wait for me there. Trust me and I'll explain later.'

'What?'

'It's just that I've suddenly remembered a bit of urgent business. I'm sorry,' I said lamely.

'You're sorry ....' I felt her stiffen, then she got out from under my arm and moved away into the corner of the seat. 'I don't believe this,' she said. 'Here I've just made you an offer you can't refuse, and now you're pushing me out into the night like some trollop you picked up. You can't really be serious.

Can you?' I could feel her staring at me through the dimness.

I glanced in the rearview mirror as a car honked behind me, but all I could see was a blaze of lights. I fumbled my keys out of my pocket and offered them to her. 'Here, take these and let yourself in,' I said. 'You know Marty and Kate. 'They'll be delighted to see you ....'

'Sure they will. They'll make me a cup of hot chocolate and a mustard bath for my cold feet. And tell me fairy stories until Daddy Bear gets home. You bastard ....'

With a swing of her arm she knocked the keys out of my hand and they clinked away into the back seat. She pulled at the door handle, then half fell out into the street. With the rain pounding down on her, she looked in at me. 'You know what you can do with your keys,' she hissed. 'You can stuff them so far up your rear you'll need a pneumatic drill to get them out.'

I was ready for the slam of the door, but it still set my teeth on edge when it came. She ducked around the front of the car and got into a taxi, and I was amazed when a shot of flame didn't spout out of the roof.

I waited for it to draw away, then followed on after it. In the distance thunder rumbled, but then again it might have been the reverberations of Annie's wrath still tumbling about inside my head.

25

I DROVE THROUGH the sloshing rain, cold, wet, alone, and definitely not feeling groovy. Taking tea with nuns who were being exploited by a land grabber and following furtive husbands about had not prepared me for dealing with gangsters and a modern Jack the Ripper. I was a little out of my depth — a little? I was going down for the third time holding onto a lifeline that was anchored to a puff of wind.

Turning into Parnell Street, I saw a flashing green light that signalled there were spaces in the Ilac Centre lot. It was as good a place as any to pause for a moment of meditation, so I wheeled the car up the ramp, took a ticket from the dispenser, waited for the yellow and black barrier to rise, then went on through. Most of the slots on the ground floor were unoccupied, but I continued on up to the third and nosed the Renault into a space against the far wall.

I had a cigarette lit and had taken the first puff from it when the Bluebird quietly shushed across the floor and nestled in beside me. I glanced across at it and saw Humphrey and Sid, looking as though they had recently been stuffed, sitting in the front seats. Humphrey was in the driver's seat, Sid in the navigator's. They had the quiet settled look of undertaker's assistants waiting for the corpse to be wheeled out.

I continued puffing at the cigarette. I tried to blow a smoke ring and after a couple of attempts I succeeded in forming a large fat one that wobbled and bounced against the windscreen. Then I examined the fingers of both hands. There was a little dirt under the nails, and the nails themselves needed cutting and buffing. I resolved to see to them the first chance I got.

Eventually someone must have activated the console that brought Sid to life, for he opened his door, got out, bent down, and stood looking in at me.

I gazed back at him, then I reached across and rolled down the passenger window. 'If you're hoping for a banana, Sid, I haven't got any,' I told him. 'No nuts either.'

He blinked, and a frown furrowed his half inch of brow. Then he raised a paw and batted my remarks away. In time-honoured fashion he said, 'The boss wants to see you.' He indicated the Bluebird with a thumb that he could have pounded a nail into a wall with. 'Get in and don't give me no trouble.'

I considered arguing the point, but my head won over my heart. With a sigh I stubbed out my cigarette. I rolled up the window, got out of the car, locked the door, and moved across and climbed into the back of the Bluebird. It was nice and roomy in there, although a bit muggy. I settled myself comfortably and watched Sid swing back into the front seat.

With practised ease, Humphrey reversed the car and took off across the parking lot, the tyres making only a slight suspicion of a squeal. A tall thin man and a short fat woman had got out of the lift and were making for a Morris 1000 sitting in solitary splendour in the middle of the lot. When they saw the Bluebird bearing down on them they froze, the woman appearing as if she were about to scuttle up the long length of her companion. At the last moment Humphrey turned the wheel, and the big car swerved past them so close that I could see the whites of their terrified eyes.

The encounter served to put both of the dummies in the front seat in good humour, and they chortled all the way down to the pay booth. Humphrey was so pleased with himself that he even passed a pleasantry with the attendant, asking him how they were hanging and if he used it for any more than stirring his tea.

The rain had eased a little but was still gusting down enough to keep the streets bare of humanity. Humphrey turned into Capel Street and then along toward the quays, but I didn't bother watching our progress. I had a pretty good idea where we were heading for and how to get there again if the need should arise, which I hoped it would not.

To pass the time I lit another cigarette and blew smoke at the two thick necks in front of me. After a while Sid turned around and glared at me. 'Cut that out,' he muttered. 'Don't yeh know smoking is bad for yeh ....'

'A short and a happy life is my motto,' I told him. 'I read a story once where a guy was passing under a balcony and a pig fell off it and killed him. He probably didn't smoke but what good did it do him?'

Sid did the trick of furrowing his brow again. 'You're puttin' me on, Sunshine.'

'Honest to God.' I crossed my heart. 'You never know the day nor the hour. Like the boy scouts, you should always be prepared. Tell me, Sid, are you in the state of grace?'

'Huh?'

'Come on,' I said in a coaxing tone, 'you can tell me. Have you had any impure thoughts lately? I hope you haven't been pulling your plonker? Let me see if there's any hair on the palms of your hands.'

Sid looked across at Humphrey, then back at me again. 'I could come back there,' he offered threateningly. 'I could come back there and pull your ears off and make you eat them.'

I blew some more smoke in his eyes. 'I thought ears would be a sore point with you,' I reminded him. 'Seems to me you had a bit of a jug handle the last time I saw you. Lean in here and I'll twist the other one.'

He made as though to climb over the seat, but Humphrey put out a restraining arm. 'Let it lie,' he told him. 'He's only trying to get it up for you, alrigh'? The boss didn't order any damaged goods. Maybe afterwards though ....'

'Yeah, afterwards,' Sid said, licking his lips. He relaxed but stayed twisted around looking at me.

I blinked my eyelashes at him, but we left it at that and rode the rest of the way in silence. The streets got narrower, the houses smaller and residential. This was part of old Dublin, once a teeming hive of humanity but in recent years the little leaning dwellings that had housed many a large family had been done over and refurbished by speculators and sold as town houses to upwardly mobile couples with mid-Channel accents and Gucci mentalities. Where before neighbourliness was the norm and a helping hand a byword, now keeping up with and surpassing the Joneses was the invigorating factor that kept the flag flying and the sweetly sour ache of ambition flourishing.

We took one final turn and, as I glanced up through the rain-spattered window at the street sign, I saw, as I had already guessed, that we were moving into Old Shop Street. Someone — probably the new inhabitants thinking it quaint — had interceded with the Corporation to have the original cobblestones left intact, and the Bluebird winced as it passed over them. A car was parked at the head of the street, the inside light on and two men sitting slumped in the front seats. As we went by they both looked out at us, and one of them appeared to write something down. 'The local gendarmes?' I inquired of my companions, but neither of them deigned to answer.

We pulled up halfway down the street, outside a house that bulged like a face with a prognathous jaw. It stood out like the proverbial sore thumb from its neighbours, the frontage iced in black and white synthetic bricks, a brightly lit, large bay window downstairs, the upstairs windows arched and made vaguely church-like by the stained glass filigree embossed into them. An ornamental railing ran along the front, bordering a tiny rectangle of very green grass, and two spotlights, one at each corner, caressed the face of the building and illuminated it in a muted pink glow. It looked like a cake that had been baked by a demented chef for a mad hatter's tea party.

'Nice, huh?' Sid said, nodding at it. There was a child-like glaze of admiration in his eyes as he sat regarding it.

'I dunno,' I said critically. 'It looks a mite rich for my taste.

Maybe if you cut me a slice I could take it away in a doggie bag. Although if I were a dog I'd prefer to piss against it rather than eat it.'

That didn't go down well with Sid at all, he obviously considering it the ultimate in architectural beauty. I wouldn't like to think what would happen to him if he ever got to Disneyland.

We climbed out into the rain and Sid carefully prised open the little curlicued gate. I walked in past him and then stood back while he rang the bell. Inside a musical number started up: 'Be It Ever So Humble, There's No Place Like Home' — the Carnival of the Animals might have been more appropriate.

A shadow imprinted itself on the frosted glass and an eye appeared at the spyhole. The three of us stood stamping our feet and trying to look unconcerned as we were scrutinised. I turned up my collar and attempted to guess the password — Mickey Mouse, no doubt.

All must have been in order for there was a snicking of bolts and a clanking of chains before the door opened wide and we were allowed into a narrow hallway lit by an overhead bulb in an old-fashioned glass globe. The woman who stood back to let us past her looked to be in her fifties or early sixties. She had blue-rinsed hair set in a frosted perm and it framed a squat, sallow, and seamed face that owned a sour expression that was probably habitual. She was wearing a twinset and a string of pearls, her bosom as solid as the front of a tank and just as ironclad. If she was someone's mother, it had happened a long time ago, and the experience had not served to make her look maternal. She looked as tough as rhinoceros hide.

'Wipe yer feet,' she instructed us, and we all dutifully rubbed away like mad on the rope mat provided.

She backed us along the hall, and I could feel Sid leaning on me as we stiff-legged our way along and then took a ninety degree turn through a door to our right.

We were in a room that was as cluttered as a pawn shop just before Friday night closing. Luckily only the woman and myself went in; if Sid and Humphrey had joined us then at least two out of the four would have had to swing from the chandelier.

The woman barked out a further order, telling me to sit down. My bottom was about an inch from the surface of an ornately carved number with a fretted back and pencil-thin legs when she jerked her head and said, 'Not there, lumphead. Tha's not for sittin' on. Can't yer see it's an antique. Some people' — this last accompanied by a loud sniff.

I settled myself on the edge of a buttoned leather armchair and looked around me. The bric-a-brac took up every available surface. At a quick glance I beheld brass fire irons, Chinese vases, an inlaid fire screen with a glowering dragon and a bemused knight, tables, chairs, a coat stand, a glass-fronted cabinet lit up from within and full of silverware and glinting crystal, a number of oriental footstools, a grandfather clock — only the Venus de Milo was missing and she was probably out having her arms seen to. It reminded me of Mrs. Walsh-Overman's parlour museum, only on a smaller scale and with cheaper artefacts.

The woman lowered herself into a wingback chair that dared to creak under her weight and sat regarding me balefully. The sleeves of her cardigan were rolled up to show arms mottled with the liver spots of age. Her hands were large-knuckled and knobby, and the rings on her fingers were sunk deep in the flesh and looked as if a spanner would be needed to get them off.

'A bit damp out,' I tried on her, by way of breaking the ice. 'The angels are weeping.'

'It's pissin',' she said nastily, her very white, very false teeth clacking.

I tried again: 'Some people like the rain, they like to think it makes their hair grow. Or that it's good for their complexions. As for me, I can take it or leave it. Give me a high starry night, with a touch of frost and your heels ringing like iron on the pavement.'

I watched, fascinated, as her eyebrows climbed up towards her hair line. 'Are yeh jerkin' me off or wha?' she asked, the words clotted with barely suppressed rage.

I recoiled in mock horror. 'God forbid. I wouldn't even presume to lift the hem of your skirt, never mind venturing up further.'

That one brought on a high-pitched sound like a kettle about to boil, but we were both saved from what might have been a nasty eruption by the opening of the door.

A man came in slowly and stood regarding me over half glasses perched low on his nose. At least I presumed they were perched on his nose: he was wearing a ski mask that obscured his face, with horizontal white lines painted across it to give it the appearance of a skull. The effect was startling or laughable, whichever way you wished to look at it. I didn't wish to look at it at all.

However, my tongue got the better of me as usual and I said, 'My God, it's the Phantom of the Opera.'

'Yeh've got a wise arse here, Billy,' the woman interjected. 'Maybe yeh should get the boys to put some manners on 'im ....'

Without turning his head in her direction, Billy said, 'Tha's alrigh', Mamie, yeh held the fort. Now fuck off and go an' do yer knitting or sumthin'.'

Mamie seemed inclined to argue, but then changed her mind, got up and shuffled over to the door. With her hand on the knob she said, 'Don't yeh go breakin' anny of my knick-knacks now. The las' time yeh entertained company in 'ere it wus like a storm hit the place. Bate 'im into chicken shit, if yer like, but don't step on the gee-gaws.' She laughed harshly and went out.

Along with the ski mask, Billy was wearing a tee shirt with Donald Duck emblazoned across the front, his large beer belly stretching it to breaking point. A charcoal cardigan sagged in two wings on either side of his gut. He was short and heavy, his large feet encased in wool slippers. His hair was sandy, and what there was of it was brushed carefully across the top of his head.

This then was The Waster, the man who was rumoured to be the leader of a gang of villains who had the centre city crime sewn up and tightly packaged. Drugs, prostitution, protection rackets, robberies — you name it, they were into it. It was popularly believed that his people had been behind the Central Bank hold-up two years before that had netted a cool million pounds. They had kidnapped the Governor and his Special Branch minder and held them while the vaults were cleaned out over a Bank Holiday weekend. They had also been involved in a shoot-out with a rival gang on a mid-winter night down in dockland that had left two dead and a couple more fit only to eat bread and milk through a funnel for the rest of their lives.

Now as I watched him take up the heavy brass tongs and poke at the coal fire glowing in the hearth I found it hard to see him as a godfather of crime. He looked like a clown. I remembered reading how, after his last court appearance, he had come out in his mask and funny shirt, had lowered his trousers at the Special Branch men shadowing him, and had gone cycling off down the quays pursued by an expectant band of baying reporters. He was by way of being a legend in his own lifetime. The public loved him, ignoring the fact that he could be as ruthless and vicious as a cornered rat when the need arose. He was responsible for more horrors in Dublin than an outbreak of the Black Death.

When he was finished with the fire, he went over and sat down in the chair vacated by the woman. Then we both took to brooding, like the rest of the clutter. I nibbled a fingernail and thought about the rain, wondering if as Jimmy Joyce said it was 'falling gently and gently falling; all over Ireland'. Clanton rattled the poker against the bars of the grate: rat-a-tat-tat, rat-a-tat-tat — was he tapping out a message in Morse code to someone hiding up the chimney?

Eventually my nerves began to get the better of me. I looked at my watch. I cleared my throat. My right knee began to develop a twitch and I had to put my hand on it to hold it down. 'You know,' I suddenly said, my voice sounding like a boy soprano's, 'Mrs Clanton didn't seem to like me very much.'

'Who?'

'Mrs Clanton. Your wife. Mamie.'

'She's not me wife, she's me sister.'

He turned his head and looked at me. He looked at me as if I had crawled out of the woodwork and he was debating whether or not to bop me with the firetongs. Then he sighed. Reaching up, he untied the ski mask, then took it off. He had a florid red face with watery eyes, a snub nose and a rose-bud mouth: an unremarkable face that one would never pick out in a crowd.

I felt like telling him to put the mask back on, that it suited him better than the one he had been born with.

'I've been told yeh appointed yourself middle man between a certain Marty Lynch and ourselves,' he now said, getting down to business. 'Not a very clever move, what?'

I swallowed a couple of times, then I said, 'Marty's a friend of mine. I just thought that maybe a third party with no axe to grind might smooth things over ....'

'Oil on troubled water, like?'

'Precisely.'

He nodded. He held the ski mask up and squinted at me through the eyeholes. 'Tha's a good word,' he said. 'Precisely.' He turned back to the fire and let go a wad into the grate. He watched it sizzle. 'Yeh know,' he said, apparently talking to the poker, 'there's all kinds of people in this world. Doctors, lawyers, teachers, judges, politicians. I could have been anny one o' them. Instead I'm a crook. I'm wha' yeh'd call a necessary evil. If I didn't exist, yeh'd have ta invent me.'

'I won't argue with you there.'

'Wha I'm sayin' is' — he took up the poker again and rattled it against the grate — 'there hafta be crooks. So there can be good guys and bad guys. Stands ta reason, wha?' He looked at me slyly. 'Then again,' he went on, 'Pop Clanton wus as honest as sixpence. And Ma brought us up to be God fearin' as church mice. I wus an altar boy, yeh know.'

'Don't worry, your secret's safe with me.'

'Naw, yeh don't understand.' He shook his head. His voice had a Satchmo hoarseness like nails rattling in a drawer. 'We were always a close community around here. In Old Shop Street. Four brothers and three sisters there were. All gone now except Mamie and me.'

'That Wyatt Earp,' I said musingly, 'he sure was a deadly marksman.'

Ignoring me, Clanton continued, 'We were all fambly though. All along the street. You scratch my back, I'll scratch yours. The Mitchells, the Wilsons, the Smiths, the Chandlers ....'

'The Mordaunts?'

For a split second the rheumy old eyes were no longer hooded: 'Now tha's a thing, isn't it?' he said. 'Poor old Bernadette. She shouldn't oughta've ended up like tha. We stepped out together once or twice, Bernie and me. Then she got ideas above her station. But once a Liberties girl, always a Liberties girl. Tha's why I owe her, yeh see ....'

'You set her up in that lodging house you own?'

'It wus the least I could do.'

'Considering the state of the place, yeah, it was.'

He turned that one over and examined both sides of it, but then decided to let it lie. 'Who coulda done that to her now, I wonder?' he asked me. 'I heard yeh called on her. Maybe you wus the party responsible?'

Suddenly the room had gone chilly, in spite of the fire. Clanton might look like an old fart, but to all intents and purposes he had the power of life and death over me at that moment. It was time I sat up and took notice.

Cautiously I said, 'If you thought that and were going to terminate my contract rather than offer me a new one, you wouldn't have brought me here. Especially not so openly past those two Special Branch men at the end of the street.' I tried grinning at him. 'You need me for something, don't you?'

We sat and eyed one another, but he lost interest before I did. 'Have yeh anny idea who killed her?' he asked me, mildly enough.

I thought about it, letting the silence build, then I realised that subtleties like that would be lost on him. 'Yeah, I've got a good idea who killed her,' I told him. 'But I can't prove it.'

'Proof me arse.'

Again he banged with the poker, harder than ever, against the grate. I was sure this time that someone would appear down the chimney, but it was the door that opened to admit Sid with an anxious look on his face. 'Get me a cigar,' Clanton ordered. 'And while yeh're at it, bring in the case.'

'The case?'

'Yeah, the case. Wha's wrong wi' yeh?'

'You're sure?'

'Get me the fuckin' case and stop actin' the prick.'

Sid blanched and hurriedly withdrew his head and closed the door. To fill the pause, I said, 'It's hard to get competent help nowadays. It's the go-slow drugs the Russians are putting in our tea.'

Clanton stared at me, the hardness at last beginning to show through. 'Did anyone ever tell yeh yeh talked too much?' he asked me.

'Frequently. But I'm cursed with a hyperactive tongue.'

'Yeh should take it out some time and give it a good whippin'.'

I took out a cigarette instead, waved it at him and, when he nodded, I stuck it in my mouth and lit it. I blew smoke at a grinning ebony effigy on a lacquer table near me. A thought struck me. 'How come with all your contacts you can't find out for yourself who killed Bernadette?' I asked him.

'That's none of yeh're fuckin' business,' he said automatically, then remembering that he wanted something from me, he went on: 'Tings're dicey at the moment with the Fuzz doin' one of their regular clamp-downs. They get like that every so often. Someone's been slashing tyres in the area, specially on squad cars. My boys haveta step careful. It's bad enough she had to snuff it in a house owned by me.'

'I can see that must've made your heart go pitter-patter.'

'The Branch were onta me like a dose of salts.'

'But of course you could account for your movements down to the last syllable of recorded time?'

'Natch. Me and Mamie were entertaining my solicitor and his wife to a quiet little supper. We played solo until dawn. Cast iron. Ye wouldn't break that with a sledgehammer.'

'Your solicitor, eh? And his wife. Sitting around playing solo and sipping the best brandy. The Brandenburg Concerto on the hi-fi. I can just picture it.'

'It pays to have a pillar of society on the leash.'

'Take care he doesn't piss up your leg sometime.'

This time I had gone too far, and I saw Clanton's knuckles whiten around the poker. Like W.C. Fields on his deathbed, I suddenly wished I was in Philadelphia. It was with relief that I saw the door open once more and Sid coming in complete with cigar box and suitcase.

Not sensitive enough to be aware of the tension in the air, he gave Clanton a cigar only slightly smaller than a rolled umbrella, watched fondly as he put it in his mouth and then lit it for him with a flourish. Unfortunately the lighter was not regulated properly, and the flame bellowed out as though shot from a blowtorch, and Clanton had to pull his head back smartly to prevent his nose turning into a burning bush. As a double act I'd pay money to get in to see them.

'For fuck's sake!'

Clanton made a swipe at Sid with the poker, missed and fell over on his knees. Sid had to help him up and put him sitting back in his chair. Then he stood back and did an Oliver Hardy tie twiddle. When he saw me grinning at him, he let go the tie as if it too had become red hot.

'Open the case,' Clanton told him. 'And don't knock over anny of the gee-gaws while yeh're doin' it. Mamie'll have yeh lynched if yeh break anything ...'

Sid hefted the case, an executive-looking job, hand-tooled and with silver mounting. Balancing it on his knee, he snapped the catches, then held it so that I could look into it. I suppose I was hoping that it would be full of money: it wasn't, it was full of guns.

There were handguns of every description: revolvers and automatics — although I also recognised a Beretta 9mm machine pistol — all snugly reposing in fitted compartments and oiled and gleaming and ready for use. There was a fascination about them, like a dream of toy guns surfacing out of childhood games of cops and robbers. These were no toys, however; they were the real thing and they caused the roof of my mouth to become dry and parched, and when I tried to swallow my throat was as moist as the Gobi Desert.

'Yeh like them?' Clanton asked me. 'Corpse makers. Only the best. Some guys collect stamps, I collect guns.'

'So,' I said, doing my best to sound nonchalant, 'I'm impressed. So would the Branch men outside be if they came tooling in about now.'

'Wouldn't they but?' Clanton sniggered. 'They've been tryin' to hang sumting like this on me since the day before the Flood.'

'Then why show it to me? I've done a bit of hunting and I could tell you the difference between a Citori-Browning over-and-under 12 gauge shotgun and a lollipop stick, but where hand guns are concerned I'm about as knowledgeable as a nun in a whorehouse. And if you're trying to frighten me, Sid and Humphrey can do that by snapping their suspenders at me ....'

'Really?' Sid said, looking pleased.

'Will yeh leave it out,' Clanton muttered, glaring at him. 'Give him a shooter,' he instructed him, then turning to me: 'What'd yeh like? The Smith and Wesson .32 with the three inch barrel? Snug and easy to hide and deadly at close quarters' —he might have been a salesman trying to convince a dubious customer.

'What would I want a gun for?'

'For picking yer teeth with, what else? Although it might come in handy when you take out the git that did for Bernadette.'

'What?'

'Yeh heard me.'

'You want me to shoot whoever killed Bernadette?'

'Got it in one.'

'I didn't exactly intend killing him.'

'Then wha?'

'Hand him over to the forces of the law?'

'Fuck that. He'd cop a plea of manslaughter and be ou' swannin' it up Grafton Street in five to ten. I want this guy put six feet under with a plaster angel sitting on his head to keep him down.'

I lit another cigarette, taking my time and forcing my hands not to shake. I was finding it difficult to come to terms with the fact that I was sitting there in that gingerbread house listening to a guy who looked like a candidate for a funny farm telling me go out and shoot someone. The scene had all the reality of a kid's cartoon.

'Let me get this straight,' I said. 'You want me to take a gun from your collection and find the bozo who bashed in Bernadette's head and do a Dead Eye Dick on him? Fill him full of lead and then go riding off into the sunset?'

'Now yeh've got it.'

'Are you not even curious to know who he is?'

'He's a shithead, that's all I need to know.' Clanton looked at me, his crumpled face earnest. 'It's a debt of honour,' he said. 'Bernadette was a member of my extended family, no matter how far she strayed. She was a good ole girl, even if she did throw a wobbler by marrying that rich git. I can't let whoever killed her go about boastin' about it, wha?'

'But why me?'

'Because yeh're clean. No connection with me. Those chumps outside only note the cars, not the people in them.

Anyway, they're always half zonked on the hash they keep stealin' from the station pound.' Clanton paused, then he went on persuasively, 'And it'd cancel out your sticking yer nose into my business. We'd be back at square one. I don't know yeh, and yeh don't know me. Am I righ'?'

'Supposing I go to the Guards with this?'

'With wha?'

'Oh, I see. I suppose your solicitor and his wife, not to mention Mamie, are lined up and ready to swear that you weren't even here tonight? You're probably down in the local church right now telling your beads and beating your breast ....'

'Give him the gun, Sid,' Clanton said, interrupting me. 'All this bollixing around is giving me a headache. I've a weak heart. I shouldn't have to concern meself with all this bullshit.'

'Which one?' Sid asked.

'Good Christ.' Clanton raised his eyes to heaven, or at least to the ceiling which was painted a fetching shade of sunflower yellow. Even in the midst of my predicament the awful thought struck me that Mamie was probably up there somewhere, maybe attired in a see-through silk nightgown and with her hair in curlers.

Her brother signalled for the case and Sid moved and offered it to him. Clanton extracted the snub-nosed .32, hefted it and then showed it to me. I took it gingerly by the barrel.

'Is it loaded?'

'Yeah. All yeh haveta do is point it, pull the trigger and Bob's yer uncle.'

'You mean Bob was my uncle.'

'Whatever.'

I dropped the gun in my side pocket, watching Sid watching me. Quite plainly he did not approve. For that matter, neither did I. 'I presume it can't be traced to anyone in particular?' I asked.

Clanton shrugged. He put the cigar in his mouth and then said around it, 'What d'you think?'

Now it was my turn to sigh. 'I guess not.'

'The serial number's filed off. The gun is as pure as the driven snow ....'

'That's very reassuring. D'you want it back when I'm finished with it?'

'What kinda question is that? Get rid of it. Bury it. Put it in a plastic bag with a rock and throw it in the river. Eat it ....'

I knew it was a case of spitting into the wind, but I made one more try. 'You're taking a lot for granted,' I said. 'What if I don't know who the killer is? Maybe I've just been stringing you along, playing for time to avoid a beating or worse.'

Clanton blew a cloud of cigar smoke, then batted it away impatiently. He looked at me, his watery blue eyes flat and expressionless. 'Yeh've got till the weekend,' he said. 'After that yeh'd better wrap yourself in cotton wool, dig a hole and pull it in after yeh. Yeh know me. I don't promise one thing, and then do the other.'

I gazed from one to the other of them, then I put out my cigarette on the ebony gargoyle and stood up. 'That appears to be it, then,' I said. 'I'll leave you and love you.'

Clanton nodded. He looked at Sid and said, 'Drive him wherever he wants to go, then pick me up a pizza. No olives or mushrooms.'

'What size?'

'Have yeh ever known me to order any excep' the large size, yeh knucklehead? Now, on yer bike ....'

I started moving, then I stopped and looked back over my shoulder.

'Tell Mamie I said goodbye,' I said. 'She's some gal, if you like them quarried out of a cliff.'

'Get him outta here, Sid,' Clanton said. 'Get him outta here before I forget me manners and stick this cigar in his eye.'

26

WHEN WE GOT back outside I stopped and took in a few lungfuls of cold moist air. The rain had blown away and the sky was clear. Sid did his business with the gate again and bumped me along, and we had just got to the pathway when the Bluebird came out of the shadows and pulled in beside us.

The rear door swung open and I climbed in. This time I wasn't alone. Whacker Whelan was huddled in the far corner, wrapped in an expensive-looking check coat. His head was bare and his blond curls glinted in the half light.

'Well, look at who we have here,' he said. 'I've been meaning to give you a call, and now you've saved me the trouble. I can't tell you how glad I am to see you.'

'But I bet you're going to try.'

'Sure I am. But I'd like a little more privacy to do it.' He leaned forward and told the back of Humphrey's head: 'Take the long way round. Up through the Phoenix Park. Nice and quiet there at this time of night. Give us a chance to become reacquainted. You'd like that, wouldn't you?'

'I can think of things I'd like better.'

Sid, who had taken up his usual position in the passenger seat, turned and looked at us. 'The boss wouldn't be too happy if Sunshine here had an accident,' he said. 'He's got something to do for him.'

'Oh yeah?' Whelan took a comb out of an inside pocket and ran it through his locks, then studied it as though suspicious he would find foreign bodies. Apparently satisfied, he put it away. 'What's he gonna do?' he asked Sid. 'Rob a bank? Swim the Liffey? Climb Liberty Hall? Am I getting warm?'

'He wants me to catch him the bluebird of happiness,' I said.

'He's been a bit down lately. Comes from mixing too much with dickheads and nose browners ....'

'Yeh hear that, boys?' Whelan splayed his hands in mock horror. 'I think this man is trying to insult us. And not for the first time either. He'll surely have to be taught a lesson.'

'Easy on,' I was glad to hear Sid caution him again. 'He's got a bad dose of the gob scutters. He don't mean nothin'. He just likes to hear himself talk.'

'Well, I'm going to put a sock in it.'

Whelan took something out of the voluminous pocket of his coat, something that shone in the dimness of the car's interior. It was a set of brass knuckles.

'You're kidding,' I said. 'Those went out with Trilby hats, striped waistcoats and spats. George Raft you ain't.'

'George who?'

'A better crook than you'll ever be.'

Humphrey revved up the engine and we lurched off down the wet, cobblestoned street. The Special Branch car was still parked at the corner. The occupants had the inside light off and were probably taking forty winks. So much for the cavalry.

We turned in through a number of narrow streets and came out on the river at Ussher's Quay. The Liffey was high and sullen-looking under the street lights. No one said anything as we moved upriver and then crossed over at Heuston Station. The siren of a train keened eerily through the darkness, and I wondered where it was bound for and wished I was on it.

Parkgate Street was as tightly shuttered as a Presbyterian Sunday. Inside in the Conyngham Road bus terminus there were lights and noise, and I could hear the wasp buzz of tinny radio music. Outside, dark and empty buses were tethered tail to tail like a herd of sleeping elephants. We drove up the main road into the park and then turned right towards the Zoological Gardens. Sid and Humphrey probably had quarters in the ape house.

'Stop anywhere here,' Whelan suddenly said. 'I want to take a piss.'

The car slowed down and then stopped. Whelan got out and stood with his back to us and in a moment we could hear the drone of his water as he hosed it out into the night. To finish, he let a rasper of a fart.

'Hark, hark,' I said to Sid, where he was twisted around watching me, 'the voice of the turtle is heard in the land ....'

Instead of getting back in, Whelan leaned down and gestured for me to get out. 'This is the end of the road for you, chummie,' he said. 'You'll have to find your own way home from here on in.'

I made the mistake of getting out on his side. I was about to put my feet on the ground when he hit me in the kidneys, possibly with the knuckle-dusters. The breath whooshed out of my lungs and I fell to my knees in the road. I had enough sense to roll and the next blow glanced off the side of my head and whirled me against the back wheel of the car. I continued rolling and then scuttled on my hands and knees around behind the vehicle. The surface of the road was hard and gritty and I could feel it scraping against my skin. It was the least of my worries.

I kept going, moving crab-fashion into the sheltering darkness. Pain and anxiety, in about equal amounts, drove me on. Behind me I could hear Whelan say, 'Where the fuck is he?', then the car bumped across grass, did a u-turn and moved back in my direction. The headlamps cut a swathe through the night, pin-pointing me in their twin spotlights.

I made it to my feet and started running. Getting some wind into my lungs was like drawing in liquid fire. I cut away to the right, holding onto my gut and weaving like a drunk on the trail of the magic whiskey fountain. There was grass under my feet now, mushy and wet and sucking at my feet as I ran. I dodged as the big car came right up behind me, and I could hear the yells of glee from its occupants as the side of it hit me and knocked me flat.

I lay for a second, then I pushed myself up and made off in the opposite direction. Behind me there was a clashing of gears, the headlamps jumped crazily, and then they were on my trail again. Running, I vowed to myself that if I got out of this I'd retire from the detective business and take up a nice safe vocation like steeplejack or explosives expert. I had not forgotten the gun in my pocket — it had nearly castrated me the second time I had fallen — but I knew that by the time I'd get it out of my jacket, turn and fire the Bluebird would have squashed me flat as a sand dab.

I knew I was getting near the end of my tether — a combination of the blow in the kidneys, the sideswipe from the car and the heavy underfoot conditions was causing me to flag. I was pretty sure they would not kill me, but there were various degrees of pain that could be inflicted, and, where pain is concerned, I have a very low tolerance level.

My vision was becoming blurred and I was about to give up the ghost, turn and sing a hymn, when I saw a barrier looming up in front of me. It was a section of metal fencing, about five feet in height and topped with arrow points that in daylight would have appeared decorative but now in the murkiness of the night looked ball-piercing in the extreme.

I could have cut away again either to right or left, but desperate measures call for desperate remedies. It was a case of shit or bust, so, gritting my teeth, I went for it. I soared up and over that railing like a record-breaking Olympic high jumper — I even experienced the crazy desire to stop and admire myself as I flew through the air.

The landing wasn't half as successful as the initial achievement of clearing the fence, however. I hit branches at the beginning of my descent, then caromed off the parent trunk of the tree, bounced a few times and did a nosedive into the ground at its foot.

Once again I lay on the ground, this time nodding in rhythm as the full cast of the Dublin Grand Opera Company, complete with hammers, thundered out the Anvil Chorus. When this eventually died down, I felt a great desire to stretch out against the spongy earth and go quietly to sleep. Tempting as this was,

I knew that even a modicum of rest was not for me. The Bluebird's headlights were thrusting curious fingers of light through the fencing and I was possibly still visible.

To get to my feet was out of the question, so once again I rolled. This was not a good idea. I must have been parked on the crest of a hill, and as soon as I started moving I gathered momentum, so that it was in a wild tangle of arms and legs that I went down the slope to end up with a whop in something decidedly splodgy and evil-smelling at the bottom.

This time I prayed a little, for Clanton, and Whelan, and for Sid and Humphrey — I even remembered good old Mamie in my aspirations. I prayed that they would all have long and painful lives, and when they finally died that they would burn in hellfire for eternity and a day. Then I must have become delirious, for I started laughing out loud, and it was only when I had snorted my fill that I realised that what had sparked me off was the thought that for the first time I understood fully the meaning of the phrase, 'As happy as a pig in shit'.

Eventually the time came, as it does for even the drunk lying in the gutter, to get up and walk away. I did it in a series of small, uncoordinated movements, trying to fool my body that it wasn't really me that was putting in all this effort.

The stink was woeful and, as the relief at escaping my pursuers began to recede, I started wondering uneasily where I had landed. I did not have to wonder long. The clouds had all gone off to rain down on someone else's parade, and the sky was embellished with a tingle of stars. As my eyes grew accustomed to the halflight I perceived a couple of odd shapes at a little distance from me. As I watched, they began to quiver and then to trundle towards me, making very unpleasant snuffling sounds. If I didn't know better I'd have imagined them to be a couple of large black bears.

Then it struck me that I was, after all, in the zoo. In my flight I had obviously vaulted one of the boundary railings — but bears in such an accessible place? No, it was impossible. My vision was playing tricks on me. I was distraught, hallucinating, the victim of a mirage.

I went back up that muddy hill like a shot off a shovel, with some kind of animals huffing and puffing after me. They might have been bush babies, koala bears, giant friendly pandas, Zig and Zag — I did not wait to find out. Lacking the proper take-off for a repeat of my record breaking performance of hurdling the railing, I had to settle this time for an undignified scramble up and over. Cloth tore as part of my trousers refused to accompany me, but I left it to fend for itself and continued on my way.

Back on the far side of the fence again I was relieved to see no sign of the Bluebird or its occupants. I hitched myself up and started walking. It didn't matter where. There are times when just going is enough, to hell with the destination.

27

THE MAIN ROAD through the Phoenix Park is wide and straight and very, very long. At one stage on my odyssey I flagged down a prowling taxicab, but as soon as the driver saw the state I was in he took off like a scalded cat.

I walked on, feeling more and more sorry for myself. The moon had risen and a light breeze was wafting across the acres of open ground. My right trousers leg from the knee down was gone, but not forgotten: its absence, for some reason, caused me to limp, even though the leg itself was all present and accounted for. I considered tearing the other one off so that I might look like a midnight jogger, but then I thought, what the hell, there's no one to see me anyway.

I finally made the dip in the road that brought me back past the silent buses, up Infirmary Road — well named, considering the condition I was in — and then onto the North Circular. I was now in flatland, and quite a number of the big old houses still had lighted windows. I passed a courting couple dug into one another up against a gatepost, and the stink wafting from me served to pull them apart like a plaster coming off a hairy chest.

I cut across onto the New Cabra Road, past Clarke's Bakery and along by Massey's funeral parlour. Like the shops across the road, Massey's frontage was also guarded by a steel grill: obviously even the dead were not safe from plunder in these troubled times.

I was surprised to see a light in the sitting room of my own humble abode. Who could the midnight watcher be? A wise virgin? An unwise one? Sid and Humphrey? Uncle Tom Cobley? I didn't give a tinker's curse.

I had to take the gun that Clanton had given me out of my pocket in order to find my keys, and I was still holding it by the trigger guard when I looked into the sitting room. Annie was sitting sprawled in a chair eating a strawberry yogurt. She stared at me, the spoon poised in the air.

'So you came after all,' I said, as breezily, I hoped, as though I'd just dropped in to look for my hat.

She closed her mouth with an audible snap, then opened it again to say, 'Not yet, but I have hopes ....' She stuck the spoon into the plastic container and laid it carefully down beside her. 'What happened to you?'

'A bear shat on me.'

'Don't tell me .... You ate his porridge?'

I crossed the room and stared at myself in the big mirror over the mantlepiece. I looked like one of the Mudmen from the old Flash Gordon serials. A pair of wild, red-rimmed eyes glared at me out of a mask of stiffened gunge. My clothes were so weighed down with it that I felt as if I were carrying a sack of potatoes under each arm.

'Pee-hew,' Annie said, holding her nose. 'That bear must have swallowed something that didn't agree with him.'

'He'd have swallowed me if I hadn't hightailed it like the Roadrunner. And Mrs Bear was with him in case she was needed to suck the bones.'

'You poor lamb ....'

Without touching anything except the trigger guard, I put the gun on the mantel. We both gazed at it, then Annie said, 'Did the bear give you that?'

Suddenly indignant, I said accusingly, 'You're laughing at me, aren't you? I've been beaten up, run down by a car, chased by a couple of bears, and had to walk for ten miles dragging a ton of muck, and all you can do is laugh at me. Where's your sense of Christian compassion? Can't you see I'm all shook up? The embarrassment alone has me so traumatised I'll need a month in an enclosed monastery to get over it.'

'I'll tell you what I'll do,' she offered. 'While you're peeling off your clothes I'll run a bath. Then when you're in it, I'll bring you strong tea laced with whiskey. How does that sound?'

'As if all my birthdays had come in one go.' I turned to march off, then I looked back at her. 'How'd you get in?' I asked her. 'As I remember it, you threw the keys in the back of the car.'

'Those were yours. I still have mine.'

'Ah ....'

'What does that mean?'

'Nothing. Just ah ....'

I went upstairs, struggled out of my duds and stuffed them into a rubbish sack. Either Mrs Walsh-Overman or Marty was going to get a hefty bill for expenses. Then I made my way to the bathroom, where, true to her word, Annie had the tub three-quarters full of warm, Radox-impregnated water. I eased down into it, its welcoming embrace as close to being orgasmic as made no difference. It was almost worth everything that had gone before just to experience such a feeling.

I was lying there, up to my neck and with the tiredness draining out of every pore, when Annie came in and sat on the edge of the bath. In one hand she held a mug of steaming tea, in the other a lit cigarette. These she administered in alternate doses, a sip, then a puff, and when I had finished she took off her clothes and got in with me. She washed my hair, massaged my aching muscles, tickled my toes.

When the water began to grow tepid, we got out and dried each other off. Then we went into the bedroom and made love, slowly, with infinite patience, as though afraid to damage the fabric of something so precious as only to be offered once. All the occasions I had made love with Annie, and yet on each occasion it always seemed to be for the first time.

It took us an age to come back from wherever we had been. I lay in the half darkness and listened to the hum of traffic on the road outside. It imparted a sense of distanced inviolability, as though we were in a high tower and had pulled the ladder up after us. How we had just behaved needed no rationalising:

it was a moulding of instinct that was as natural and perfect in its way as a filigree of frost is on a winter window pane.

And as fleeting. Annie had suppressed her curiosity for long enough, and now she was eager to hear what had happened to me. I gave her a condensed account, providing the meat and leaving out the trimmings.

'So that's why you got rid of me,' she said. She leaned over and kissed me on the lips. 'You were protecting me. And to think that I hoped you'd meet up with an accident, a tiny one, and have holes in your underwear when the nurses came to take it off ....'

'You sadistic person.'

I sat up and switched on the bedside lamp. Annie had brought up the bottle of Bushmills, so I poured some of it into a glass and offered it to her. She declined.

I lowered an ounce or two and waited for its warmth to travel southwards. The room was in a mess, with clothes strewn everywhere. What a kip to bring one's beloved into, I thought.

'Do you really know who committed all these killings?' Annie asked me. 'It makes me shiver inside to think you do ....'

'One person did the throat cutting. Bernadette was murdered by someone else. Although maybe I shouldn't call it murder.'

'What d'you mean?'

'It was more a kind of retribution for past wrongs. And it wasn't premeditated, like the others.'

'Are you going to tell me?'

'No.'

'Why?'

I turned to look at her. Her hair was all fluffed out, making her face appear smaller. In the golden glow of lamplight her skin had a honeyed hue, burnished almost. 'For your own safety,' I told her. 'There's a very vicious and cold-blooded killer moving around out there ....'

'Out where?'

'In the canyons of the city.'

'Is that a quotation?'

'Naw, I just made it up.'

Annie leaned over me and took the glass and drank from it. The raw whiskey made her shudder. I put my arm around her and hugged her. 'And that reminds me, remember what I asked you about finding Redmond? Well, I've changed my mind ....'

'You don't want me to look for him?'

'No, it's too dangerous. I think we're coming to a resolution of sorts, and Redmond is in more jeopardy now than ever before.'

'You're not really going to kill someone for that Clanton, are you?'

'Of course not. I'm only stringing him along.'

'I think it's me you're stringing along.'

'Only as far as my bed. And now that you're in it, I've thrown the string away ....'

I drank the rest of the whiskey, put out the light and let her cuddle into me, but she was breathing quietly in a deep sleep long before I made it down that same dark tunnel.

28

THE NEXT DAY I woke up feeling as though I had been crucified. I was lying in the cruciform position on the bed, my extremities felt as if six-inch nails, in diameter as well as in length, had been driven through them, and I had a pain in my side that could only have been put there by a centurion's spear.

There was no sign of Annie, the bed on her side disturbed but empty. With no small amount of effort I manoeuvred my trembling legs out from under the sheets. As soon as my feet hit the floor, it tilted like the deck of a ship. I made it to the window, although a drunk on roller skates would have done it more gracefully.

Applying an eye to the gap in the curtain, I looked out. The morning looked as if it had crawled on hands and knees out of the night and then fallen over and expired. It was dull, grey and comatose, the sky bleary, the street soiled, the trees that yesterday had appeared spring-like now aged and dispirited. Then again, it could have been me.

Aimlessly I walked around the room, finding underwear here, a shirt there, my one remaining suit hanging in the gallows of the wardrobe. Then I remembered the gun. I made it down the stairs in a hop, step and a jump. I had use for that gun; it had come to me sometime in the night, either in a vision or as the result of inspired cogitation. Martin Luther King might have had a dream, but I had a plan.

It was where I had left it on the mantlepiece. I went out to the kitchen and got a soft dusting cloth, then I went back into the sitting room and lifted the gun, using the duster. Gently and lovingly I rubbed the barrel and the triggerguard, being careful not to touch the butt or the chamber. I rooted around and found a cellophane freezer bag, and I dropped the .32 into it and sealed it with the twist of wire provided.

After that I made some coffee and drank it black and highly sugared. I tried a cigarette but when the smoke went down it made me feel as if someone was polishing the back of my throat with size six sandpaper. I stubbed it out and drank some more coffee. The ache in my gut had subsided to what could euphemistically be termed a throb, and the palms of my hands and my knees where the gravel of the road had grated only hummed where formerly they had sung a full high C. One of these mornings I would wake up feeling fresh and blithe and young, and the shock would probably kill me.

I was still sitting at the kitchen table, doing my imitation of a zombie, when the phone rang. After my nerves had returned to normal, I picked it up and cradled it at my ear. Annie's voice came through sounding excited, her words garbled. 'Hold on,' I protested, 'and slow down. I can't make out what you're saying.'

There was a pause, then she said, 'It's Victoria. She's found Redmond for you. I've just had a call from her.'

'Where is she?'

'Up near Christ Church. There's a parking lot beside the Tailor's Hall. Redmond's been living there in an abandoned car.'

'An abandoned car?'

'Yes, an abandoned car. You know what an abandoned car is, don't you? It's a car that nobody wants anymore.'

'Is that a bit like an abandoned husband?'

'Oh, we're feeling sorry for ourselves, are we?'

I scowled at the phone. 'I'm feeling rather fragile this morning,' I said haughtily. 'I had a harrowing night.'

'Oh, forget that,' she said dismissively. 'I'm going up there now ....'

'No, wait.'

'Why?'

'Where are you?'

'I'm in the office.'

'I'll pick you up in ten minutes.'

I hung up on her protestations, grabbed the gun, my keys, then suddenly remembered that my car was still down in the Ilac Centre. Hurriedly I phoned for a taxi, then stood at the front door biting my nails until it arrived. I promised the driver a tip that would keep him in Woodbines until Christmas if he got me down to the quays before I had finished counting to a hundred. I was at eighty-nine when we drew up beside Annie where she was waiting at the kerb in front of her office block.

This morning she was wearing a black and red patterned sweater under her pea jacket, a denim mini-skirt and red tights. Sitting well forward on her head was a flat, Spanish matador's hat held by a knotting thong under her chin. She was a splash of colour against the sombre aspect of the rest of the morning.

She climbed in, and I gave the driver further directions. Our sense of urgency must have communicated itself to him for the taxi wheels burned rubber as he took off. 'You'll get us there safely, won't you?' I asked him, 'rather than dead on time, I mean.'

He was a fat, sallow-skinned individual, with a Pancho Villa moustache, long sideburns and what remained of his lank hair glued to his skull with Brylcreem. A stub of a cigarette was worked into one corner of his mouth. He used the other corner for talking out of and, I presumed, eating, sneering and spitting. Now he assured us that he was fully in control, that I wasn't to worry, and that we'd be at Christ Church before the bell for Mass had ceased ringing. I didn't bother to tell him that they didn't have Mass in Christ Church, it being of the other denomination.

Although his Mexican appearance might have put him more appropriately astride a mule, he handled his Volvo as if it were an extension of his body. He stitched it in and out the eyes of more needles than any rich men ever wriggled through. And he seemed to possess some in-built sense of timing that caused him to hit every traffic light just as it was turning amber.

We went past Dublin City Hall, caught a glimpse of the portico of the Castle, swung into Lord Edward Street, and screeched to a halt, having made a u-turn on a sixpence, outside Christ Church Cathedral.

'Yeh want me to wait?' Pancho asked me. 'Is it a wedding? A christenin'? Not a funeral, wha'?'

That last one stopped me in my tracks, a little premonition of unease stirring in my breast. 'I wish you hadn't said that,' I told him.

Annie caught it — I could see it by the look she gave me. She hurried away while I paid off the taxi driver, and she was already across the road and going hard towards the vacant lot before I managed to overhaul her.

The parking area was of the most rudimentary: some tubular steel railings enclosing a gravelled stretch with more humps and hollows than an acne-scarred face. There was an entrance and an exit, and a galvanised shed afforded a haven for the attendant to shelter in against the elements. The shed was shuttered, its erstwhile occupant probably off somewhere drinking his breakfast. Every available space was taken, the cars silent and closed under the lowering sky. In the background the arched windows of the Tailor's Hall were blind eyes that would see no evil.

'There's no sign of her,' Annie said, her unease apparent. 'I thought she'd have waited for us here at the entrance.'

I climbed up on the bonnet of a brand new BMW and looked around. In a far corner I could see a dilapidated blue van, tilted sideways and with its rear doors hanging open. I got down and set my hip against the side of the car.

'What is it?' Annie asked me.

'I can't see anything,' I lied.

I pointed to an aisle that led away from where I had seen the van. 'You go down there,' I told her, 'and I'll go in the opposite direction and we'll meet in the middle.'

'You think ...?'

I nodded. 'Go on. She's probably sitting on Redmond trying to keep him from taking off.'

Reluctantly Annie moved away in the direction I had indicated. I waited, watching her. We were beside a main artery and the traffic noise was very loud, but underneath it the silence of the parking lot was as palpable as a prickling itch across the shoulder blades. I quickly ran down the tunnel formed by the parked cars, then, as I got closer to the corner where I had spied the van, I slowed. I was afraid of what I was going to find, yet resigned to it at the same time.

Someone had indeed been living in the vehicle, for there were dirty rags serving as curtains hanging in the apertures where the windscreen and the side windows had been. It was jacked up on concrete blocks, but some of them had crumbled and this accounted for its lopsided appearance.

I needed the familiarity of doing something ordinary, so I took out my cigarettes. Then I found I had no matches, so I put them back in my pocket again.

Slowly I went around to the rear of the van, my feet crunching on the uneven surface of the lot. One of the doors creaked as I brushed against it, the noise startlingly hard and shrill. I put an eye to the crack. Inside was a jumble of pots, pans, a broken chair, pieces of old newspaper. Taking up most of the floor space was a stained mattress, its stuffing protruding as though someone had been pulling at it. Victoria was sitting all scrunched up in the space between where it ended and the back of the driver's seat began. She was staring at me, but she was not seeing anything. She would never see anything, ever again. She had come to this place on this grey morning on an act of mercy, young, vibrant, alive, and wishing no one any harm, and an act of violence had been perpetrated against her that had left her broken and useless as a discarded doll. Only her blood, which was everywhere, served as a reminder of the freshness and enthusiasm that had been so abruptly taken from her.

I stepped back and breathed deeply, then I looked around.

No-one shouted or screamed, or did anything out of the ordinary. The traffic noise still pulsed, the cars and the buildings were silent. No snare drum rattled a slow march, no band played 'The Flowers of the Forest'. There would be a time and a place for that. For the moment there was merely the mind-emptying dislocation of sorrow, the horror of loss. And all I could think about was the lack of a match to light my cigarette.

The sight of Annie turning the corner of a row of cars and then heading in my direction startled me back into life. With a great screeching of metal I managed to push the doors closed, the right one sagging and almost coming off its hinges. I put my back against it and faced Annie as she moved towards me. There was no need for me to say anything, my face told her all she really did not want to know.

'Vicky?'

The single word was a question and an accusation all in one. I nodded. She stopped some little distance away and gazed from me to the van. 'I'm sorry,' I said. I spread my hands, palms outward, the gesture as futile as the prosaic unoriginality of my words.

Her reaction was just as commonplace. Refusing to accept the awfulness of finality she said, 'Has she been injured? We'll call a doctor, get an ambulance ....'

I nodded again. 'Yes,' I said, giving her the balm of being able to do something, to remove herself from what she did not want to see. 'Find a telephone and get some help. And call the police. I'll stay here until you get back ....'

She didn't move, then she came towards me in a rush. 'Oh, Annie,' I said, as I enclosed her in the circle of my arms. I held her tight, an anger that was elemental in its ferocity suddenly taking hold of me. The thought had just occurred to me that it could as easily have been her lying with her throat cut in the back of the van.

29

WE WERE STILL in the same position, me holding her, neither of us saying anything, when a scrawny character wearing an official-looking cap with a shiny peak came sidling up the aisle of cars towards us. He had a nose long enough to poke a dog out from under a bed, a pair of rheumy eyes and a down-drag of mouth that was made for sneering. 'What's up, chief?' he asked me, looking us up and down but keeping his distance.

'Go and phone the Guards,' I told him. 'There's been an accident. The van ....'

Looking highly dubious, he said, 'Pull the other one. That van hasn't moved from there in years. How could't have been in an accident?'

Gently I moved Annie to one side, then I fumbled in my pockets for change. I proffered the coins. 'Go and make the call.' I held up my hand when he looked like arguing. 'Tell them they'll need an ambulance.'

I watched his eyes widen, then I followed the direction of his gaze. A thin trickle of blood was dripping out from under the door of the van to form a small puddle on the pitted surface of the lot. It was very bright against the surrounding greyness.

The attendant took the money and scampered away. I forced Annie, who was looking grim and sick, to walk with me back to the entrance. There was a public house called the Sheaf of Wheat across the road and we went over there and I ordered two stiff whiskeys. At first Annie refused to drink, but I made her persevere. The glass clicked against her teeth and she gagged, but she got most of it down. The alcohol brought the colour back to her face. She smiled at me wanly and squeezed my hand.

'Why don't you go ahead and talk,' I said. 'It helps ....'

She shook her head, and then the tears came and that made me at least feel better. I gave her my handkerchief and patted her back and made some soothing sounds. There was a residue of anger in me that refused to lie down. I knew now what I had to do. The pity was that I had not done it sooner and possibly prevented this latest killing.

'It didn't have to happen, did it?' Annie asked me, as if reading my thoughts. 'You've more or less told me Redmond is responsible ....'

'There's a difference between knowing and making it stick,' I said lamely. 'I've no evidence. It's just a feeling, a certain train of events, some things that were said, or half said ....'

'Vicky was so full of life. She was planning a holiday. Why did she have to die?'

'She was in the wrong place at the wrong time.'

'As simple as that?'

'I'm afraid so.'

'That's not really good enough, though, is it? A loss of a life shouldn't be that random. All the plans, all the expectations ... cut off so abruptly.'

I shrugged uncomfortably. Some things can't be explained away. 'Would you like another drink?' I asked, gazing at the empty glasses.

'No.' She gave me a level stare out of eyes that were still tear-stained. 'What kind of person would do a thing like this? What kind of mind ...?'

'Twisted. Vicious. Inhuman.'

'Those're just words. Explain them for me.'

'I can't, Annie. Maybe a psychologist could. We're all capable of violence, I suppose. It's probably a thin veneer that separates the good guys from the bad guys.'

'Oh, I can understand someone striking out in defence of home or family. But cold-bloodedly killing people just to see them die ... That's an abomination.'

'I've often wondered if I could kill someone.'

'If I had the opportunity to slaughter whoever did that to Vicky, I'd do it.'

'Would you?'

'I would right now ....'

I thought of the gun in its plastic wrapping in my pocket. I thought about pointing it, holding it at arm's length in the accepted manner and pulling the trigger. Then I put Annie instead of Victoria in the back of that soiled van with her throat cut and I kept pulling that trigger until it clicked on an empty chamber.

There was movement at the front of the pub and Superintendent George Quinlan and Detective Constable Hanley pushed their way in and strode purposefully towards us. They were both wearing long beltless tweed coats, their hands in their pockets, their faces set and watchful.

Quinlan came over to us, while Hanley leaned an elbow on the bar and nodded at the dumpy blonde woman behind it. She had been regarding us curiously since we had come in, but she now gave up on that and went off to wash glasses at the far end of the counter.

I greeted Quinlan with an 'Hello, George', bringing a twinge of displeasure to his craggy features at the familiarity. This was official business, there would be no time for such pleasantries.

'You shouldn't have left the scene of a crime,' he chided me. 'Or is it force of habit?'

'What d'you mean by that?'

'Never mind. And I'll ask the questions.'

He looked at Annie. He obviously recognised her, although to my recollection he had only met her once before. Trained eyes and trained mind. They nodded at one another but didn't shake hands. Quinlan looked about him, then sighed, hitched up his coat and squeezed into the seat across from us. He put an elbow on the table and scratched his ear. Behind us Hanley cleared his throat and shuffled his feet.

I told Quinlan about getting the call from Annie, of how

Victoria had told her she had found Redmond and how we had journeyed up the quays to find her already dead in the back of the van.

'Redmond Walsh-Overman?'

'That's right.'

'You knew we were looking for him. Why didn't you call us?'

I gave him one of my sincere looks and said, 'I had that in mind. But I also had a commitment to his mother. She's my client, after all. She's hired me to try and talk him into going home. I had to tell him that before calling down the law on his head.'

'I talked to her this morning. She's terminated your contract.'

'Says who?'

'The old lady told me she fired you last night. Says she's changed her mind about having Redmond found.'

'Not so. That's not how it happened.'

'Whatever.'

Quinlan hunched himself more comfortably into the seat. He took his right hand out of his pocket and ran it over his chin. There was an audible rasping sound as though he had shaved himself that morning with a blunt razor. 'Did you ever consider that if you'd called us first that girl might still've been alive?' he asked me, his eyes steady and unwavering.

'You wouldn't have got here any quicker than we did.'

'Maybe.'

To change the subject, I said quickly, 'What about the parking attendant? Did you talk to him?'

Quinlan deliberated, then he said, 'He told us some old guy had been kipping down in the van at night. Said he chased him away, but he kept coming back.'

'Did he see Victoria?'

'The dead girl? No. Who is she anyway?'

'She worked with Annie. A fellow social worker. She'll be able to tell you about her better than me.'

I left them while Annie filled him in. Bellying up to the bar beside Hanley, I bummed a match from him and lit up. He took the matchstick back and chewed on the end of it. He looked morose and bored. 'A killing doesn't brighten up your day?' I asked him.

He squinted at me. 'Dunno as I should talk to you. I might be arresting you in a minute. Maybe I should search you for offensive weapons.'

'You're just dying to get your hands in my pockets.'

'I'll bet you've got a hole in your trousers pocket to account for that secret smile you've always got on your kisser.'

'Nice one, Hanley.' I winked at him. 'Takes one to know one.'

He scowled, took the matchstick out of his mouth and dropped it on the floor. We both looked down at it.

'You daring me to step over it?' I inquired.

He stuck out his lip, then gazed over my shoulder at Annie and Quinlan. 'Nice bit of crackling there,' he said. 'You humping her regularly?'

I kept my temper. In a level tone I said, 'She's my wife.'

He had enough human feeling to appear disconcerted, but not sufficient to apologise. 'What about the bint that was snuffed?' he asked, changing track. 'What about her then?'

'A friend of Annie's.'

'Dead about an hour and a half,' he volunteered. 'One lateral cut with force from a very sharp instrument. Across the throat from left to right. Presupposes an unknown right-handed person did the cutting. Or at least unknown to me.'

'Me too.'

'Yeah?'

'Did you find it?'

'What?'

'The weapon.'

'Not so far. We're looking for maybe a cut-throat razor. Or a very sharp butcher's knife. Probably the former.'

'Why?'

'Easy to secrete on one's person. What d'you use?'

'To shave?'

'Naw, to shape your toe nails.'

'I use a very sharp butcher's knife.'

'Thought as much.'

We glared at each other for a while, shifting from foot to foot like two prizefighters sizing one another up. I would have liked to have asked him why he acted the bastard all the time, but it didn't seem like the time nor the place. Anyway, he probably wasn't acting.

I went back over to the table and sat down again beside Annie. They had run out of conversation here too. 'So what d'you think, George?' I asked him. 'Can we go?'

He gave me that level stare again, the one that reminded me of a winter's day on the side of a bald mountain. For a second I thought he was going to say no. Then he pursed his lips and told us, 'I'm allowing you to go for the moment. Your wife has told me all she knows. I wish I could say the same about you. We'll let that ride for now, but I'll need you — you in the plural — to come down to the station, say tomorrow morning, to make full and complete statements. Now get out of here ....'

We did just that.

30

ANNIE HAD THINGS to do and phone calls to make, so I tucked her into a taxi and saw her on her way. She was still in a state of shock, but fighting back. I didn't know if she intended coming up to my place later and it did not seem the time to ask her.

It was past midday and the streets were crowded with people on their lunch breaks. I decided to leave my car where it was and collect it later. I strolled down Dame Street, enjoying the hustle and bustle of ordinary, everyday life. In the past few days I had come across enough of the other kind to make me feel soiled and ill-used.

But there is chicanery everywhere. I saw a couple of teenage girls with coats over their outstretched arms pushing and bumping into people. The coats hid their busy fingers as they investigated inviting pockets and fumbled with the flaps of bags. I could have called a policeman, brought them to his notice, but if he took them in, which was not certain, they would be out in a matter of hours, once more plying their trade.

As I walked, I thought about Redmond. It was beyond me how he was able to stay hidden for so long. It was as if some dark deity were lending him a hand as the consequence of some Faustian bargain perhaps. Then again, as with nuns, no one ever bothers to look closely at tramps. Most punters avoid them, probably with the thought that there but for the grace of God go I.

I made the street where my office was a little after three. Batt was on his high stool behind the counter of the Roxy. I had a favour to ask of him, so I went in and let him throw some film questions at me. I even pretended not to know who said,

'I was a fourteen-year-old boy for thirty years,' just to put him in a good mood. It was Mickey Rooney.

When I could get a word in, I asked him if I could borrow his keys when he closed up that night: 'A little matter of surveillance,' I told him, with a nudge and a wink.

He looked at me warily. 'Oh yeah, what're yeh going to be watching?'

I considered that one, then I answered, 'You know Swan's across the way? The all-night chemists? They've had a number of break-ins recently and they think it's the same party that's rustling their stock. They've asked me to look into it. Your place'd be ideal as a hidey hole.'

'Why can't you use your own office?'

'By the time I'd get down the stairs I'd have woken up the whole neighbourhood. Come on, Batt, it's not as if I'm asking you for your other arm.'

'What's in it for me?'

'How about a fiver for a one night stand? Maybe a little extra if I catch anything more than a crick in the neck.'

He thought about it. It was like watching a mouse circling a piece of cheese and wondering if it would explode. In the end greed won out over caution, as it usually does, and he agreed to let me use his place as a stakeout.

I went up to my office. As usual the outer room was bare of human habitation, although the spider who was building his summer home across the ceiling was diligently spinning away. I let myself into my inner sanctum, sat at the desk, took out the bottle of Bushmills and poured myself a stiff one. Then I took up the phone and made a call. There was no answer.

I sat there and thought about George Quinlan and of the number of dead bodies he had to go and look at in the course of his work, and I wondered if he ever got used to it. After thinking about it for a while I came to the conclusion that he probably did not. I lowered the whiskey another couple of inches and tried the phone again. Still no answer.

During the course of the next hour I tidied my desk, let the blind on the one and only window up and down a few times, gazed down into the alley behind the building, saw a small, piebald dog wander along and fastidiously pee against a row of dustbins, taking them one at a time as though it were his duty not to miss any.

I took off my jacket and got down on my knees and examined the bottom of the visitor's chair. The only thing I learned was that there were some woodworm holes under the seat. Next I examined the Walter Osborne print on the wall. I decided I did not like the way it was hanging, so I loosened the cord and let it fall away at a wider angle.

I sat down again, rummaged about in the bottom drawer and found a roll of masking tape. I placed this on the blotter in the middle of the desk. Next to it I put the gun that Clanton had given me. I sighed, scratched my head, had another snort from the Bushmills bottle.

My black-faced Seiko watch told me it was four thirty, so I tried the phone again. This time it was picked up on the fourth ring and a voice that I knew said, 'Yeah' cautiously into it.

I took a breath, then said, 'This is Blaine. I've got something for you.'

A pause, then, 'What?'

'Redmond. I've got Redmond.'

'Oh yeah?'

'I'm willing to give him to you if the rest of it stops now. Someone very close to me nearly got killed this morning and I don't want to take any more chances. Redmond is nothing to me. He'll be here tonight at eleven all trussed up and ready for the pot.'

'Here meaning where?'

'In my office. He'll be all yours, no strings attached.'

'You must think I came down in the last shower.'

'You want him badly enough — and you do — you'll come take a look.'

'How do I know the place won't be crawling with the law?'

'That's a chance you'll have to take.'

'Will you be there?'

'You must be joking ....'

Gently I placed the receiver back on its cradle to cut the connection. My hand holding it was clammy with sweat. I also had difficulty breathing, the air not wanting to go down any further than the back of my throat.

Dispensing with the glass this time, I put the bottle to my head and threw back a walloper. It made me gag, but its fiery warmth did wonders for my circulation. I nursed the bottle in my lap and let time crawl by and comfort me.

After a while I got up and stood by the window. An early dusk was pulling the shades down over the city. I looked at my reflection in the glass. A strained and worried face stared back at me. 'Pretty hairy,' I told it, before lifting the bottle and toasting it one final time.

31

I WENT DOWN to the Ilac Centre, got my car and drove it home. There was noise, light, the stop and start of evening traffic, but it was being run past me just out of reach of my sense perception. It was a bit like the serial effect one gets travelling in a fast train at night through the outskirts of a large town. Everything trailed streamers of itself into something else, distinctness and outline blurring into the wavering insubstantiality of a dream world.

My mind was also running in the fast lane, an accelerated tick-tocking of images, disconnected scenes, snatches of conversation all banging together and bouncing off one another, and then sliding away as I was about to get hold of something I could home in on. I thought of a line from Eliot's 'The Wasteland': 'I will show you fear in a handful of dust' — its full impact had never been clear to me up to now.

The house was quiet, damped down by a lack of company. Where was everyone? Marty seemed to have gone into hiding, Kate to have disappeared. Who needed them anyway?

I went upstairs, stripped down to my underwear and lay on the bed in the dark. I willed myself to sleep, but it would not come. Behind my eyelids my pupils seemed to be revolving like the fruit symbols on a slot machine. Also the twitch was back in my leg, knocking out a juddering beat to suit my whirling thoughts.

I switched on the bedside lamp and counted the cracks in the ceiling. I stopped when they began moving. The whiskey I had drunk was giving me heartburn, so I went downstairs and filled a pint glass with water and forced myself to drink it.

I had a bath. I shaved my face so closely that my skin tingled. I put on clean underwear, broke open the plastic wrapping on a new shirt, shrugged it on. Around my neck I carefully knotted the silk tie that I'd bought myself in a fit of extravagance the Christmas before. I brushed my suit and climbed into it. Then I took the trousers off again because the legs were too tight, and put on bell-bottomed jeans that had gone out of fashion ten years before.

Maybe I was trying to kid myself that I was a knight of old, fitting on his armour for the joust. Maybe I wanted to be the best dressed corpse that George Quinlan had seen this week. Maybe I should have gone out and got into my car and driven down the coast and breathed in some sea air and waited for the dawn to come up in a gleam of purple and gold.

Down in the kitchen again I opened my gun case and took out a shotgun that I'd been trying out on loan. It was an Ithaca M & P handgrip, the five shot version, with an eighteen and a half inch barrel and weighing just over five pounds. It was a beautiful gun, but for someone like me who did a lot of trap shooting it wasn't of much practical value. The dealer had been so lost in admiration of it that he had insisted on my taking it for a week or two. Now I was glad that I had.

I wrapped it in padding and brown paper, took it out to the car and locked it in the boot. A light sprinkling of rain was making its presence felt, but not enough to wet the pavement. I went back inside and extracted the .32 that Clanton had given me from its bag. With great care I padded the grip with cotton wool, then I did the same with as much of the body of the gun as was practical and still permit it to be fired. I taped all this into place and hefted it. Then I put it back in its plastic sack and dropped it into my jacket pocket.

I was as ready as I'd ever be. One last glance in the hall mirror on the way out, which was a mistake. The grim and pinched face that stared back at me made me hope someone was looking over my shoulder.

To put in the time before I met Batt, I dropped into Destry's and watched the piranha gobble up his supper. That was mistake number two. The sight of those teeth opening and closing only served to set my own choppers rattling.

Eventually Batt came in and passed me over his keys and I thanked him and left.

I went down to the shop and let myself in. Batt's stool was about four feet in height, so I moved it in behind a stand and arranged it so that when sitting on it I had a view of the street without being visible myself. Then I climbed the stairs to my office and made a few preparations that might enable me to see the dawning of another day.

By nine thirty I was back on the stool, chewing my nails and agonising over whether I could afford to light and smoke a cigarette. The need for one gnawed at me like a rat with his breakfast. I counted the cassettes on the stand, then recounted them to be sure I'd got it right the first time. I hadn't. I was out by one. Resignedly I started all over again, but I was never destined to get that bit of accounting signed, sealed and delivered. I was halfway down the second row when I glanced up, and there he was, standing in a shop doorway across the road.

I hadn't seen him arrive, but it was undoubtedly my quarry. He was making no attempt at concealment, he was just lounging there nonchalantly like a guy on a date waiting for his sweetheart to turn up. I could even see his lips pursed in a whistle as he gazed up at the window of my office.

He stayed like that for a few minutes, then he moved diagonally across the street until he was out of my vision. I listened, but I heard nothing more until suddenly the boards in my anteroom began to creak. Mentally I followed the trail of sound across the floor. There was a dull click, some more footsteps, then silence. The fish was hooked, now all I had to do was reel him in.

I took my time about going up there; I did not want to be out of breath or show any of the fear that was stuttering up along my backbone. This was the time for a cool head, steady hands, and the kind of bluster that would do justice to a lover caught by a jealous husband in his wife's bed chamber.

I don't know why I bothered to cross the outer room's creaking boards on tippy-toe, but I did. I reached in around the office door and switched on the light. Saunders was sitting behind my desk with his hands clasped together on the blotter. He was wearing a nice, pin-striped suit, his white hair was neatly combed, his face was composed. He did not at all look like someone who had horribly slaughtered five people and was entertaining notions of adding a few more before the night was out.

He made no movement, his eyes merely following me as I came in and sat down in the visitor's chair. He stared at me silently for a long minute. He didn't even blink.

'So,' I said, opening negotiations, 'here we are. Just the two of us. No sirens, no heavy tread of approaching flat feet. We could play pat-a-cake all night and no one'd be any the wiser.'

He narrowed his eyes. 'Cut the cackle. Where's Walsh-Overman?'

'All in good time. I'm going to reach into my pocket and take out my cigarettes and matches, so don't go all nervous on me.'

'Who's nervous?'

I lit up and blew a thin stream of smoke in the direction of the electric bulb. I could have told him who was nervous, but I didn't bother. He probably knew anyway.

'It was a nice neat plan to begin with, wasn't it?' I said. 'Was it you or Bernadette who thought it up?' He didn't say anything, so I went on: 'At first I thought Charles and yourself were in cahoots. There're not too many motivating factors that lead people to murder, and money is nearly always tied in there somewhere. In this case an awful lot. How much is Mrs Walsh-Overman really worth? Ten million? Twenty million? And no one to inherit it except a candidate for the funny farm or a fat man with an atrocious taste in clothes. I reckoned Charles had hired you to get rid of Redmond and that you were killing the other tramps to cover up your real intentions. The second part was correct, but I was off line with the first. Then I began to think of the one and only conversation I had with Bernadette. When I met her first and she awoke from her little reverie she called me Larry. You and I are about the same height and build, and with her fading eyesight ....'

I took another drag from my cigarette, hoping he would not notice how my hand shook.

'I didn't put it together, though, until I sorted through your room and found your writing case,' I told him. 'Laurence V. Saunders, a nice solid name. She also told me that when she was living out in Howth and beginning to tire of Redmond that she'd started playing around. Who could she have begun to knead flesh with, I wondered? Not the old man, not Charles, and I presumed she wasn't into unnatural practices. That left you. You with the eyes of blue, your bird's nest hair, and your greedy mind. Am I hammering out the right tattoo?'

He said nothing, but his knuckles were getting whiter where he held his hands clasped on the desk top.

'Then Charles turned up dead, his throat cut, and my wondering began to crystallise into certainty. Bernadette was still legally married to Redmond. If he died before her, why lo and behold, she'd find herself rolling in the old legal tender. And just as importantly, very well disposed towards you. The old lady had one foot in the grave, but if necessary she could be given a push. That wouldn't have cost you a thought ....'

I had allowed the cigarette to burn down to a stub, and now I pretended it was burning my fingers and I dropped it on the floor. I bent down to put it out, and when I surfaced again Saunders had the Ithaca M & P shotgun in his hand, the masking tape where I had fixed it to the bottom of the visitor's chair still adhering to it.

'Looking for this?' he inquired. He placed it on the top of the desk, within equal reach of both of us but with the muzzle pointing in my direction. 'Pretty amateurish move,' he sneered. 'I could've been sleep-walking and still found that.'

I let a little of my fear show, but not enough to make him

feel too secure. Keep them jumpy, that was my motto. He looked about as jumpy as a pole-axed kangaroo.

'Well, imagine that,' I forced myself to say, 'so you found it. I've been looking for that gun for weeks. Now, where could it've been? No, don't tell me, let me guess.'

All that that got me was: 'Stop beating around the bush. Where's Walsh-Overman?'

I started pushing a little. 'Come on, Saunders — or may I call you Larry? Be a bit original. You didn't really think I'd have had Redmond here, did you? You must be pretty desperate to have come here at all. As far as I know, the police know nothing about you. And your meal ticket is gone, now that Bernadette's passed over to the other side. Could it be professional pride in your work that's driving you on? And for that matter, why'd you get me involved in the first place? Too many cooks ... you know what I mean?'

'You're the one with the answers. Why don't you tell me?'

'I think I can at that.' My nose itched, so I scratched it. The gesture made Saunder's hand involuntarily reach out for the gun so maybe he was not as calm as he appeared. 'The old lady was getting restive,' I continued. 'Somewhere in that icebox of a heart of hers there might have been a suspicion of a thaw. Maybe she really did want to see Redmond one last time. She probably started hinting at bringing in the law to find him, and you had to head her off. I'd say it was you who convinced her to hire the private kind. When you saw me you thought I might be a little too efficient, so you tried to get me to jump to your hand signals. Was it you sent Charles to buy me off? What kind of story did you spin him?'

Something showed in his eyes and once again his hand moved towards the gun. He was also beginning to sweat, a fine glinting of moisture just under the hairline.

I pressed home my advantage, trying to rattle him a little more: 'Bernadette's death must have come as quite a shock to you. It had to be Redmond. What'd she do to bring it on herself, I wonder? Maybe taunted him with what you and she were up to? Redmond's temper was always on a short fuse. He may even have killed before. It can become a habit.' I forced myself to grin at him. 'But then you should know ....'

'Yes, I know.'

With his right hand he reached inside the breast pocket of his jacket and took out a six-inch razor with a mother-of-pearl handle. With practised skill he flicked out the blade. Twisting it in his hand, he caused the light to swirl off it. It was merely an old-fashioned barber's tool, but in his hand it became something repellent, an instrument of death.

'Quieter than an angel's kiss,' he said, weaving figures of eight with it in the air. It plainly fascinated him. Me too. I hoped his hand would slip and that he'd cut off his nose.

'I was fond of old Bernadette,' he said. 'She had these fantasies. She talked about a foreign specialist giving her back her sight. She dreamed about being up on a mountain in a clinic in Switzerland, and having the bandages taken off one morning and seeing the hard white glare of snow. She really believed in things like that. It was only make-believe, but sometimes, listening to her, I really wanted to make it come true for her.'

'Yeah, you're a regular knight on a white charger,' I said.

His hand holding the razor paused in the air. 'So where is Walsh-Overman?' he asked me. Then for the first time he smiled. He had small, even, white teeth, startlingly so against the redness of his lips. 'You don't know where he is, do you?' he said. 'You couldn't find him either.'

I lifted my shoulders and spread my hands. 'Afraid so.'

He clicked the razor open and shut, open and shut, while continuing to smile at me.

'Why'd you kill the girl?' I asked him.

'She saw me prowling around.'

'So what? She wouldn't have known you from the President of Turkey. I presume Redmond had skidded off before you arrived. I think you killed the girl for sport, for the kick you got out of it. You didn't really feel that much for Bernadette, or for the money for that matter. It was the killing, wasn't it? The power you'd gained over life and death ....'

He looked at me out of eyes that were flat and blank and possibly quite mad, and I realised he was a stranger to me. I knew nothing about him except that he had killed at least five people. Where had he come from? Did he have a family? A father, a mother, sisters and brothers? What had caused him to be as he was? Was he born with the seeds of wickedness in his heart?

I said, my voice beginning to tremble, 'There's someone that I love. Her name is Annie. She was also helping me look for Redmond. Both she and Victoria, the girl you killed, were looking for him because I asked them to. This morning it could have been Annie who was in that parking lot, and you'd have cut her throat. You'd have cut her throat and left her to bleed to death in the back of that filthy van. My Annie ....'

He must have recognised the look in my eye, and for a moment we were united in the feral atavism of one of man's most basic instincts: the need to kill. Then something quite absurd happened to break the spell. My always unreliable window blind suddenly decided to take a hand by snapping itself shut with a loud thwack. Saunders hunched his shoulders, but couldn't prevent himself from glancing around. Immediately I bent down and pulled Clanton's gun free from where I had it strapped to my lower leg, the pain as the tape came away from my skin acting as a spur to make me go faster.

Saunders saw it coming and reared up in the chair, but he was too late. I shot him twice in the chest, putting a brace of steel-jacketed bullets into his breastbone as close together as the recoil would allow. They arrested his forward motion, imparted a rictus of surprise to his face, and took away his life force as abruptly as it had been given to him in the first place.

For a moment he stayed suspended in the air, then he sat straight back into the chair, loose, sagging, weaving from side to side. Finally all motion ceased and he hung there, his mouth open, his eyes staring, his race run.

Shakily I placed the gun on top of the desk. I could feel my head moving from side to side, and the skin of my face was drum-tight and itchy. Frantically my mind hunted about for an antidote to the horror suffusing it, but the only thing I could come up with was a childish rhyme which I surprised myself by reciting out loud:

'Twinkle, twinkle, little star,
How I wonder what you are,
Up above the trees so high,
Like a diamond in the sky.'

This struck me as being so incredibly sad and beautiful that I felt the hot prickle of tears sting my eyes. But I still did not have the strength to move.

I sat on, listening to the silence and smelling the acrid odour of cordite in the close confines of the room. Then a small sound began to pit-pit-pit into my consciousness. I bent down and looked under the desk, and I saw Saunders' bright blood dripping drop by crimson drop onto the highly polished toe of his shoe.

32

IT WAS A LONG night. I rang George Quinlan, but he was out at an official function. They contacted him and he arrived, resplendent in full uniform, on the heels of a couple of car loads of his men. I was glad that he was there in person; he may not have been a friendly face, but at least he was willing to sit down and listen to what I had to say.

My story, and I refused to budge from it, was that Clanton had hired me to find Bernadette's killer — she had been his sweetheart once upon a time, I informed a highly dubious Quinlan. I was hoping that part of my tale would be validated by the fact that the Special Branch sentry box at the bottom of Old Shop Street should have a report on my visit to Clanton's house.

I said that I'd already had a suspicion that Saunders was the one responsible for the killing of the tramps on the instructions of Charles Walsh-Overman. When George asked me why I thought that, I told him that Charles had let slip a few innuendoes to the effect that he had hired Saunders to kill his brother so that he himself would inherit his mother's money.

After that it seemed logical to me, and I hoped to Quinlan, why Saunders, if he was working for Charles, should murder Bernadette: as Redmond's wife she was in line for a large slice of the inheritance. It was not quite as easy to come up with a plausible story as to why Saunders had changed his method of killing: I skated over it by saying that he probably wished to blame it on Redmond. I don't know why I went to so much trouble to protect the selfsame Redmond — maybe it was out of some misguided feeling of being honour-bound in my duty to his mother. As for not implicating Bernadette, that was the true chivalrous spirit in me.

When Quinlan asked me why Saunders had killed Victoria when Charles, the money man was already dead, I asked him who could look into the mind of a psychopath and find a balanced sequence of thought.

Bringing the story up to date, I said that Saunders had broken into my office, presumably in the hope of finding something there that would lead him to Redmond. I had stumbled on him, then Clanton had arrived; there had been an argument, and Clanton had shot Saunders.

The gun was intended as my clincher. In the interval between my phone call and the arrival of the Gardai, I had unwrapped the strapping from the .32 and laid it carefully on the floor. There should still be enough of Clanton's prints on it to back up my story. Or so I fervently hoped. The shotgun I had hidden down in Batt's emporium. The weakest part of my story was what I told Quinlan in reply to his querying why Saunders had killed Charles: that it was probably a falling-out among thieves.

George pretended to believe me because it suited him to. Being delivered the serial killer dead and so saving the complication of a trial was not to be sneezed at, and having Clanton implicated was a bonus. George was nothing if not a pragmatist.

We all went home, and over the next few days I signed so many forms in triplicate that I developed writer's cramp. The blood samples taken from Saunders' razor matched up with those of the victims, and hairs from the mattress in the van were found in his clothes. It was not as easy to break down Clanton's alibi for the time of the shooting; not so surprising as it was probably the first time ever that it was genuine.

It was only my word against his, but the prints on the gun helped, and the Guards brought him in for intensive questioning. Quinlan worried about my safety, but I assured him that if anything were to happen to me it would be conclusive proof of Clanton's guilt. That made George happy and me sleep with the Ithaca M & P under my pillow.

On the Sunday, Annie, my father and I went to Croke Park for the big hurling match. It was one of those bright, newly hoovered spring days, with the sky high, wide and a handsome blue. The cherry trees were fluffed out in curls of white and pink, and the crowds converging on the stadium were in smiling good humour.

Outside the Hogan Stand my father insisted that we all buy Wexford favours. Annie, in jeans, a canary yellow shirt and her ever-present navy pea jacket, tied a knotted purple and gold string Willie Nelson fashion round her head; I had to pin a dinner plate sized badge on my chest; and my father donned a large crepe sombrero that drooped around his face and gave him the appearance of a squirrel looking out of a head of cabbage.

Thus attired, we took our seats. The stand was full, the atmosphere electric. Wexford and Cork rivalry went back a long way — some said as far as the 1798 rebellion when the North Cork Militia had invaded the Model County and laid it waste with fire and sword. When the hurlers engaged in combat it was as if those ancient times were being reenacted all over again.

When hurling is played well, it is the very game of the Gods. It demands from the participants the ultimate in sacrifice, and out on the green sward of Croke Park in front of thousands of eyes there is truly nowhere to hide.

On that glorious spring day we were treated to a classical exhibition of all that is good in the sport. It was as though the players had been lifted onto a higher plane than the ordinary, to a field of endeavour where grace and beauty, speed of movement and mighty clashes of man, ball and hurley stick all came together in a synthesis of flowing perfection.

Often in the past the men of Wexford had been found wanting — no one knew that better than I did — but on this magical Sunday they had one of their finest hours. They were behind until the last minute of the game, and then a soaring shot from one of the midfielders swung in from over ninety yards' range, deceived the Cork goalkeeper, and ended up in the net. The goal gave Wexford a one point victory.

My father, hat erect with static electricity, made the historic statement that if he were to die at that moment he still would not stop cheering until the end of the following week. Annie was also caught up in the excitement of the moment; the finer points of the game might be a mystery to her, but the overall cornucopia of colour, movement and highly-charged display won her over.

As for me, I felt a pang for old times, for the immediacy of involvement, and for the plaudits of the crowd. But I did have my memories.

We were still standing outside the stadium talking and watching the crowd ebb away when an ancient relic of humanity came towards us, hand out and toothless mouth working. I caught Annie's eye, and it was obvious that she was thinking the same as I was.

'You never did find Redmond, did you?' she asked me.

I looked at her, then I put my arm around her and the other around my father.

'No, I never did,' I said.

Epilogue

REDMOND WALSH-OVERMAN came from the direction of Ringsend, across the hump backed bridge, then down the hard packed clay slope that bordered the River Dodder. He moved along at a leisurely pace in the afternoon sunlight, his bowler hat firm and square on his head, his hands swinging at his sides.

He came to the Grand Canal Docks, where the river, the Grand Canal and the Liffey all converged. There were three locks, two narrow and one broad enough to admit even the widest barge. The lock keeper's house had white and black painted window frames, and a grey, pebble-dashed frontage.

Across the Liffey the squat shape of the Point Depot Centre was visible, arches below, windows above. To the right a slipway looked pitted and unused, the walls leading down it covered in graffiti: Joycer, Pullo, Shay, Fizzer, Shake a Leg, Sailor. Further out the twin white- and red-striped chimneys of the Pigeon House Sewage Plant made a rude sign against the sky and the plumes of smoke issuing from them seemed painted into immobility.

Redmond had the place to himself. He crossed the lock gates and stood where the canal formed a smooth rectangle of water between stone restraining walls. In his mind's eye he could see a rowing boat out on it, the lone occupant a girl of about seventeen. Idly she trailed her hand in the small ripple caused by the slow progress of the craft.

Redmond smiled and raised his hat, then he stepped off the edge and plunged straight down into the murky, grey-green depths. The hat stayed bobbing on the surface, then it too disappeared as though he had reached up and pulled it down after him.

Overhead, the sun went in behind a cloud, but it soon reappeared. The afternoon became calm and unruffled again, and nothing stirred to disturb its serenity.